HIDDEN CITY

ALAN BAXTER

Hidden City by Alan Baxter

This edition 2026

ISBN 13: 9781940095783

Cover Design by Christian Bentulan

13th Dragon Books

WHEN THE CITY IS SICK, EVERYONE SUFFERS.

Steven Hines listened to the city and the city spoke. Cleveport told him she was sick. With his unnatural connection to her, that meant Hines was sick too. But when his friend, Detective Abby Jones, comes to him for help investigating a series of deaths with no discernible cause, Hines can't say no. Then strange fungal growths begin to appear in the streets, affecting anyone who gets too close, turning them into violent lunatics.

As the mayhem escalates and officials start to seal Cleveport off from the rest of the world, Hines knows the trouble has only just begun.

PRAISE FOR ALAN BAXTER AND HIDDEN CITY

"A grim and gritty fantasy noir with razor-sharp humor. I loved it!"
Tim Waggoner, author of *Teeth of the Sea*

"Hidden City is a delicious supernatural noir, the song of a city of the lost with both Chandleresque and Lovecraftian undernotes... razor sharp, dark, compelling, cosmic and strangely touching all at once. Highly recommended."
William Meikle, author of *The Ghost Club*

"Poisonous fungi? Check. Murderous transformations? Check. Deep-down, bad-to-the bone evil? Check. Good old-fashioned horror? Check. Enter Hidden City at your peril."
Angela Slatter, author of *The Bitterwood Bible*

"Creepy. Visionary. Catastrophic. Apocalyptic. These are words occurring frequently in discussions of horror. Hidden City encapsulates them all !"
Michael R. Collings, Collings Notes

"Alan Baxter is Australia's master of literary darkness."
This Is Horror podcast

"The Lord of Weird Australia and all-round good bloke."
Talking Scared podcast

"Good stuff… Alan Baxter can write like a m***********"
Gail Simone, best-selling author of DC's *Birds of Prey*

"Alan Baxter is an accomplished storyteller who ably evokes magic and menace."
Laird Barron, author of *Swift to Chase*

"…Baxter shows off his impressive versatility and range... At turns creepy and visceral, Baxter delivers the horror goods."
Paul Tremblay, author of *A Head Full of Ghosts*

"Master of the slow build, master of insidious horror, master of multiple points of view…hell, Alan Baxter is simply The Master… one of the best horror writers working today."
Tim Lebbon, author of *The Last Storm*

"Alan Baxter is one of the best horror writers in the business."
Kealan Patrick Burke, Bram Stoker Award-winning author of *The Turtle Boy, Kin*, and *Sour Candy*

"Baxter is one of the greats. He feels next level."
Well Read Beard

ALSO BY ALAN BAXTER

BLOOD COVENANT
SALLOW BEND
RECALL
DEVOURING DARK
HIDDEN CITY

BOUND (Alex Caine Book 1)
OBSIDIAN (Alex Caine Book 2)
ABDUCTION (Alex Caine Book 3)

REALMSHIFT (The Balance Book 1)
MAGESIGN (The Balance Book 2)

SERVED COLD – Short Stories
CROW SHINE – Short Stories
AND FIRE POURED FORTH – Short Stories

THE GULP: Tales From The Gulp 1
THE FALL: Tales From The Gulp 2
THE RISE: Tales From The Gulp 3

THE LEAVES FORGET
THE ROO
THE BOOK CLUB
GHOST OF THE BLACK: A 'Verse Full of Scum
GOLDEN FORTUNE, DRAGON JADE

Co-authored with David Wood

PRIMORDIAL (Sam Aston Investigations Book 1)
OVERLORD (Sam Aston Investigations Book 2)
CROCALYPSE (Sam Aston Investigations Book 3)

SANCTUM (Jake Crowley Adventures 0)
BLOOD CODEX (Jake Crowley Adventures 1)
ANUBIS KEY (Jake Crowley Adventures 2)
REVENANT (Jake Crowley Adventures 3)

DARK RITE

1

Steven Hines listened to the city and the city spoke. Its streets whispered secrets its curtains tried to hide. Its walls, damp with rain, hinted at lives their occupants were embarrassed to admit. Hines let the undercurrent of over four million lives piled one on top of another wash through him.

His was a jealous city. He had always loved her, but had no idea until far too late that she loved him back. His city was a psychopath. Death walked its byways, hatred roamed its corridors, murder stalked its alleys. Their closeness afforded Hines unique skills and he was intrinsically tied to Cleveport.

His mind drifted like a dry leaf on a cold wind, searching the buildings and alleyways, as his fingers rubbed the clothing the client had sent him. He sensed hints of people almost like the one he sought everywhere, but nothing close enough to give him hope. From the relative safety of his apartment in a small brownstone on a quiet edge of town, he stared through the grubby glass pane and astrally slipped from window to window, swept the usual haunts, the drug corners and sex worker hangouts. Ten dollar blowjobs and fifty dollar baggies were the currency of the street and if he found this kid anywhere, it would probably be in that economy.

The sprawl of the city was overwhelming, impossible to cover in several nights of searching. But the client had paid and he would do his best. He would seek more as he was out and about, the legwork of the mundane PI tied together with his particular talent.

With the quarry's psychic signature floating in his mind like a scent he searched for a match in the rain-slick thoroughfares. He toured missions and soup kitchens, trawled a dozen seedy bars and twice as many clubs, and his back began to ache from immobility in the scruffy armchair. His right knee throbbed, the old injury never letting him fully forget its existence.

The phone rang, momentarily startling in Hines's small, gloomy home. It vibrated insistently across the coffee table.

His voice was rough, like the sleep-thickened tones of a smoker in the morning, though he hadn't touched a cigarette in years. "Hines."

"Mr Hines, it's Mrs Parker. Any news on Grant? Anything at all?"

"I'm working on it right now, but I'm afraid I don't have anything for you yet."

"Nothing?" Her tone was strained with the inevitability she refused to admit. Always there was hope, until a corpse proved that hope dead. *If* there was a corpse. More often than not there was no closure at all.

Hines favored her with a gentle smile she couldn't see. "It's not easy, Mrs Parker. Missing persons are tricky at the best of times, but a city this size... Leave it with me. I have a lot of possibilities to investigate." He stretched out his right leg, wincing at the painful stiffness in his knee.

Parker's crestfallen silence spoke volumes.

He opened his mouth to offer further empty reassurance when she said, "You'll call me though? With even the smallest news?" Grief were obvious in her voice.

"As soon as I know anything. And I'll check in from time to time." She already knew his strike rate was low, he'd been honest with her.

"Thank you." Parker sighed. "Grant's just a kid, Mr Hines. Lost in the big city."

"We're all lost in the big city, Mrs Parker."

The phone clicked dead.

As dead as his chances of finding Grant Parker, most probably. Although he meant it when he said he wouldn't give up and he had found people before. It was what he did and where his reputation set him apart. Most PIs didn't have the ability to search the way he did. Trouble was, most people who went missing for more than a few days were either long dead by the time he discovered anything, or had no desire to be traced. More than once he had found someone who resented his success. He'd had to tell those clients he couldn't give any details on the missing person's request. Which hurt more than the dead, the lack of closure always worse than grief for those left behind.

Hines sank deeper in his armchair, dragged a hand across his face. Just once it'd be nice to land a result quickly and clearly. Something in the aether this night gave his talent a potency he wasn't used to. Perhaps he was in the zone, could maybe give Mrs Parker good news yet. But seventeen, fatherless, drug-user, this city. The odds were not in young Grant Parker's favor.

The telephone rang again. He scrabbled for it, found his glass on the way and picked that up too. He sipped burning scotch and checked the screen. Abby. "Hey, buddy."

"Too busy masturbating to answer right away?" she asked.

He grinned, swirled the amber liquid in the tumbler in his hand. "Just seeing a client out, actually."

"Sure."

There was a moment's pause. Steven sensed some discomfort. "Everything all right?"

"Yeah, it's a work thing," she said, reluctantly.

"Oh, and here was me thinking you wanted to go out for a drink and a bite to eat or something."

"We could do that. My date last night was a disaster anyway."

He was genuinely sad for her. This last guy had seemed like a decent sort. "What happened?"

"Fucking married."

Hines barked a sound of disgust. "Scumbag."

"Why do I get all the fuckknuckles, Steve?"

"It's not you. Pretty much everyone is a fuckknuckle. You notice because you're one of the few who isn't."

She laughed and he felt better, like he'd relieved her melancholy, if only briefly. He really cared about Abby, had done since they met in school at eight years old. He was an orphan, growing up in care, and ridiculed for it because kids are mean; she had a West Indian mother and red-haired Irish cop father, which made her exotic to some, but not enough of one or the other to most. Their mutual dislocations drew them close and the bond never broke. It pissed him off when the world was cruel to her.

"So I might need to ask you some stuff," she said.

"Sure, shoot."

"Off the record. The department can't know I'm divulging..."

"Yeah, yeah, usual rules apply. What's the deal?"

There was a pause. He heard a clicking, knew she was nibbling at her thumbnail, like she always did when she was worried, indecisive. He let her think.

Eventually she said, "Fuck it. You wanna get pissed?"

He grinned again. "You never have to ask me twice."

"I'll meet you at Murphy's in an hour. I can ask you about this stuff then."

Steven nodded, then felt foolish because she couldn't see it. "Sure thing," he said. "And when we're loaded we can track down this married fuckknuckle and kick his ass."

Her laughter came again. "I love it when you get all big brotherly."

"I might not be your big brother, but I do see it as kinda

my job."

"I know." Her voice was suddenly soft. "I appreciate it. See you in an hour."

She hung up and he cradled the phone for several moments while he sipped twelve-year-old malt. Like a big brother. He really did feel that way. Perhaps that's why the brief fling in their late teens had felt so weird and they'd gone straight back to being buddies. They'd needed to try the lover thing, it became unavoidable, but it had been a fumbling comedy of errors and just not right. If you know someone long enough, they're as good if not better than family. Steven and Abby worked best that way and it was something they both valued pretty much above all else.

Knowing Abby's appetite for drinking, he decided he'd better line his stomach. Thankfully Maeve Clemens had been by the day before. His friendly neighbor, her tiny body preceding her round behind everywhere she went, like she was a half-human, half-bumblebee. She was the sweetest woman Hines had ever known, and often "accidentally" made too much of one meal or another and dropped the leftovers by. Yesterday it was chicken and rice, and it served him well as ballast.

He smiled as he ate. He was the youngest resident in the building by a good thirty years, not yet forty, though he was showing a little gray in the tight curls above his ears, bright strands against his dark skin. But he liked what Abby called his old folks' home. It was peaceful and he was looked after.

He finished the food, downed the last of the glass and stood, limped to the door. He tied scratched and faded Doc Martens to his feet and dragged a long, dark coat over his jeans and dark blue, heavy-knit sweater as a shield against the autumn cold and seemingly endless rain.

Janusz was in the lobby checking his mailbox as Steven headed for the doors. The old man's papery white face was screwed up, a dripping cap clutched in one gnarled hand.

"Hell of a day to be going out," Janusz said.

"Ain't it always?" Hines asked with a grin.

He left the Pole's wheezing laughter behind and paused at the top of the short flight of stone steps leading to the street. He flexed his right leg a few times, warming it up for walking. Sometimes it was worse than others, but just lately all the wet weather seemed to be making the old injury more of a hindrance than ever. Well, he didn't need to hurry and he'd still get to Murphy's well before Abby. It was better than drinking in his apartment alone.

2

A dank, slick alleyway on the edge of Cleveport City. Rain drips from fire escapes, runs down the walls in grimy sheets. A man, wrapped in ragged, filthy coats and socks but no shoes, stumbles into the gloom between the tall buildings, seeking oblivion. His grizzled face is twisted, permanently on the verge of collapsing into hysterical tears. He shakes the brown paper-wrapped bottle in his dirty hand. It sloshes encouragingly.

In the deepest shadows at the alley's end he finds comfort on piles of broken garbage bags, vomiting their contents onto the old cobbles. He sinks to the ground, stifles an insistent sob, swigs. The cheap liquor burns and the pain begins to numb. He swigs again. And again.

His blurring gaze falls on a dark greenblack patch among the trash, shimmering faintly. The man leans forward, blinks. The patch is a miniature phosphorescent sea with a strange forest of minute mushrooms gently waving on dark stalks mere millimeters tall. The man cocks his head, his tired ears catching a sound like bells, like the distant voices of angels. The bottle clinks dully against the cobbles, forgotten, as he moves forward on hands and knees. He leans in, the softly glimmering domes draw him forward with glowing green, with mysterious song.

The man cries out as every mushroom top bursts, his face scant inches away. Clouds of swirling particles swarm up through the air like green smoke and engulf his head, invade his mouth, nose, eyes, burn his skin.

He stumbles backward, wailing softly as he claws the flesh of his cheeks, gouges knuckles into eye sockets. He collapses onto the garbage sacks, more rotten detritus pulsing out. For a moment, he's still, but for the rapid rise and fall of his chest as he gulps shallow breaths.

He calms, a smile flickers the corners of his crusty lips. His eyes blink open, solid greenblack glistening orbs in a pale, filthy face. He pulls himself to his feet, strips off layer after layer of clothing until his scrawny frame stands naked in the gloomy rain. He laughs, deep, phlegmy. He stalks out into the night, a hunger like he has never known even in his deprived lifetime chewing at his soul. Car horns blare and people shout and laugh as he staggers across the road and into a small side street, hidden from the crying night again in the shadows of tall buildings.

3

Hines sat nursing a beer. When Abby arrived they would hit the scotch. He'd long ago learned to pace himself against her capacity. People in Murphy's were a strange mix of lowlifes and losers, mostly harmless, sometimes dangerous. Most importantly there were no cops, which was why Abby liked the place. *I have to spend all my waking hours with the bastards, I don't want to drink with them too.*

She knew the hypocrisy of her words, admitted she could be the most bastard cop out there sometimes. Steven smiled at the memory of her lambasting the force she was married to. The force that had made her, living up to her father's legacy despite her gender and her skin. Her mom had died of breast cancer when Abby was sixteen, she'd largely taken care of herself, in awe of her dad, until she was eighteen and then ran straight to the Academy.

"What are you grinning about, fuckwit?"

He looked up, shook his head. "Lovely to see you too, Abs."

She wore tight jeans and a tailored black blazer over a white button-up shirt. She threw the jacket on the seat beside her, slumped down on the opposite side of the booth and put a shot of whiskey in front of him. "Get off the fairy juice, we have serious drinking to do."

He skulled the rest of the beer and toasted her with the whiskey tumbler. "To fuckknuckles everywhere."

"And their dumbass wives." She slammed the shot without a wince and waved at Sal across the crowded room. Sal gave her a nod, knowing all she needed to from the gesture. Abby stared at the glass. "I had meant to make that last a bit longer."

"It's all right, you'll have another one soon enough."

"I promised myself I wouldn't let this asshole get to me, Steve."

He saw a glisten in the corner of her eye. No way she'd cry in public, she was too much of a hardass for that, but it showed how much she really was hurt. He squeezed her arm. "Fuck him. And the wife he rode in on."

Abby grinned, sat up straighter. Sal arrived and put four doubles on the table. "Saving myself some shoe leather. You two look like you're in for the night."

"You're an angel in an apron, Sal," Abby said, pushed two glasses across to Steve. "Come on, pussy, catch up."

"I'll keep an eye open for empties," Sal said as she set sail through the sea of flesh and disappeared.

Steven downed the first whiskey, picked up the second. The third sat threatening him on the table. He could already feel tomorrow's regret nipping at his heels. "So what's the secret business you're not supposed to be telling me?" he asked.

"We've got some unexplained corpses."

"That's not unusual for Cleveport City."

"We get un*known* corpses all the time in this city. These are un*explained*. We don't know how they died."

Steven sipped, frowned. "Coroner no use?"

She gave him a patented Abby Jones look. "He can't figure it."

"How many?"

"Six so far. They all seem to have died completely inexplicably, no recognizable cause of death at all. They all share some strange similarities though. I've got a hunch there's going to be a lot more."

Steven had learned to trust Abby's hunches. Most of the force had. She'd made sergeant in no time based on her tenacity and skills and a lot of that came down to a powerful sixth sense for the job. She was about the most magical untalented person he knew. Her father had been the same, which only made it harder for her now to see him in a care home, often not even able to remember her name. "So what do you think I can do about this?" he asked, his intuition already buzzing.

"I have no way to be sure, but I think all six victims were… you know. Like you. Three I *know* were. Thought you might help with the others."

Steven raised his palms, surprised at her openness with something she did her best to disbelieve despite the evidence that came in the form of *him*. "Happy to help, but the police don't officially recognize anything arcane. How's it gonna be of use?"

Abby drank again, frowned. "Officially I call it hocus pocus bullshit, Hines. But I've seen enough from you since we were kids to know there's more in the world than most people admit. Three of these guys were associated with people or societies that you've told me are arcane or arcane-connected. I need to know if the rest were."

Not officially recognizing his bullshit was an understatement. For everything they shared in explicit detail, his talent and the existence of talents in others was something she blatantly ignored, usually changing the subject as soon as it came up. It was the only thing about her, about their friendship, that bothered him. She knew it was all real, maybe one day she'd admit it. "Okay," he said. "Got something to show me?"

She pulled six manila folders from her bag, spread them out on the table, two lines of three. She pointed to the top row. "These three I know are… you know." She waggled her fingers at him.

"Some connection with talents," he offered.

"Yeah, exactly. I've kept up my lists over the years." Her voice carried her skepticism far better than her expression. She indicated the three nearest Steven. "These I don't know."

He opened the first folder. A young face stared back at him, paper-clipped to a sheaf of notes and a coroner's report. Male, maybe twenty years old and completely unfamiliar. He read the name, a few details. "Not a clue on this one."

He opened the next. A woman, early thirties, long auburn hair and a sneer that could freeze hot soup. One side of his mouth curled up in distaste. "This is Yvonne Veloitte. She's a technomancer from Johnson's crew. Nasty bitch. Can't say anyone is likely to miss her."

"Technomancer?" Abby's eyes narrowed, her face fixed in the expression she wore when she had to admit to stuff beyond the normal. Hines had never understood why she resisted so much, but at heart she just wanted to see more justice and less cruelty in the world.

He nodded. "You know, uses magic to enhance tech and vice versa. All about melding mind, body and machine, new wave of human evolution, all that shit."

Abby tipped her head to one side. "You don't approve?"

"I don't really have an opinion. They're usually a weird bunch and I don't want to be a cyborg. And Johnson's lot are some of the whackiest."

Abby shook it off, nodding at the files. "But she's got talent, you're certain?"

"Definitely."

He took the third folder, opened it. A man in his twenties, fit-looking, kind of angry around the eyes. He didn't recognize the face or name, but there were a few familiar people in the Known Associates list. "This guy is a stranger to me, but half the goons he hung out with have talents or talent connections."

"So it's likely this guy does too?"

"Well, that's not a given. Look at you and me. But the possibility is strong, at least."

Abby pursed her lips, stared at the folders across the dirty, scratched tabletop. "Bit too much to be coincidence?"

She was onto something. "There are a lot of folk with skills and interests beyond the mundane in this city. Well, everywhere else too, but Cleveport attracts more for some reason. But there aren't *that* many talented people compared to the general populace, even here. We're a tiny fraction in the grand scheme of things. So yeah, this does seem to be a strangely coincidental collection."

Abby leaned back, quietly sipped scotch. She was on her third, so Hines quickly finished his second to catch up, felt the buzz rising. He let her ruminate. Eventually she said, "Still gives me fuck all though, eh?"

He shrugged. "I guess so."

She looked up, her eyes a little reddened. He wondered if that was the drink or the hurt. Or both. "Could they have died...?" Her question petered out.

"What? Magically?"

She nodded.

Steven drank, thought about it. "I guess so. There are millions of ways to kill a person including lots of magical ones. But any kind of death usually leaves a trace."

"Can you look at them for me? If I get you into the morgue, can you, you know...?" She waved her hands like a stage magician.

Steve laughed. "I'm a citymage, not some kind of magical surgeon. And really, I'm a bloody average citymage."

Abby looked crestfallen. "Do you know anyone who is?"

"A magical surgeon?" He smirked and leaned over to pinch her cheek when she scowled.

"Fuck you, Hines!" But a half-smile tugged at her lips. "Seriously though, do you know anyone who could look at the bodies and see if there's been something weird at work?"

"It's possible, yeah."

She nodded once, decisive, raised her glass. "Good. And after a lot more of these we'll crash at your place and in the morning you can take me to see this Johnson technowanker guy."

"Technomancer."

"Whatever. Drink up."

"But I don't really know him well, I just know that Yvonne..."

"Shut the fuck up and drink, Hines." She waved at Sal for more whiskey.

4

Steven staggered from his bed, driven by a desperate need to piss. He walked past Abby on the sofa, mouth open and sucking air like an industrial machine. Her long black, wavy hair, usually tied back, lay spread across the couch arm in a messy fan. He half-smiled, trying to ignore the axes pounding his brain. She would wake without a hangover and then insist on a massive fried breakfast and yet still maintain her athletic curves. She also busted her ass on a regular basis to maintain them. But he could always see the little girl he grew up with hiding behind her skin, scared and vulnerable. Then again, perhaps that was him projecting and doing her a disservice with his own weaknesses. He absently ran a hand over his slowly increasing pot belly. His own youthful athleticism was beginning to soften up.

He relieved himself and turned to splash water on his face. The mirror above the sink mocked him, hiding behind its curtain of black cloth. He ignored it, pretended it wasn't there. He hated mirrors. His bad knee pulsed painfully in sympathy and he grimaced. He dried his face and stumbled back across the small lounge room, planning on another few hours of sleep. He cried out as his shin connected with the edge of the coffee table and Abby chuckled. "Well done, Nureyev."

"Screw you, lady."

She swung her legs off the sofa, holding the blanket around herself, wearing nothing but undies and a t-shirt she kept in his dresser and always wore when she crashed at his place. "You look like shit."

He sneered, rubbed his face. "You up now then, are you?"

"Yep. Breakfast time."

He sat in the armchair opposite with a groan, one hand absently rubbing at his knee. "Let's do some more sleeping first."

"No, come on. Bacon and eggs on me, then we go and see this technowanker."

He looked up to correct her and shook his head at her stupid grin. "You're not human, you know that?"

"Superhuman is the word you're looking for, weakass. Come on, get dressed."

They sat at a bench facing out the large plate glass window of Berloni's Cafe, drinking mugs of coffee and eating greasy food. Steven reluctantly admitted he was feeling better, though he feared for his heart. The almost perfect riff of Stevie Wonder's *Superstition* persisted over the clatter of crockery and the hubbub of conversation at their backs.

Rain pounded the sidewalk outside, made everything a slick darkness under a heavy slate sky. The cement and aged stone of the buildings, reaching gothically for the storm clouds, seemed to hem them in, adding shadows to the wet grime. Traffic cruised slowly by, moving lights enhancing the glow from offices and stores along the street. Steven chewed lazily, mesmerized by the downpour. He let his mind drift out through the glass, searching for young Parker, the lost drug-addict. Every window was an eye in the city, and if he blinked one he could look out of another. His magic was simple, and not well-developed beyond his strange affinity with the urban sprawl. He barely deserved the name citymage, but since his rude birth onto the cold stone of a Cleveport alley his connection had been undeniable. He used what small amount of magic he had casually, flicked his vision from one pane to the next, saw snapshots of Cleveport, like clicking through an old 3-D View-Master. And again, he felt more in tune than ever, more potent. Disconcerting, but he chose to enjoy it while it lasted.

He skipped from one glass-paned cityeye to the next, scanning.

"So this Johnson," Abby asked. "What do I need to know?"

Steven jumped, distracted from his search. His mind snapped back to Berloni's. "I told you, I don't know him well."

"Sure. But what *do* you know?"

"Well, he's head of a crew called Cyberdawn. They're just a gang really, ragtag bunch of weirdoes who all share a passion for mixing magic and tech. They enhance computers to be super fast and stuff like that. They enchant hard drives and bond with them biologically to have massive amounts of mental storage, like the mother of all eidetic memories, bind cameras to their eyes, embed iPhones into their arms. All kinds of freaky shit. They sometimes get contracted for work by various groups, but they're usually self-contained. Self-obsessed, really. And very secretive, obviously, so they don't get what they call "lab-ratted". They're just waiting for their time. When you think you're the evolution of mankind, everyone else is kinda beneath you, you know?"

"They sound charming. Can they really do all that stuff ?"

Steven gave her the look. She rolled her eyes.

"So how do you know them?" she asked as she mopped up egg yolk with a chunk of toast.

"I've run across them a couple of times. Had a missing person's case once and the kid had joined Cyberdawn. Asked Johnson to make sure the kid's parents knew where to find her. Apparently Johnson sent her a maged photograph showing the kid happily waving with the note, 'All is well, I've evolved' scrolling across the image. It disintegrated once both parents had looked at it, according to them."

"Nice."

"Yeah. Parents were talented, so it was okay in the long run. The only reason Cyberdawn would have done something so blatant, I guess. Untalented kids run off to join some strange religious cult or the army or something. Talented kids run off and become walking computers."

Abby looked at him, eyebrows raised. "Anything else?"

"Nah. I've used them and they've used me over the years, little things. Nothing much. Johnson lives in a big old place out near the commercial docks, courtesy of the proceeds of his unique skills. A lot of his crew live there with him, others blow in and out."

"Off we go then."

"You're springing for the cab. I'm not waiting for trains or buses in this weather." He waved out the window at the persistent and torrential Pacific North-West autumn.

Abby blew him a kiss and pulled on her jacket, headed off to the counter to pay for breakfast.

5

Many bars in Cleveport City open around the clock and many patrons care little for the hour. *Clarence's* is a dingy place in a dingy alley and home to a collection of people doing their best to forget all kinds of things when a naked man staggers in. His stench precedes him, despite the rain washing down his pale, scrawny form. The drinkers laugh, raised from their despondency by the moment's absurdity, until they see his shining greenblack eyes. Those flat orbs, no white, no pupil, scan the room as the man weaves gently as if in a soft breeze. Around his eyes are tiny lumps. As he opens his mouth to groan, hair-like filaments seem to flex and wave forwards.

"The hell is your deal, buddy?" the barman says, voice quavering with concern as he reaches below the bar for Justice, his trusty pump-action shotgun. It's saved his bacon before.

The hobo stumbles to the nearest patron, an overweight man somewhere between fifty and seventy with a face a Bassett hound would call sad-looking. The man's name is Ted Griffin, everyone calls him Griff and to his ears it always sounds like Grief. "Get the fuck away from me, man," Griff says, nose wrinkling in disgust.

The hobo reaches out and Griff sees the palms of his hands are covered in tiny, black hairs. Or spines, too thick for hair. Similar spines bristle around the hobo's eyes, ring his lips. They writhe across his cheeks, chest, arms. Disgusted, Griff notices the filthy flaccid cock, forested with sharp black needles. Before he can move, the hobo grabs Griff by the forearms and the agony in Griff's flesh is blinding. He howls like a whipped dog as a million thin spikes worm into his flesh.

A nearby drinker jumps up, swings a heavy punch at the side of the hobo's head. The punch connects with something that feels more like turf than bone. The drinker pauses, stares in pain and shock at his suddenly bristled knuckles, and the hobo drops Griff to the floor and staggers into his attacker. He grabs throat and hand, sinks a wide bite into the man's neck where it meets his shoulder. The man squeals.

A shot rings out, deafening in the tiny bar. The hobo's shoulder explodes in a bloodless burst of fibrous matter, like an old doormat blown apart. The elderly woman holding a Magnum in a trembling hand stares dumbfounded. The hobo falls towards her. She screams in the hobo's spiny grasp as the barman makes it around the bar, puts the barrel to the naked man's head and Justice roars. That fetid head explodes like a hay bale, tiny filaments of green and black bursting out, no flesh, no bone, no brains, no blood. Still the hobo grabs at the woman even as he falls, still she howls in pain.

The barman pumps and fires, pumps and fires, point blank range blowing the hobo to pieces that scatter the floor in fibrous lumps that eventually fall still. The barman stares, shaking.

Griff stumbles groggily to his feet, collapses into a chair. He looks at his arms, still burning like they've been doused in acid. Those tiny black spines bristle from his flesh, hundreds of them, searing before they burrow away.

With a sob, he plucks at them, tries to pull them out, but they shiver and vanish into his saggy skin. The other man and woman touched by the strange attacker are wailing and scratching at spiny infestations of their own.

"The fuck is going on here, man?" the barman says, still staring at the lumps of hobo on his floor. They're breaking down, becoming piles of scattered vegetable matter like half-rotted grass, threaded through with waxy, pale fibers. "I'm calling the cops." He rushes back behind the bar, scrabbles for the phone.

Griff is light-headed, like he's been drinking for twelve hours rather than six. He stands and heads groggily for the door. Outside. He just needs to be outside, fresh air, away from… away from here.

"Where you going, Griff?" the barman shouts. Griff doesn't respond and a voice at the other end of the line distracts the barman. "I need the police out here right now!" he says.

Griff shuffles into the rain, turns his face up to the sky's tears, revels in their cool touch, and walks away.

6

Hines sat in the back of the cab and watched rain streak the windows as they headed for the port. He half listened to Abby complaining about something procedural at work while he let his mind skim the streets and alleys, scan the smaller buildings, seeking poor young Parker in the big metropolis.

He knew it wouldn't matter if he paid little attention to Abby. He was unlikely to understand the details anyway and sometimes she just needed to talk, to vocalize things that got under her skin. She didn't expect an answer or a solution. Just an ear. They turned onto older streets, heading into the original port settlement of Cleveport, old stone and wood, and still the real heart of the city no matter what the business district or executive elite suggested.

As they turned at the giant memorial statue of Samuel Cleve, atop his pedestal, pointing out to sea, Hines twisted in his seat, looked out the back window. "Stop the cab!"

The driver braked hard, his face concerned in the rearview mirror. "You're not gonna puke in here are you, buddy?"

"No, no, sorry. I just… I saw something. Can you wait a moment, please?"

"You're on the meter, pal. I'll wait as long as you like."

Steven turned to Abby. She had one eyebrow raised, lips a flat line of tolerant disapproval. "Is it work?" she asked.

"Yeah. Young kid, been missing a couple of weeks. His mother came to me and I took on the contract."

Abby nodded. "You can, what? Feel him out there?"

Steven frowned, chewed his lower lip. "Yeah. Really clearly. Too clearly. These things are always hit and miss, but this is strangely intense. Can you wait here while I do a quick run?"

Abby laughed. "Fuck no. I know you, you might be gone for hours." She checked the meter, handed the driver a few dollars extra. "Thanks."

The driver shrugged, took the money with a nod.

"Come on then," Abby said. "We'll go together."

The cab crawled away from the deep, worn curb as they stood in the pouring rain, collars pulled up.

"This fucking weather," Abby grumbled.

Steven looked into the leaden clouds, squinted against the downpour. "When was the last dry day we had?"

"Who knows? Cleveport's always been one wet and miserable shithole, but just lately it's worse than ever." Abby caught Hines's look. "What?"

He shook his head. "You sound more like me than yourself right now."

She laughed. "Screw you, Steve. Come on, do your thing. I'm getting soaked out here."

She deliberately looked away, staring into nothing up the busy street as Hines turned to the nearest window. It was an empty shop, peeling *For Lease* signs covering the grimy pane, but there was enough uncovered for his purposes. He looked into a patch of smeared glass, saw the rubbish and dust of the abandoned shop inside. A pile of coupons and junk mail sat like a tumor inside the door. He blinked. His mind merged with his city and Cleveport cooed softly in his mind, pleased to feel him with her again, instead of simply passing over her parts. He sensed something unusual in her presence, an uneasiness he couldn't quite define. *What's up, girl?* But her communication was never as simple as language. She vibed him with discomfort. He frowned, vowed to take some time to commune with her more deeply, to figure out what this sensation was. Meanwhile, the sensation of Grant Parker dragged at his attention.

Through the window now he saw a small street, a couple of cars cruised by. The threads of connection to Parker snaked through his mind, overlaid his mental map and physical vision, stronger than any he had experienced before. He blinked again, followed the aether-bound filaments of Parker's psychic signature. He saw a broken down townhouse, one of the old, narrow workers' cottages from the boom days of the harbor industry. Some of those places were fixed up beautifully, modern desirable residences for the city's elite. Others, on the smaller streets, the ones still under the purview of the bureaucrats that had yet to go up for public auction, were often squats and drug dens. Steven looked into one of those, saw four or five young people lounging on battered furniture. One of them glowed with relevance. Grant Parker, sucking hard on a bong. The dirty water bubbled and his face disappeared in a cloud of thick, bluish smoke.

There was a broken mirror on the wall above Parker's head. Gritting his teeth, Hines looked into it. Ignoring *her* shadow, always trying to ignore her gossamer presence in silvered glass, he looked at the reflection of the room instead. It showed a window opposite. Hines bounced his talented vision off the mirror, back out into the street. A sign was screwed high on the wall: *Carters Lane*.

He'd found him.

"Well?" Abby's expression did nothing to hide just how unhappy she was as she sheltered in the shop's doorway.

He gave her his most impish grin, one he knew would soften her. "We need to go to Carters Lane."

Abby pulled out her phone, tapped up a map and squinted at it. "Three blocks that way." She pointed towards the port.

"Okay. Let's go."

"We were in a cab going that way before."

Steven took her hand, pulled her into the rain. "Come on, grumpy pants. I didn't know where it was going to lead. When I catch a thread like that, I have to grab it wherever it is."

"Is it usually this clear? Sounds pretty specific."

Steven frowned as they walked. "No. I don't think I've ever had such an obvious snag before. And the vision was so easy to pass from here to there. Parker must have been this way recently, but it's still like my talent's far stronger than usual."

"Does that bother you?"

"Yes and no. I'm not going to complain if it earns me money. I don't get many jackpots."

They walked for five minutes, giving up on any possibility of staying dry. When they reached Carters Lane, Steven said, "Can you wait here while I check?"

Abby scowled. "You don't trust me or something?"

"No offense, but you reek of cop. These kids would bolt. I just need to confirm this is where he's staying."

Abby nodded and stepped into a clothing store doorway, an expensive harborside boutique aimed at the wealthy tourist or the label-conscious elite. "I'll be in here then."

Hines headed along the small lane until his senses pinged again, the thread clear as day so close. The house had boarded up windows on the second story and a roughly patched front door. Only a single front pane of glass was intact, which had been lucky for him, but it was mostly obscured by cardboard taped up on the inside. The few gaps, including the ones he had looked in and out through remotely to see the street sign, emitted a weak light. He stepped up to the door and knocked.

Scuffling and tight voices from inside and a couple of slams and shifting furniture. Hines imagined the squatters quickly hiding bongs and baggies and whatever else they might have on display. Grant was into way harder stuff than weed. The boy's mother had admitted it. The door cracked open and he grinned. Grant Parker himself. He'd hoped it would be, it made things easier.

"What?" Grant's eyes were sunken in his skull, red and wet. His skin was sallow across his cheekbones, pale and sweat-sheened. He gave off the acrid odor of the dedicated junkie.

Steven shook his head. This kid was most likely well past saving. The world had a habit of chewing people up, fucking them over and then they died. Why would this kid be any different? Salvation wasn't really his job. Just finding them if he could. "Dave Callow here?" he asked, affecting the rough voice of a fellow user.

"Dave who?"

"Callow. Used to squat here."

Grant shook his head, started closing the door. "Not anymore, he don't."

"Do you live here?"

The door stopped, opened again slightly. "The fuck does that have to do with you?"

Steven raised his palms. "Just making sure, you know? If you live here, then you know for sure Dave doesn't. You don't live here, maybe Dave's out and you just haven't met him yet or something."

Grant laughed, shook his head. "You fucking idiot. Yeah, I live here. And no, there's no Dave Gallows or whatever here and ain't gonna be."

The door slammed shut, but Steven had all he needed. He missed Dave Callow. It was no random bit of imagination using that name. Dave had been a good friend until the world – this city more specifically – had chewed him up and left him for dead too. Hines had found him, cold from an OD.

He shook off the memory and pulled his phone out, went back to the corner, dialing. "Hello, Mrs Parker? It's Steven Hines… Yes, actually, good news of a sort. Grant is staying in a squat, number four Carters Lane, down near the port… Yep… No, it's no problem… Yes, just deposit the finder's fee into the same bank account. Thanks very much, I appreciate it." He listened to the woman's effusive thanks, how other PIs had been useless, but he had found Grant so quickly. "Yes, ma'am. I guess I have skills other PIs don't. Feel free to recommend me to anyone who you think might use my services." She didn't need to know his services were magically enhanced. He tried to keep that secret from pretty much everyone.

He took a deep breath. He should warn her. "Mrs Parker, your son is staying with a pretty wasted bunch of people. His drug habit is quite extensive… Yes, I hope you can too. Bye, ma'am."

He tapped on the window of the clothing store and Abby looked up from examining a rack of jackets. She looked quite relieved to see him.

"I was getting close to buying some shit from that awful place, just for something to do."

"You can pretend all you like, you love a bit of clothes shopping."

Abby sneered, refused to rise to the bait. "Success?" She gestured back down the lane.

"Of a sort. He's there and his parents will be able to find him. His mother was ecstatic that I'd succeeded, but she'll be pretty disappointed when she sees him."

"Too far gone?"

"Almost certainly. Still, you never know."

Abby squeezed his shoulder, gave a soft smile. "Yeah, you never know. You've done your bit. Well done."

"Thanks."

"So where's this Cyberdawn place?"

Steven pointed down towards the old original harbor, which stood more as a tourist attraction than anything functional. Impressive stone structures that might once have housed goods for shipping or bunks for stevedores were now home to high-end restaurants and bars. The only traffic afloat was a mixture of bright orange water taxis, sightseeing boats, and a huge replica three-master moored up for photo opportunities and the occasional wedding reception for a particularly well-off couple or extravagant corporate junket. Over the old three and four story buildings, tall cranes arced in the distance like giant insects, lifting rectangular containers on and off huge ships. That was where the industry happened, the real business of distribution well out of sight of the heart of Cleveport's public face. "Not too far down there. We may as well walk the rest of the way."

As they strolled, hunched against the downpour, he thought about how easily he had found Grant Parker. Was it just a piece of luck? Right place, right time? But the magic had felt stronger, clearer than ever. It bothered him. Why were his average skills suddenly so much more effective?

7

Gina Baker smiles at her boyfriend, lifts the tiny ampule in a toast. Trev grins back at her and raises his own. They tap them together like miniature champagne flutes.

"Been a while," Gina says. "I'm looking forward to this."

"I already hit one of these, you wait and see how damn good it is!"

Gina grins. "Let's go." She concentrates, lets her magic out. Just a simple illusory manifestation, she's never been a particularly powerful mage. But she's only nineteen. Plenty of time to get better, stronger. So Trev assures her anyway, with his worldly twenty-seven-year-old knowledge. Let him think he's wise and that she idolizes him. It's doing no harm. Not while he scores the good stuff and she doesn't have to pay. Plus, he's an animal in the sack. Her gentle enchantment buzzes through her and the clear liquid in the small vial shivers and swirls, turns multi-colored like oil on water and twists into the air like smoke.

Gina leans forward and sniffs, sucks it all up. Colors burst behind her eyes, a rush washes through her from toes to crown and back again. Her body lightens and her mind swims. An involuntary smile curls her lips as she sinks back into the cushions of Trev's oversized, overstuffed sofa. She becomes aware of him snorting his own hit, hears his soft, drawn out, "Wooooaahhh!" of appreciation.

She's never felt the mis as strongly, as deeply. This is some of the best stuff she's ever known. She had no idea it could be this good.

"You feelin' dis?" Trev slurs. "S'like a freight train of cotton candy through my eyes."

She giggles, tries to speak but just splutters softly.

"Seriously, Geenie, this stuff is mad. Best I ever had, you know. Can you feel the colors?"

Gina giggles again. "Yeah," she manages. "It's a trip."

She senses movement, realizes her eyes are closed and flutters them open. Trev is standing over her, something in his hand, the touch of his magic in the room. He holds another hit. She waves a hand, but it barely lifts from her lap. "Nah nah, n'more. Not yet."

Trev laughs, puts a hand behind her head. "C'mon, Geenie, this is the really, really good stuff."

The vapor crawls up her nostrils, its metallic, multi-hued tendrils snake swiftly through her brain. She huffs out most of it, can't help taking back some and Trev laughs. He stands back, activates another one and sniffs hard. She wonders what's the point, it's so strong she's only going to pass out. She'll sleep it off and wake in a few hours, groggy and cotton-wool brained, gasping for a drink and with a dull headache. Not like a hangover. Trev calls it a sadache.

But a subtle fear passes through her, because this is like nothing else. She's done way more than two bangs of mis in a row before and never felt this way. Hell, she's done a half dozen through the course of an evening before and eventually passed out, but never from being as totally wasted as this.

She blinks rapidly, her vision hazy. Trev stands right where he was when he snorted, only he seems frozen. His eyes are wide, absolute terror on his face, like he can see the maw of the monster opening right in front of him, about to bite down and swallow him whole. Drool runs from his slack lower lip.

"Trev!" she says, but it comes out like a high-pitched croak, not a word at all.

Trev claws clumsily at his face, drives a finger one

knuckle deep up a nostril. He begins to mutter and stammer, spittle flying. He drops to his knees, right in front of her, but she can't even sit forward to reach out to him. Her mouth hangs open, saliva dribbling over her chin. A weak sob escapes her as Trev tips over sideways, eyes still wide open but blank and empty. She knows, deep inside, in the last clearly thinking part of her brain, that he's already dead. What the fuck have they done? What is this stuff, this stronger than ever stuff?

Her brain fades out in a kaleidoscope of euphoric rush, swirling colors and bone-deep fear as everything goes dark.

8

Jerry Rundle was the kind of cop people called a grizzled veteran. He was a cliché, seen it all before, never surprised by the depravity of the common man. Or woman. He also prided himself on being one of the few cops in the world without a drinking problem, but he was overweight and smoked a pack a day, so who was he to judge? Though right now, he could really use a drink. He'd insisted on light duties while his partner, Maloney, was recovering in the hospital from three gunshot wounds. Rundle had been through a few partners already in his decades in the department and he wasn't about to start with a new one. And he wasn't going to be tied to a desk in the meantime. Maloney would be okay in a few weeks. It'd take more than a street punk drug runner to end that big guy's career. Rundle could sure use the man's calming presence beside him now, but he was flying solo for the foreseeable future.

"Mind if I smoke in here?" he asked the white-faced barman.

The barman shook his head. "Against regs, but what the fuck do I care? You're the law."

Jerry smiled crookedly. "No, I ain't. I'm the law's servant, trying to enforce the unenforceable. But I cede your point." He pulled a pack of Luckies from inside his long, dark trenchcoat, tapped out a smoke and lit it, stared at the lumps of damp black grass on the floor, woven through with pale threads like dental floss. "This was a guy?" he asked, sure the man had been enjoying too much of his own supply. He pulled out his notepad.

"Yeah, yeah, he came stumbling in here stark naked, filthy and stinking, scrawny as a chicken. All dirty beard and matted hair, gross hobo, you know?"

Rundle nodded. "Name?"

"I don't know his fucking name, man."

"No, your name. For my report."

"Oh, Callahan. Pete Callahan."

"And you run this place alone?"

"I have help on the weekends, but we're quiet during the week."

"You own the bar?"

"I lease the building, but the business is mine."

"And business is good?"

"Sure, I guess."

Rundle looked up from his pad. "You guess? You owe anyone money, Pete?"

Pete's eyes widened. "The hell are you going with this?"

"Building a picture, that's all. Gotta get the whole thing in perspective."

"For fuck's sake, man…"

"You owe any money, Pete?"

Callahan sighed, slumped onto a bar stool. "Sure, I got some debts, credit cards and shit. But I'm not in any trouble, nothing with the mob or anything like that. Just usual shit. I do okay here. People always want a drink, you know? And a certain type of person likes this type of bar."

"And what type of bar is this, Pete?"

"Quiet. Discreet. The type where people know they'll be left alone."

Rundle nodded, pencil scratching at his notebook. This guy seemed to be pretty straight up and down, honest in his appraisal of his own life. And he seemed sober enough. Which was a shame, given the report he was making. It sounded like something only a person very drunk or very high would make up. "Tell me again how it went down. Every detail."

Jerry made more notes as Callahan repeated the story. It was consistent with the first rushed telling when Rundle had arrived. More detailed, but consistent. And those details were insane. When Callahan stopped talking, went to pour himself two fingers of bourbon, Rundle crouched and poked the end of his pencil at the fibrous lumps on the floor. They were damp and appeared to be breaking down. Melting away. He looked up to Callahan. "These were dry before?"

"Yep. He just burst apart when I shot him. He kept moving for a while even after I'd blown his head off, so I shot him til the fucking twitching stopped."

Rundle nodded. "Right." He pulled an evidence baggie from his pocket and used the pencil to scrape a sample in. He looked up, scanned the ceiling, the corners. "CCTV?"

Callahan frowned. "Kinda let that lapse a bit."

"Lapse?"

"My old system broke down and I got a bunch of quotes for replacements, but didn't get it fitted yet."

"How long you been without it?"

"'Bout a month."

"What if you got robbed?"

Callahan shrugged. "Just hoping I wouldn't. I've got a guy coming week after next to put a new system in, friend of my cousin's. He's doing me a good deal, but it meant waiting til he was free."

Rundle stood, grimaced as his knees cracked. "So you've got no footage of this morning. Nothing to prove your story?"

Callahan shrugged again, looked at the floor.

Rundle knew a nutcase when he saw one, and Callahan was not in that league. The man believed what he said and Jerry's internal sensors told him something really strange was happening here. Another cop might write it off as beyond the job description, but Jerry didn't operate like that. He wasn't about to simply drop it. Although he had nothing much to go on. "You said three people were here, and they all got attacked."

Callahan poured another bourbon. "Yeah. And they all just left. They went kinda quiet after and just… left."

"How hurt were they?"

"Hard to know really. One guy was bleeding pretty badly at the neck."

"You know these people well?"

Callahan nodded to a customer coming in. Rundle waited while the man looked at the mess on the floor, shrugged and was served a drink. Callahan returned. "The bleeding guy and the old woman I don't know. I've seen them before, maybe, here and there, but they're not real regulars. The other guy, the one who got attacked first, was Griff. He's here all the time. Works a night shift and comes in from early til around lunchtime almost every day."

"Griff. Got any more than that?"

Callahan frowned, shook his head. "Griff is short for Griffin, I'm pretty sure. He lives in walking distance because he once told me he gets the bus back here from work so he can walk home when he's drunk."

Rundle snapped his notepad closed, pocketed it and his pencil inside his overcoat. "Okay. I'll check into what I can, but there's honestly very little here for me to follow up. Not even a body."

Callahan pointed at the lumps on the floor, smaller than ever.

Rundle nodded. "Yeah." He pulled his phone out and took photos from several angles. It had dissolved by at least half since he'd first seen it. He wondered if the sample in the sealed baggie would last. "For evidence, that's not very stable. I'll follow it up. I'll call if I get anything."

Callahan nodded and went behind the bar, pulled a broom from a shadowy corner. Jerry Rundle walked out into the rain. "This city, really," he muttered as he leaned forward to shield his phone from the weather. He speed-dialed the station. "Yeah, track me down anyone in the phonebook or elsewhere, surname Griffin, within a few blocks of Clarence's Bar." He paused, listened. "Yeah, that's the one. I need addresses. Thanks."

He missed Maloney more than ever when the weird stuff happened. At least with a partner he had someone to agree it was insane. On his own, it was harder to write things off. But lacking a partner was a feature of his life these days. It started when Lois left him ten years ago for their good lady doctor, but he wasn't bitter about it. Janice had been their GP for years, he had always liked her and hoped she'd do better by Lois than he ever had. The job had always lived between him and his wife. And Lois was happier than ever now she'd accepted the truth of who she was. They caught up for dinner sometimes, all three of them, but not often. Lois wouldn't be coming back to him, but Maloney would soon enough. He was happy in his own company until then.

He turned up the street and went in search of a meatball sandwich.

9

Steven and Abby looked up at the dark brown bricks of a large warehouse on the edge of the old side of Cleveport docks. Two huge roller doors stood closed like massive hooded eyes, a regular-sized door a little further along the building up a short flight of steps. White lattice windows with dirty panes of glass ranged along high on the wall. A steep metal roof rose above them, those busy cranes visible beyond.

"Big place for a bunch of nerds," Abby said, squinting against the rain.

Steven huffed a laugh. "Don't underestimate them. They're strange, but they have a certain power and respect in the underworld. And a lot of money."

"Fair enough. Come on, let's get out of this fucking weather."

They mounted the short flight of metal steps which rang dully with their tread. Steven knocked and they waited. After a moment, a voice sounded from a hidden speaker. "Yeah?"

"Wondered if we might speak to Johnson," Steven said.

"You got a warrant?"

Steven held up a finger at Abby's outraged intake of breath. "No, it's nothing like that. Just wanted to know if he might help us out, that's all. No one's in any trouble. Tell him it's Steven Hines."

"And who else?"

"And his friend. Just go and tell Johnson, will ya?"

There was a long moment of silence, then, "Wait."

"How did he know we were cops?" Abby asked, a frown creasing her brow.

Steven laughed. "We're not cops. You are. And honestly,

look at you in your blazer and tight tied hair."

"Fuck you, Hines."

Steven grinned and she couldn't help a smile of her own.

"I'm not ashamed of who I am," she said.

The door clicked open. Steven gave Abby a wink and pushed it wide.

The room was dim, a faint greenish glow from a monitor on a desk in the corner the only illumination. "Step inside and stand still," the voice from the speaker said.

"The hell is this?" Abby asked.

Hines shrugged. "Just play along. They have… quirks."

Abby shook her head but chose to say nothing more. They walked to the center of the room and waited. The door clicked shut behind them without any apparent mechanism to close it but Hines felt the slight shift in the air of magic at work. A fan of bright green light burst out of the monitor on the desk and swept up and down. Abby jumped and turned in a half crouch.

"Stand still," the disembodied voice instructed. "The scan will only take a moment."

Steven patted Abby's shoulder. A soft beep sounded.

"You've got a weapon," the voice said.

"Yeah, I'm a cop, remember." Abby's voice dripped disdain.

"Leave it on the desk. You can collect it when you leave."

Abby barked a laugh. "The fuck I will!"

"You have no warrant, you want to parley, so you follow our rules. Or you can leave."

Hines gave Abby a look and she hissed between her teeth. Reluctantly she pulled out her service piece and put it on the desk.

"This is against every reg in the book. If that's not here when we come back…"

"Oh, please," the voice interrupted. "We don't need a

cop's pea shooter."

Another door ahead of them opened and a young man, still in his teens, stood framed in light from behind. His hair was long and wild, he wore dungarees and combat boots and a headset with a lens like a small camera lowered over his right eye. "This way." His wasn't the voice from the speaker.

Steven and Abby followed him along a corridor. Twice Abby opened her mouth to say something and twice Hines silenced her with a warning finger. This was no time for her smartassery and that's all she'd be spouting.

They passed several closed rooms, ripples of magic here and there. Throughout the building a low hum resonated, but that was electronic rather than arcane. They went through another door at the end of the corridor that led into a large room with couches, bean bags, TVs, gaming consoles, pool and table tennis tables.

"Quite a playground you got here," Abby said.

"We relax sometimes," the kid said. "When there's not work to be done."

"You busy with work a lot?"

The kid paused to look at her. "All the time."

Abby nodded. "Oh. Well. Good."

Stairs led up from the lounge area to a second story and they followed the kid to another passageway that ended in a large door, covered in red leather studded into place. The kid tapped an intercom beside it. "They're here," he said.

"Bring them in."

Johnson's voice. He braced himself.

Johnson's office was massive and ostentatious. He sat behind a huge mahogany desk with a bank of the latticed windows visible from outside casting their light over his shoulders. An ornate perch stood alongside with a beautiful russet hawk gripping its T-bar top. The hawk's eyes tracked Hines and Abby as they entered. In one corner, a large dog sat strangely still. It was black and tan, a good proportion of Doberman in its heritage, and it wore a blank expression, neither wary nor relaxed. It simply watched them. Hines found it slightly unnerving.

All kinds of tech sat on smaller desks around the room and display cases bore sections of circuit board, small devices with screens and keyboards, unusual-looking, vaguely organic brushed aluminum structures. A large glass-fronted unit against one wall had several shelves of bell jars holding preserved body parts; hands with wires extending from a stump of wrist, eyes with camera lenses embedded in them, an arm with a series of long, narrow screens along it, melded into the skin. Hines looked away before he saw any more. It all creeped him out too much. Another cabinet held figurines of superheroes, Wolverine, Batman, Wonder Woman and many more he couldn't identify.

"Are these Tamagotchi?" Abby asked, her voice low.

"The entire range, yes." Johnson stood. He was tall, thin, somewhere between middle-age and gone to seed, but he had a strong bearing and confidence. He wore jeans and an Atari t-shirt, his hair tied back in a dark ponytail showing almost as much gray as black. His face was sharp and suspicious and he sported a jet goatee beard that had to be dyed at least once a week. He wore wire-rimmed glasses, the left lens rippling with coruscating green light as if something were being projected on it from the inside. A leather vambrace covered his left forearm.

Abby stared approvingly into the cabinet at shelf upon shelf of colorful, egg-shaped digital toys, each resting on a satin cushion. "Every one? Really? I had a couple of these as a kid. I loved them, but they always died."

Johnson nodded. "The early ones would die easily. Later versions are harder to kill, but I'm sure you could've managed it."

"The hell are you two on about?" Hines asked.

Abby turned to him with a smile. "Tamagotchi. Digital pets. All the rage in the 90s. Don't you remember I had these as a teenager?"

"No, not really."

"Anyway," Johnson said, doing nothing to hide his boredom. "Much as I respect your appreciation, I know my collection is impressive. To what do I owe this visit?"

Steven walked across the room, shook Johnson's hand. "Thanks for seeing us. This is Detective Sergeant Abby Jones. We're working on a case and wondered if you could maybe help us out? Nothing official, just a few questions."

Johnson popped one eyebrow up. "Nothing official?"

"What my idiot of a non-cop friend means," Abby said, "is that I'm just following up some leads. We wondered if you might be able to clear up a couple of loose ends for us."

Johnson looked Abby up and down, as if noticing her for the first time. "Why should I help you?"

"Er… why not? What do you have to lose?"

Johnson shrugged. "Hardly the point. What do I have to gain?"

"Do you have to gain anything? How about a nice warm glow from helping out?"

Johnson chuckled, shook his head. "We're not really interested in helping out the unevolved. Does the fox care for the rabbit? Does it get a warm glow from doing the rabbit a favor before it eats it?"

Abby's face twisted into what Hines called her sneerfrown. "You planning to eat us normal folk? Should I file a report?"

"Not actually eat you, Sergeant Jones, no. Don't be so literal."

"Look out," Hines said wearily. "The Cyberdawn manifesto."

"The singularity is coming," Johnson said, ignoring Hines completely. "Technology and humans are on a collision course to a new state of being. Minds uploaded to the cybercore. But there's magic too, and that can't be forgotten. People who think the future lies only in technology are as foolish as those who think magic has had its day. We're the link. We're the vanguard of human evolution, the first ones and the creators of the new order. When the singularity comes, we will be the new gods! We will reign over that new paradigm and all of you will serve us." He walked to one wall, strangely plain compared to the rest of the office, pressed a hidden button. The wall shimmered and winked out, a hologram concealing a large window. "Look."

Steven and Abby moved to see. Below was a huge room, bank upon bank of computer servers with several technicians moving calmly among them, tending to them as if they were patients in hospital beds.

"It's starting there, right now," Johnson said. "This is where magic and tech are creating a new race as we speak."

"All very well until there's a power cut," Abby said with a disdainful laugh. "Or a big solar flare or some terrorist dumps an EMP. Then what?"

Johnson drew a long breath in through his nose, shook his head like he was addressing a child. "What's the difference, do you think, Miss Jones? Hmm? What's different about our tech?"

"The magic, presumably?"

"Yes. And where does magic come from?"

"Fucking fairy land? I don't know."

Johnson nodded, walked back towards his desk. "Exactly, you don't know. It comes from the mind, Jones. It's a result of biology. Look closer."

Steven and Abby turned back, trying to spot what the hell this strange man was on about. Hines saw it first. Tubes running between the servers, flowing with what looked like blood plasma. Lit panels that bubbled gently, clearly a contained pale liquid of some kind, a technician sprinkling a white powder from a small tub into the top of an open chamber at the end of one server bank, like a pet store owner feeding fish.

"It's alive," he said quietly.

"Well done, Hines. Yes, it's alive. So a fucking EMP or anything else will have no more effect on it than it would have on your own body and its electrical signals. Evolution, Jones. Not machine. Not human. Not magic. All three combined and infinitely more powerful as a result. We're just biding our time until the tech catches up with our skills and desires. Then we will change the world. Already the magic has started getting stronger, surely even you can feel that, Hines?"

Steven looked at him, suddenly spooked. "Getting stronger?"

Johnson smiled. "Yes, you feel it. And it only highlights what a petty trickster you really are. The singularity is coming, but the technological singularity is only one very small part of it." He lifted his arm, opened the leather of the vambrace. His flesh beneath was bonded with a screen the length of his forearm that flowed with icons and readouts. He tapped a couple, flicked one image aside and opened another. "Time's getting on," he said. "What do you want?"

Abby gestured over her shoulder as she returned to his desk. "Why are you showing us this? Isn't it better kept a secret?"

Johnson raised his palms. "No one who matters would believe you and there's nothing you can do about it anyway."

Abby nodded, shrugged. "I suppose so."

Hines knew his friend would be processing the legality of everything she saw, considering the possibility of a warrant. But Johnson wasn't dumb. He operated inside the law and certainly wouldn't show them anything he did outside those boundaries. Steven was certain the man would have plenty of activities that were not legal, hidden away. He returned to the desk to stand beside Abby. As he moved he held the eye of the hawk on its perch, then looked over at the dog, still motionless in the corner. "What's with these animals?" he asked.

Johnson shook his head, sighed impatiently. "You don't like animals?"

"Sure I do, but these ones are weird."

"Look closer. They won't bite."

Hines leaned in towards the hawk. It blinked at him and its eyes irised in like a camera shutter. Hines jerked back. "It's a robot?"

Johnson laughed. "Haven't you been paying any attention? It's a cybernetic organism. An organism *enhanced*. The army fools around with drones and mechanical toys for surveillance and struggle to make anything work right. We take what already works and turn it to our purpose."

"You use these birds like drones?" Abby asked.

"Certainly. And others, pigeons, sparrows, what have you. The dogs are excellent trackers and can pass easily through the streets, just another stray mutt. But they see everything, record it, send it back. Their intelligence is enhanced, their obedience guaranteed. And if we need to, we can take over their nervous system and operate them entirely remotely. But we find a kind of partnership, linking minds and magetech of animal and operator, works best."

Hines laughed softly. "That's really something." He was impressed, but also quite disturbed. He knew he would be considering every animal he saw with suspicion now. "Is it easy to tell which are your drone animals and which are just… regular animals?" he asked.

"It's in the eyes, Mr Hines. Always look closely at the eyes."

Steven nodded, crouching before the dog to see its artificial camera lens vision. It stared back at him without blinking. "Huh."

Johnson slumped behind his desk. "Anyway, I'm a busy man and really don't have time for the Cyberdawn grand tour. What do you want?"

"Yvonne Veloitte," Abby said. She perched on the edge of a seat facing the desk.

As Hines sat in a chair beside her, Johnson's face betrayed a moment's discomfort. Hines noticed Abby's pleasure at having caused it. She liked to drop info bombs like that, it was an integral part of her policing style.

"What about her?" Johnson asked.

"You know her?"

"Yes. You know I do. If she's why you're here, Steven here must have told you she was one of us. What's she done?"

"She died."

Johnson raised both eyebrows, shocked. But the look struck Hines as insincere. "When?"

"Sometime over the last couple of days, we're not sure exactly when or how. So we were hoping you might be able to shed some light on it."

"I'm sorry, no," Johnson said. "Last time I saw her was about three days ago. She would often blow in and out of here, sometimes be gone for several days at a time. Everyone in Cyberdawn is free to pursue their own lives and interests, I keep no tabs on them."

Abby sat forward, elbows on her knees. "Really? I would have thought you were more of a control freak than that."

Johnson's face hardened. "Then you have me all wrong, Sergeant Jones."

They sat in silence for a moment. Eventually, Abby said,

"What can you tell me about Yvonne Veloitte?"

Johnson shook his head, steepled his fingers. "Mid-twenties, bloody clever, got a moderate talent that would have blossomed well with training. A tremendous programmer. She had a lot of potential. What do you mean, you don't know how she died?"

"Autopsy came up blank."

"Poisoned?"

Abby narrowed her eyes. "Why would you suggest that, Mr Johnson?"

Johnson opened his palms again. "Just that if you found no obvious cause of death, perhaps it was something less obvious, like a poison. Not that I'm trying to do your job for you, Sergeant."

Abby sat back. "Toxicology came back negative. Any known associates other than your good selves? Any enemies? Someone who might want her dead?"

Johnson pursed his lips in thought. "Well, not that I know of. But she was a big fan of misery. Perhaps she ran afoul of a dealer. Those people tend to be less than pleasant more often than not."

"What's misery?"

Johnson chuckled. "Oh dear. And you're the police? I suggest you ask Mr Hines here to explain it to you. And before you ask, no, I have no idea who her dealer was. I told her to never bring the stuff in here and she complied, so it stayed off my radar." He stood, reached out his hand. "Sorry I can't be of more assistance."

Steven stood, shook the offered hand. "Thanks, you've been very helpful."

Abby shook as well. "Yeah, a real revelation. Thanks."

Johnson pressed a button his desk, said, "Gavin," and the office door opened immediately. The young man with the lens over his eye stepped in. "Please show Mr Hines and

Sergeant Jones out."

Gavin nodded, gestured for them to follow.

As they walked back along corridors and down stairs, Abby asked, "What the fuck was that pretentious dick on about?"

"Let's get out of here," Steven said. "I don't know if it's relevant but it might be a lead. I'll explain it all over a drink, yeah?"

Abby slapped him on the shoulder. "Now you're talking."

10

Jerry Rundle nodded to the uniform as he approached the apartment block.

"Sorry I took a while," the uniform said.

Jerry shrugged. "Eh, nothing happens fast in this town except herpes and crime."

"You got that right."

"You're Andrew Blackford?"

"Yessir."

"Call me Jerry. I can't stand formality. I'm gonna call you Blackford."

"Okay."

Rundle turned and headed for the front doors. "You been briefed?"

"Yeah," Blackford said, looking up at the building before he entered. "You're after some guy who was maybe the victim of some bizarre attack in a bar. I'm guessing you want to ask him about his attacker?"

"Yeah, and find out if he's okay, what he knows, was the person known to him, the usual stuff. This one might be a bit weird though."

Blackford frowned. "Weird how?"

"Don't know exactly, just keep your wits about you."

Rundle walked to the elevators and swore. Black and yellow tape marked them as out of order. "I guess I need the exercise anyway. Dispatch said fourth floor." He pushed open a door and started up the stairs, Blackford close behind. "He's the only Griffin within walking distance, which is why I think this is our guy. You're along for protocol, so try to stay out of it if you can, I don't want him spooked by the uniform." Rundle paused, hands on his knees, breathed heavily. "Too many damn smokes, really." He looked back over his shoulder. Blackford smiled, expression patient. He wasn't even slightly out of breath. "Don't smoke and watch what you eat, kid. You don't want to end up like me."

Blackford grinned. "You're right. I got a hot young wife and a kid to keep up with anyway." His face darkened. "Cigarettes killed my dad in his fifties. You look about the age he was when he died."

Rundle coughed out a laugh. "Thanks a lot, kid." Before it could become any more uncomfortable he forced himself to continue. He didn't want to admit that Blackford was right. He really should quit the coffin nails. One day soon. One day.

When they reached the fourth floor they paused again, Rundle taking a couple of minutes to catch his breath and compose himself. "Okay," he said. "Let's see if this guy is in and if he's the Griffin we're after." He walked to number 406 and knocked. After a moment more he knocked again, harder. The door clicked and swung open.

Tension in the hallway ratcheted up. Blackmore slipped his weapon from its holster and took a stance.

Rundle nodded. "Let's stay calm, okay?"

"You got it."

Jerry pushed the door all the way open and called inside. "Mr Griffin? You home? This is Detective Sergeant Jerry Rundle. I wanted to ask you some questions about something you may have seen this morning."

The apartment yawned silently back at them. Rundle slipped one hand inside the threadbare jacket he wore under his coat, felt the smooth grip of the shoulder-holstered revolver there. Leaving it in place, fingers resting on it, he stepped into the hall. "Mr Griffin?"

The short entrance had a coat stand and a reproduction print of a Turner seascape. Rundle smirked, proud to have spotted it. Probably one of the few artists he recognized. A bathroom on the left, empty. To the right, a small kitchen, also empty. They moved on into a lounge area, messy with dirty plates and cups, newspapers spread around the couch. An armchair sat directly in front of the TV, a well-developed ass print in the scuffed leather reflecting light from a standing lamp in one corner. A door across the lounge led into a bedroom, the foot of a bed just visible, the covers tangled up and hanging off one corner.

"Mr Griffin?" Rundle called out again. No answer.

He moved to the bedroom, Blackford right behind him. They entered and saw no one there either. A distant sound of music floated somewhere nearby, like bells. Rundle sighed, disappointed and a little relieved. "Not here. Must have not pulled the door shut properly when he left." He paused, looked around, tried to triangulate the musical sound. Was it coming from outside or just in his head from the exertion of the stairs? "We should go. We don't have a warrant."

"You hear that?" Blackford tipped his head to one side.

"Hear what?"

"Like… bells or something."

Rundle narrowed his eyes. "Yeah. My ears ain't what they used to be kid. What do you think it is?"

Blackford moved around the bed, frowning, head still tilted. As he got to the other side, his eyes widened. "Look at that. It's beautiful."

Rundle shook his head. What the hell was this kid looking at? He moved around to see what had the uniform's attention as Blackford sank to his hands and knees and crawled forward. Jerry caught a glimpse of a shining, dark pool of some viscous liquid right beside the bed, a forest of shimmering neon green pinpricks waving softly in the air atop thin-stemmed tiny mushrooms, then a dark cloud of deep green particles burst up around Blackford's head.

The uniform fell back with a cry of agony. His gun

forgotten on the carpet, he clawed at his face, gouged at his eyes. Rundle took a shocked step away, mouth working like a beached fish. Blackford tumbled to the ground, keening softly, curled up tight.

Jerry wanted to go to him, but was cautious of the pool on the floor, the particles in the air, whatever the hell all that stuff was. He swallowed, moved forward to grab Blackford by one arm and haul him away when the uniform cop leaped upright.

Rundle staggered back again, heart racing. He cried an incoherent noise of shock when he saw Blackford's eyes, solid shimmering greenblack, all trace of white, pupil and iris gone. "Kid, are you..?"

Before he could finish, Blackford began tearing at his clothing, stripping down. He laughed as he worked, no longer acting as if he were in pain, more like he was high.

"Hey, Blackford. Andrew, what the hell are you doing?"

The young man got quickly naked, his hard, muscled body, smooth and shaved, gave Rundle a moment of jealousy even in his shock. The kid laughed maniacally and lunged forward.

Rundle leaped away into the lounge and pulled the bedroom door closed between them. Blackford hit the door and started hammering, still laughing. "Pull yourself together!" Jerry shouted. "I'll get you help, but you gotta calm down!"

The kid was too strong and wrenched the door open. Rundle stumbled, drew his revolver. He kicked out, caught the young officer in the groin and doubled him over briefly. Rundle made it to the hallway and saw, stark in the light of the standard lamp, strange black bristles sprouting around Blackford's eyes and mouth, from the palms of his hands as he stood up and reached forwards.

"Andrew, I'm goddamned serious, I will shoot you!" he

yelled.

Still the kid came on.

Rundle ground his teeth. "Shit on me," he snarled and squeezed the trigger. Blackford's left knee exploded, a burst of blood and bone and something else with it, black and fibrous. It barely slowed him as he dragged the injured leg without any signs of pain. Rundle howled, blew out the other knee.

Blackford fell, used his hands like claws into the carpet and kept coming. More bristling black spines emerged all over his body. His face was twisted with effort and pure rage. He reached up between hauls, spitting with the exertion.

Rundle backed into the apartment's front door and it swung to click closed behind him. He hit it with his shoulders, trapped. "Oh, shit on me!" he hollered and emptied the final four rounds into Blackford's head and torso. Every bullet tore flesh and bone, blood burst out, but with it blasts of wet, black fibers like matted grass and writhing white threads that spattered around the floor.

Blackford fell, twitching and trembling, vibrating almost, against the thin carpeting. Rundle stared and panted, heart threatening to leap from his throat and run for the harbor. Blackford convulsed once, then again, even though most of his head was blown away, then finally, thankfully, fell still.

Rundle sat and stared, the emptied revolver hanging loose in his hand. "What the hell just happened?" he whispered, and fumbled in his pocket for his phone.

11

Steve and Abby sat at the window seat of a dockside bar, looking over dark gray, turgid water and passenger ferries coming and going from a row of wharves. To their left, the tall cranes and multi-colored shipping containers of the industrial port were just visible, more wharves and warehouses out of sight around the small head. Beyond it all, the harbor opened into the ocean proper, two tall headlands like sentinels watching over everything that came or went from Cleveport by sea. They sipped overpriced beers, mesmerized by the rain making rivulets down the glass in front of them. Hines was careful to look through the pane, not into it. He'd seen enough of the city for now. He felt her, Cleveport, clamoring for attention. *Look at my alleys and seedy bars,* she cajoled. *Slip your mind along my rain-slicked streets.*

He would try to learn more about her discomfort later, but he couldn't be on all the time. His relationship with this town was unhealthy as hell and he knew it, but he simply couldn't leave. Even after what had happened to Jenny. Perhaps especially after what happened to his fiancée. And it seemed the city's grip on him felt tighter than ever. He remembered something Johnson had said, *Already the magic is getting stronger, surely even you can feel that, Hines?*

He *could* feel that and it bothered him. Deeply, viscerally, it perturbed him but he wasn't able to quite figure out why.

"You look like you dropped a diamond and found a turd." Abby's gaze was genuinely concerned.

He half-smiled, not able to pull out a full grin. "Rain always makes me melancholy."

"You were thinking about her again, huh?"

Not only her, he thought, but nodded. He didn't want to talk about it, but it wasn't something he could hide from his best friend.

"I won't say time heals all wounds or any shit like that," Abby said quietly. "But time does help you get used to living with scars. I can't imagine how much you miss her."

Steven swallowed. "Yeah. I'm always going to have a Jenny-sized hole inside me." It had been three years. Would the hole ever get any smaller?

"You'll get used to it. I'm sorry." Abby put a hand on his shoulder, squeezed. She left it there, turned back to look out the window and silence hung warm and comfortable between them for a while. She got it even if there was that one aspect of his life, his talent, that she avoided, managing to live and talk around it, a blind spot in her love for him. Given everything else she meant to him, he reluctantly forgave her that blindness.

After a few minutes she got up, went to the bar. When she came back with two fresh beers she said, "So, what the fuck is misery? Other than this entire town and everyone in it, I mean."

Steve saw her grin. This time he managed a full smile in return. "You're actually close to the truth right there," he said.

"Johnson talked about dealers. Is misery a drug?"

"Yeah, magical drug. It's something only people with a talent can use. It takes a little eldritch energy to… activate it."

Abby frowned into her beer. "So how come I've never heard of it?"

"Outside your purview, I guess. It's not illegal because you guys don't know about it and no law is passed on it. If you found some on a person, you'd test it and find an inert fluid. It comes in little vials, like ampules, you know? Most people, if they are caught with it, tell the police it's a homeopathic remedy."

Abby snorted. "Homeopathic?"

"Yeah. Dickheads spending a fortune on water and enjoying the placebo effect. But it works in favor of mis users. All the components in the solution are untraceable without a talent, until they're activated. So they have nothing to get caught with."

Abby nodded, sipped beer. She looked out over the harbor and Steven could almost see her brain at work, collating, cataloging, hypothesizing. "So, it's something we know nothing about and only magical people can use it. What does it do?"

"Gets you high."

"You ever tried it?"

"Yeah, once. Didn't really agree with me. It's a little bit like pot, a little like weak acid. Kinda happy-making, slightly psychotropic. I can totally get why people are into it, but it's just not my kinda buzz."

"So what actually is it?" Abby asked. "And why does it have such a fucked up name for a happy drug?"

Steve laughed. "Well, that's the rub. It actually is misery. It's drawn from a dissatisfied populace, their frustrations and grievances, grief and struggle. It's distilled human misery, which is why it's so prevalent in a city like Cleveport. Easy to make in such a densely populated place. The distillation process, plus the activation process, converts it into a pretty potent high." He waggled his fingers and grinned. "Paradoxical! Comedy is someone else's tragedy and all that, I guess."

Abby shook her head, refusing to look at him. "How the fuck do you distill human misery? How do you… collect it?"

"No idea. I'm not a drug baron, don't have that kind of talent, never looked into it. I can use it, same as anyone with a magical skill, but I have no idea how it's actually made. I guess we could find out if we asked the right people."

Abby pursed her lips, lost in thought again. "We're missing the point," she said eventually. "Much as this is all just fucking fascinating, the point is that Yvonne Veloitte died maybe because she fell foul of a dealer. Johnson said he had no idea who her dealer was, so do we really even have a lead?"

"I could ask around," Steven said.

"Is it possible she OD'd on the stuff?"

He shook his head, drained the last of his beer. "No, it's like weed in that respect. You can keep taking it and get more and more wasted, but it's not something you can chemically OD on. You can go slowly nuts, you know, trigger psychosis or whatever if you have a pre-existing condition or predisposition, just like people do with too much pot. But it's a safe drug otherwise."

"How do people take it?"

"It comes in little vials, yeah? The user snaps the top off, does their magic thing to activate it and that makes the liquid inside react and turn into a vapor which is sniffed up. Quick and simple as that."

Abby nodded again, brain still ticking over. "So everyone knows the.. what, special spell to activate it."

Hines grinned at her obvious discomfort talking about arcane things. Even after all this time, the way she resisted amused the hell out of him. "No, it's simpler than that. Whenever any sort of magic is used it generates a kind of energy. Imagine a radioactive signature; you can't see it, but it registers on a Geiger counter, yeah? It's there as a result of the radioactivity. Magic has a resonance like that, which is what sets off the misery. It remains inert until a user targets a magical frequency directly at it. So even the most mundane and barely capable mages like me can have their fun with it."

Abby sat quietly and Steven let her think. A cruise liner

hoved out through the heads, leaving the rainy city for brighter climes. He wouldn't mind being on board, but knew from experience the painful tearing at his heart he would feel as the vessel passed into the ocean. Just like when he drove on the highway out of town or took a plane somewhere. Flying was the worst, the wrench enough to make him cry aloud. And all the time he was away, that burning, bone-deep, debilitating ache, until he finally returned into the shadows of his city's buildings, felt her streets wrap around him and the pain subsided again.

"I gotta follow up this misery angle," Abby said suddenly. "What if all my unexplained deaths were misery users? It's not much, but it's all I've got so far. How could I learn more?"

Steven shrugged. "I guess you need that magical surgeon we talked about."

"Can you arrange that?"

"Yeah, I can try. So you need me to track down misery dealers and someone with a talent to look over these corpses your coroner proved useless on."

Abby nodded, face deadly serious. "Yeah. Exactly that."

"And what are you going to be doing? Painting your toenails while I run around and do your legwork?"

Abby's face cracked, a smile pushing through. It was like she could push away clouds when she smiled like that. "I'll make sure you get your subcontractor's rate. That what you're angling for?"

Steven reclined, sighing like he'd just been given the best blowjob of his life. "Ah, you know how to please me."

Abby laughed. "God, Hines, you're a fuckwit. I'll make sure you get paid, okay. Just knock off that creepy... whatever the fuck it is!" Her phone rang and she shook her head at Hines as she answered. "Jones. Yep. Really? What the fuck does that mean? How many? *How many?* Yeah, yeah, right, I'm coming in now. Be there in thirty minutes." She hung up and stared at her cell for a moment, brow creased.

"Problem?" Steve asked.

"Apparently there's been a rash of deaths across the city. People are getting infected with something and going on the attack."

"Infected?"

"Yeah. It's driving them batshit, assault someone and then turn into fucking hay or something."

Steven tried to parse what she'd said. "What?" he managed eventually.

"Yeah, right?"

"That is not in any way normal," Hines said.

Abby raised her hands. "No shit, Sherlock Hines. I need to go in and learn more."

"The magic in the city is stronger," Steven said, brow creased. "Talented people are inexplicably dying, now this. I'm getting a very bad feeling, Abs."

"Me too, Hines Solo. Let's stay alert on it, yeah? I'll let you know whatever I learn, but I gotta go to the station for a full briefing." She slapped some money on the table. "Get some lunch on me, then do your spooky bloodhound thing, yeah?"

"Sure, no problem. Take care."

She leaned forward, kissed his cheek. "You too." She paused, growing serious again. "You wanna talk about her, anytime. You know you can with me."

He smiled, genuinely grateful. "I know. Thanks."

"Okay. Get onto this misery shit and find me someone to look at my corpses."

Steven saluted and she grinned and strode out of the bar. He looked at the money on the table and thought about lunch, then decided that maybe lunch could be a couple more beers and anything left over would get him a taxi back across town.

12

Gina Baker woke and took several seconds to remember where she was. Although the fogginess of her brain refused to shift, it all came crashing back. The massive hit from the mis, Trev forcing more on her, Trev taking a hit and… She gasped, pushed herself into a sitting position, struggling against the voluminous cushions and her slack muscles.

Trev lay on the floor, eyes wide and glassy, staring at her feet. Gina sobbed, one hand covering her mouth. She reached down, touched Trev's cheek. She whipped her hand away with another sob at the cold, clammy feel of his skin. Bone-deep trembling set in and she tried to force coherent thoughts past the mist in her head. That dull sensation of depression that always followed a misery session. What Trev called the sadache. You couldn't die from a misery OD. There was no such thing.

Gina stared into Trev's dead eyes, the skin around them already a blueish tinge in his otherwise pasty face. Not pale like Gina, what her dad called her alabaster beauty, but a kind of sickly, pasty shade. She used to like it, heroin chic, but suddenly it looked horrible. Such a fine line between life and death, and Trev wore it badly now, a mask of desecration.

Gina sobbed again, staggered to her feet and stepped over Trev, stumbled into the kitchen. She vomited noisily into the sink then ran cold water into her hands. Washed her face and palmed it over her short, dark fuck-you hairstyle.

You've such thick, shining hair, her mother used to say. *Like a satin curtain.* So she'd hacked it all off and wore it like a badge of honor. Same as the torn jeans, combat boots, little leather bomber jacket. Indie punk, goth revival, whatever the hell it was, the whole intention was mainly to throw off the trappings of her wealthy middle-class upbringing. Gina's was a very self-aware rebellion, yet she lived and breathed it utterly.

But thinking about their house in the gentrified edge-of-city urban paradise, and her mother, and Trev lying dead in the front room, everything seemed turned around. With a wince of frustration and shame, Gina realized that she really wanted to hug her mom. She'd run off, after the most blistering screaming match they'd ever had, only three weeks before. She'd moved into Trev's place, enjoyed the gritty edge of inner city squatting, sniffing misery, drinking too much, partying in warehouse gigs where the air was hot and humid and full of smoke and industrial guitar music. It suited her well, still did. But just for a few minutes, she wanted her mom. Maybe she could apologize, rebuild some bridges. She wasn't about to go home and be a good little girl anytime soon, but she'd never watched a man die before. Never seen a dead body before. She could look after herself, get her own place, keep her part-time job at the diner and survive. But maybe, just for a day or two, she should go home and patch some shit up.

She devolved into wracking sobs and bawled her eyes out. She gave herself five minutes of that, then mentally slapped herself into shape. She wanted to give Rufus a pat. She missed that dumb dog. She wouldn't tell them Trev had died, just that they weren't together anymore. It was still the truth. Her parents would be pleased. Maybe stay the night and then get back to her grown-up life.

Only overnight, that's all. Just find her center again. At the very least, she needed to be away from here, away from poor Trev. She didn't want to find herself answering questions from the police and trying to explain what she had seen.

The streets ran with tears when she stepped from the terrace squats. She squinted into the lead-gray sky and curled her lip in a sneer. Seemed like it had been raining forever. She shifted the small sports hold-all with all her worldly goods in it onto the other shoulder. A washbag, make up bag, four changes of clothes and her iPad. With her phone in her jacket pocket, it accounted for all she really cared about in the world. Her room at home, full of pointless stuff, appalled her these days. But the bed was hella comfortable, a big double thing with thick quilts and pillows that cost about three hundred dollars each. Ridiculous, but so comfortable. She hated herself all over again.

Just one night.

She cinched the collar of her jacket tight and set off along the street. She didn't really mind the rain, it suited her mood most of the time. And the cold air and open city would help to clear her head of the sadache. Honestly, after what had just happened, she'd probably never touch a hit of that again. Trev had been a big fan, had used it to help prove to her the innate talent she had for magic. But it was nothing special, her talent. She could conjure images, illusions in the air or in the mind of people, convince them they'd seen things that weren't there. She'd done it since she was about twelve years old. Always known she was different, but kept it secret. Until Trev picked her out at a *Sawed Corpse* gig and told her she was magical. "Like recognizes like," he'd said and that was the start of a beautiful few months.

Until last night.

She stopped walking, glanced back over her shoulder. Should she report his death? All she had been able to think of was getting the hell out of there, but Trev wasn't a bad guy. Could she just leave him there to rot? And would the cops come looking for her anyway? Enough people knew she and Trev were a thing.

She turned a slow circle on the sidewalk. "Shit, shit, shit."

The last time they'd been out together was two nights before at the Razor Club and they'd had a big fight. Lots of people had seen the fight and she'd stormed off. Of course, she'd gone back to the squat, he'd turned up an hour later with booze and they got wasted and fucked the argument away. But no one else knew that. She hadn't left the squat since that night and Trev had only gone that morning to score mis from Sally and Dave. She'd tell anyone that after the fight, she had had enough and went off on her own. Hadn't seen Trev since. It seemed a little cold, but Gina had always been a survivor. Always looked after herself well. That was a good enough story and he had OD'd, even if that was impossible. Let everyone think he'd been alone when that happened. Maybe the misery was cut with some horrible shit. Just as well she'd coughed up most of that second hit or she might be dead on the sofa now.

She sniffed, started walking again. "Sorry, Trev," she said aloud. "It was great, but it's over. You're on your own now." If anyone asked, she hadn't seen him since the fight at the Razor Club. Good.

The walk to the center of the business district wasn't long, but by the time she got there she was soaked and unsettled. An unease, a pervading sense of disquiet, had risen throughout her trudge, as she stared at the sidewalk and tried not to remember Trev's glassy eyes. The city seemed changed somehow.

A shout caught her attention and a naked woman ran along the road a hundred yards ahead of her, several people turning to watch, point, lift phones to snap pictures. As Gina frowned, the woman disappeared into a cross street and raised voices turned to screams and faded away. What the fuck was that about?

A news crew in a brightly emblazoned van went hurtling

past. Gina's discomfort increased. She turned away from the direction the woman had run and doubled her pace for two more blocks. As she approached the junction she needed, she saw a bus crawling along and ran to intercept it. She reached the stop at the same time as the vehicle. The driver looked at her through the glass, eyes narrowed.

"Open the door, man!" she yelled. "It's pissing down out here."

The driver stared for a moment more, then the door hissed open.

Gina stepped up, swiped her weekly pass. "What the hell, man?"

He shook his head, closed the door. "Sorry about that. City's going a bit nuts today."

"You're telling me."

He looked her up and down. "You heard about the outbreak?"

"What outbreak?"

He shook his head again, pulled away from the curb. "City's gone fucking nuts." He stared down the road, lips pressed together.

His weirdness did nothing to ease Gina's discomfort. She moved to the back of the bus and everyone on board, about a dozen bedraggled and slack-faced passengers, gave her a suspicious look as she passed. What the hell was wrong with everybody? Had they all watched their boyfriend die today?

Anger rose and she bit it down, slumped onto the seat and put her bag beside her. She rummaged for headphones, pushed them into the port on her phone and cranked up an old Mudvayne album, loud and angry music to ease her spirit.

A few people got on and off the bus during the journey, but she was on for a while, heading to the Ring of Affluence, as Trev called it, where the inner-city density gave way to larger, leafier streets. Where big houses stood shoulder to shoulder, but with backyards and swimming pools and double garages. Homes detached from each other by a few feet, but detached from reality by the wide abyss of privilege. Half an hour out – not close enough to be inner city but not so far as to be the sprawling suburbs where the vast majority of the population lived. Gina's home was on the periphery of that most desirable area before the land turned industrial, then beyond that the wide sweeps of housing estates across land that used to be countryside but had slowly been swallowed by ever-burgeoning urban edges. Thousands of identical houses still barely affordable for families, yet with a one hour or more commute into the city for work. Standing behind those distant suburbs, the mountains slowly rose, like a sloping wall of guardians as far to the north and south as the eye could see.

The streets got wider and more tree-lined as the bus rolled on, the tower blocks and apartment buildings gave way to single- and double-story homes. Bar the driver, Gina was alone by the time she reached her stop. Cleveport itself was a distant postcard on the coast, visible from the higher ground. The industrial wastes and denser suburbs rose in a gentle slope off to the west until they vanished into the foothills.

"Better think about staying home," the driver said as she passed him to get off. "I'm not going back, gonna head straight to the depot. City's gone nuts."

She frowned at him. "So you said before."

He nodded sagely and Gina left it at that.

She walked in the rain again, along the main street with its shops and restaurants, off onto Camelia Drive and down to the cul-de-sac where they'd moved when she was twelve years old. All the new houses, McMansions she called them, built for the elite. So new when they'd moved in it still smelled of paint and new carpet and freshly sawn wood. The house where she'd been so unfulfilled and discontent. "Some people see the world for what it is from a very early age," Trev had told her one night while they sat slack and wasted on the floor of the squat, eating instant noodles. "Consider yourself lucky. You see through the bullshit. And believe me, people who see through that shit know it from when they're kids. I did. You did. We see clearly, Geenie. We see what it actually is, not what the powerful tell us it is."

What did Trev see now, his blank eyes staring at the base of the sofa where her feet had been?

Her little cul-de-sac was strangely quiet. Something sat on the driveway of the Jenks's place, next door to hers, like a pile of blackened grass, slowly washing down the drive with the persistent rain. Some new gardening compost or something, delivered and left to the elements, probably. Clarisse Jenks would be pissed off, come around and talk about the incompetence of the delivery driver, no doubt.

Gina looked slowly from house to house and saw no movement. Maybe she was just spooked by her proximity to death this day, but everything felt fucked up. Like a TV not quite tuned in or something. The wrongness pressed down on her, made her tremble again. She felt like crying and shook it off. She was in shock, certainly. The drug had been stronger than ever and that always left you feeling a bit blue until you got it out of your system.

But this was different. Deeper, more total. She walked to her front door, casting a nervous glance at the weird compost on Clarisse's drive. She found her keys and opened up. She could see straight along the clean, white hallway into the kitchen and something dark and liquid sat on the floor right inside the kitchen door. Two things, in fact, like two puddles of thick oil. Tiny green lights seemed to shimmer and flicker over them both. Gina tipped her head to one side. There was a sound coming along the hall. The most beautiful music she'd ever heard, a bell-like symphony, an angelic melody.

A frantic scrabbling caught her attention and a smile began on her lips as Rufus came hammering out of the kitchen and along the hallway. She was half-crouched to greet him when her smile faltered and Rufus began to bark and slaver, his lips pulled back, eyes wide and furious.

Gina straightened, staggered back a step or two. "What the fuck, Roof? It's me, it's Gina."

She tripped and staggered again, catching her balance before she fell backward over the front step. Rufus skidded to a halt at the front door, barking rapidly, drool flicking from his baggy brown lips.

Gina took another pace or two away, still in the shelter of the ridiculous portico porch of the ridiculous house. "Rufus? What's going on?"

He stopped barking, stood blocking the doorway with his considerable bulk, at least half Saint Bernard, half who knew what the hell else. His baggy lips flickered with a snarl barely turned off. Gina reached a palm, moved towards him again. She cried out as he leaped forward, snarling and barking again like he was possessed.

Tears filled Gina's eyes. "You not gonna let me in, boy?"

Rufus barked and bounced forward, shuffled back, barked forwards again.

Gina shook her head, retreated, hands raised. "Okay, Roof. Okay." She had never seen her dog like this before. He was the most placid idiot in the world, like a giant teddy bear. He would shy away and whimper when little white terriers harangued him in the street or the park. What the hell had got into him?

Neither of her parents had appeared despite the racket, so they were presumably not home. For that matter, no one seemed to have appeared. No nosey neighbors, no tut-tuts of disapproval for the disturbance of upper middle-class peace. Gina looked at the hills looming behind her suburb, the thick trees of the national park there. She turned towards the city, its towers and bridges distant and tiny, hazy through the rain like a watercolor painting. There was a motel on the main road out of town only ten minutes or so walk.

All she wanted was to be warm and dry, and sleep. She needed to stop. Rest. She'd get a motel room, have a shower and go to sleep. When she woke up, maybe all this lunacy would have passed. She could call from the motel, hopefully her parents would be home again and she could decide then what to do next.

She glanced once more at Rufus, who crouched and growled at her. With a shake of the head, a sense of deep betrayal gnawing at her gut, Gina set off again through the rain.

13

Yegor counted to ten. Then he counted again. He watched while Mr Crater thought, elbows on the huge mahogany desk which was empty but for an ashtray with a cigar resting in it. Smoke curled gently towards the ceiling. Portraits and landscapes hung from the wood-paneled walls, heavy, red leather sofa and chairs sat brooding in one corner. Yegor knew better than to interrupt. Counting helped. Whenever he got upset, he'd learned to use the numbers to calm himself. It could stop him beating a guy to death when he really wanted mayhem, and it could stop him opening his stupid mouth and upsetting Mr Crater with excuses or apologies. You did not interrupt the boss.

"So tell me again," Crater said eventually in quiet Russian. "Tell me again how you have no idea where my merchandise is."

Yegor swallowed, shifted uncomfortably in the suit that was too tight over his bulging muscles. His merchandise? "The runner reported in that he'd collected the stuff. He said he was loading it to drive into the city and would contact us once he had arrived. But we never heard from him again."

"And how long has it been?"

"He's late by six hours now."

Crater switched from Russian to heavily accented English. "And what have you been doing for six fucking hours?" he yelled. "Why have you no better news for me?"

Yegor's English was unaccented. He was born and bred Cleveport, after all, to Russian parents, and he fell back on his first language gratefully. "We've made calls and sent the word out. We're searching all the likely places he might have gone, but it's possible…" He trailed off.

"It's possible this runner has absconded with my merchandise?" Crater said quietly, in Russian again.

Yegor replied in English. "Yes, it's possible. Which is why I thought I should come and tell you what's happening."

Crater sat and tapped his fingers against his lips, thinking. Yegor began counting again. Eventually Crater stood and walked around his desk. He was a well-built man going soft with age, but no less intimidating for it. Even though he stood a good six inches below Yegor's huge frame, his balding head shining in the overhead light, Yegor still felt a pang of apprehension. Was it actual physical fear or trepidation born of Crater's reputation? He couldn't be sure, but if he did have to fight this sixty-year-old man any day he would not underestimate the boss's potential. He was called Mr Crater for a reason, after all. If you believed the stories.

Crater reached up, patted Yegor's cheek. "You will go back out there," he said, almost too softly to be heard. "And you will take however many men is necessary and you will search every street of Cleveport until you find my merchandise. This stuff, this misery, it's a mystery to me, but it is so very profitable, according to you. I want to see it and I want our agreement met. I lose my money on this shipment I will be very unhappy, you understand?"

"Yes, boss."

"I have *invested* here. I trusted you, came through for you. I need a return on my investment. If it has gone missing in transport from one side of the city to the other, I will be very annoyed."

"Yes, boss." *One, two, three, four…*

"It was made in the suburbs. It was inspected by you and confirmed, yes?"

Yegor swallowed. "Well, it was inspected by someone I trust. I can't… it's not a drug I can use." How much did he explain? How much did he even understand? Human growth hormone he understood. Creatine he understood. This stuff was just weird.

Crater turned the pat into a slap. "You confirmed for me that this stuff was real and you explained the profit margin and that you had a supply chain and a market for it and you simply needed capital investment. This is on you, do you understand?"

Yegor nodded, teeth clenched. *One, two, three, four…*

"And you arranged for its delivery here," Crater went on, "so that I could see my investment before we together turned it into profit. So if that does not happen, I need to get a return on my investment from somewhere, yes?"

"Yes, boss."

"And that may mean making a new crater in the skin of this earth and lining it with something. You know what that something might be?"

"Yes, boss."

"What is it?" Crater hollered.

"Me, sir. You'll fill it with me."

"With parts of you, Yegor. Bit," he slapped Yegor's cheek again, "By." *Slap*. "Bit." *Slap.*

Yegor nodded. "I understand. I just wanted to you to know what was going on. I'll find out what's happened to the merchandise. If it is truly missing, I'll bring you the hide of this runner and I will absolutely make sure your investment is returned to you."

Crater's eyes narrowed. "With my promised profit on top, of course."

"Of course." Yegor couldn't believe the trembling in his legs, but there it was. He badly needed to hurt someone. How would he raise the kind of money needed to balance things with Crater?

The boss returned to his seat behind the huge desk. "Off you go then."

"Yes, boss. I'm sorry, this will be fixed."

Crater smiled, a predator grinning at its prey. "Oh yes, I know it will. One way or another."

Yegor left quickly, counting all the way along the corridor, down the metal steps from Crater's office into the massive car mechanic's workshop and out into the rain-swept streets. He breathed deeply of the wet air, clenched his fists a few times then pulled a phone from his pocket. He dialed. "Tommy? Get the crew together. Whatever they're doing can wait, this is more than urgent. We are potentially in deep shit. I need everyone at the gym in thirty minutes."

Without waiting for an answer, he hung up and slipped into the driver's seat of his silver Mercedes C-Class, sniffed the aroma of soft leather. He drove the few blocks to his gym, parked in the bay marked *Manager*. He looked up at the black and red sign, *Yegor's Muscle & Fight*, and sighed. If only this paid enough to keep him and he didn't have to maintain it as a front for other business. He'd genuinely be happy if only it made enough money. He was too old at forty-one to compete anymore, but even when he'd made a living in the cage, he'd still had to supplement it with less above-board endeavors. He was good, but had never made the really big time, the television events with the massive purses. Politics it was, certainly no lack of skill on his part. But he'd used other means to enjoy the lifestyle to which he had aspired. Life could never be simple once you got used to a certain standard of living. And he wasn't about to downgrade now.

He strode in through front door, through the shop with overloaded shelves of supplements and MMA gloves, books and videos, racks of tracksuits and Muay Thai shorts. Gary looked up from behind the sales desk, half lifted a hand in greeting, then dropped it as Yegor barely spared him a glance.

Yegor went into the gym and the odor of sweat and *Deep*

Heat, leather and metal. A class was taking place on the mats, several effort-soaked people practicing cover-ups in a corner, sparring matches in both the full-size boxing rings. The lifting area was fairly busy, free weights clanging, cables hissing as they hauled stacks of iron plates. The thwack of glove on bag and glove on flesh punctuated the air along with the songs of training and Def Leppard, though blaring, was almost lost in the racket of people getting fit, strong and learning to fight.

Yegor smiled, glad to be home. In his office in the back he changed into training gear. He had twenty minutes to pump some iron and punch the shit out of some bags before his crew arrived. Long enough to tire him. Or he might be tempted to punch the shit out of them.

14

Hines sat in his apartment looking at the reporter's notepad in his hand. His scrawling, barely legible handwriting covered one page, a list of names and numbers. All but the top two had question marks after them. He was not into misery so knowing who might be a dealer was tough. All the names listed as questions were worth following up, but the top two he was fairly sure were pushing the stuff. Or they at least knew people who were. He'd give those two names to Abby first and take it from there.

He tore the page from the spiral top binding and folded it in half, slipped it into his hip pocket. Now to find someone who might be able to help out with these corpses. He went into the bathroom first to take a piss. As he washed his hands he looked up at the canvas covered mirror. Against his better judgment, he lifted one corner, revealed a tiny amount of reflective surface. Ghostly movement swirled across the glass and he dropped the canvas with a gasp before he caught a glimpse of her face. Her pained expression. The same expression he saw as the life slipped from her as she lay crushed by fallen masonry. As he reached for her, desperate to help but unable to move, his own leg trapped by a chunk of wall. As he watched her die. "Jenny," he whispered, suppressing a sob.

He reached down, absently rubbed at his knee, throbbing as much with grief as with actual pain. He drew a deep breath, blew it slowly out. Time to commune with his jealous city.

He left the apartment and stood on the steps leading to the street. A low brick wall marked either side of the half-dozen stairs, a round, cement ball mounted at the end of each.

He laid a palm on one ball and closed his eyes.

Cleveport slipped into him. She stroked his consciousness, purred at his touch. "Hey there," he said quietly. "What's up with you, eh? You don't feel right."

His mind washed with images and sensations, but nothing clear. Sometimes Cleveport communicated with him quite clearly, but she never used language. She was sentient, like all cities, but she was not a person. Not even a being, really. And now her discomfort was evident, but unformed, unfocused. Hines got the impression she didn't know what was wrong herself, she just felt off, something amiss at the very roots of her. Like someone with the start of a cold, things were just a bit out of whack. He would help if he could, but there was little he could do now.

To business, then.

"I need your help," he said quietly under his breath. "Show me where Mary is, please?"

A soft rush tingled through him. His mind slipped away along the street lined with parked cars and crawling traffic, past stop signs with sparkles of rain flickering past them, sparkling green and red. He was drawn along roads and alleys, past towering edifices of glass and chrome, under railway lines that marched on latticed steel legs over and along the edges of streets. On towards the big intersection of highways crossing over each other, leading in and out of Cleveport from everywhere else. Before his mind stopped he knew where he was being led. In the dry, cool shadows of a huge overpass on the southern side of town, his consciousness came to rest on a group of people gathered around steel barrels with fires burning in them. The people were ragged and hopeless, broken and full of despair. Or most of them were. Mary moved among them, looking as much a hobo as any other there, but with a clarity of mind and purpose quite different to the rest.

Hines pulled his consciousness back, opened his eyes. If only it was as easy to find missing persons as it was to find people he knew, people with whom he already had a personal connection that he could communicate to the city. He'd make a much better living if that were the case. But something else nagged at him. Even though looking up someone he knew well was always pretty straightforward, this time it had been a breeze. No hitches, no confusion. The magic was stronger and smoother and more potent than ever. It bothered his gut, made his balls tighten in consternation, almost as if he expected a sudden, solid kick to the groin from out of nowhere. The eldritch air of Cleveport was buzzing in strange and unusual ways. Perhaps that was the source of the city's dis-ease. Maybe she sensed it too and it bothered her. He patted the cement ball. "Thanks." She sighed with pleasure.

It took a few minutes to find a cab. They were all busy, doing good business in the seemingly endless rain, but eventually one stopped. He told the driver where to go and sat deep in the seat, closed his eyes. Music like a Bollywood soundtrack filled the car. Those lunchtime beers had left him a little lightheaded. He really should have eaten something too. Maybe he'd pick up a burger on the way back.

"So how about this disease, then?" The cab driver's voice was high and pleasant, a singsong sound with a strong Indian accent. Or Pakistani, or Bangladeshi. Hines had no idea how to tell the difference. The guy wore a turban, which made him a Sikh. At least, he thought that was how it worked.

"What's that?" Steven asked.

"This disease that's sweeping Cleveport."

Hines frowned, remembered Abby's call in to the station. "There's a disease sweeping the city?"

"Oh, yes, sir. You haven't heard? People are catching something and it makes them crazy. Makes them lose their minds, they run around naked and attack anyone they see."

"Sounds like someone took some bad acid to me."

The turbaned man laughed. "You are not wrong, sir. But this is not an isolated case. There are dozens of reports from all over."

"Dozens, really?"

"Yes. On the radio earlier they were talking about a pandemic! The police have said not to worry, the mayor has come out and told people not to panic. If you ask me, that sounds like there's every reason to panic."

Hines nodded, lips pursed. The man made a lot of sense with that assumption. "They make any suggestion what it is?"

The turban in front of him shook and nodded at the same time, a strange, spiraling motion that didn't convey affirmation or negativity. "They still deny there's anything happening. But then the news said that citizens should avoid any strange substances they see spilled in the street and avoid anyone naked in the city." He laughed, sudden and high, absolute hilarity. "Can you imagine? The news telling us to avoid naked people? I can tell you, sir, if an undressed person came running up to me in the street, I would most certainly avoid them without needing the news to tell me so!"

"Even if it was a hot woman?"

The driver laughed again. "Especially so! I would be most suspicious. Even my wife doesn't run to me like that anymore, sir."

Steven laughed along with the man, but the knot of worry and trepidation in his gut only grew larger and tighter. They didn't talk for the rest of the twenty-minute drive. When they reached a nondescript road surrounded only by chainlink fences and other roads, shadowed by flyovers crossing above, Steven asked the driver to stop. "Any chance you could wait for me? Leave it on the clock. I'll need a ride back to the city in about fifteen minutes."

The driver narrowed his eyes. "Pay me for this far and give me twenty up front and I'll wait for half an hour. Deal?"

Steven grinned. "Good businessman. Sure." He couldn't blame the man's caution, handed him the money, and headed off under the massive gray highways arcing above.

The roadway was wet and littered with gravel and the detritus of too much humanity in one place; plastic wrappers and broken toys, chunks of wood and cardboard, bottles and cans and other things to which he didn't want to pay too much attention. This side of Cleveport was lacking in homes, but not in people. Huge industrial warehousing and business parks covered the landscape in the distance, with easy access to highways. Traffic from the outlying suburbs vibrated every roadway, thousands of people with thousands of purposes coming and going like lines of worker ants. Hines made his way along one chainlink fence until he found an opening cut in it and pushed his way through, careful not to catch skin or coat on the rusty wire. He strolled casually, non-threatening, to the enclave where so many of the city's homeless sheltered under high, concrete-cathedral roofs, slept on cardboard and squabbled over cigarettes. Two dirty, skinny men broke into a fight as he passed, a woman screeching at them unintelligibly. Hines felt he should intervene, but knew better.

Others watched with various levels of disinterest. An elderly woman with a shopping trolley walked past, muttered something about the neighborhood going to the dogs. Hines headed towards the burning braziers, shaking his head at the repeated requests for loose change, a cigarette, offers of blowjobs from men and women alike. He ignored the aggressive challenges of some, defending their territory from the suspicious interloper.

A man sat smoking a cigarette in the open passenger

door of a burned out car. Hines had no choice but to walk right by this one.

"You're in the wrong place, buddy," the man called out in a voice like barbed wire. "The wrong fucking place."

Steven cast a disdainful glance at him. "Bring it if you think you've got it."

The man stared at him for a moment and Hines hoped his shaking legs weren't visible. He was no fighter. He hated this stuff, felt terrible for these poor souls, being eaten alive by life, by Cleveport. The man grimaced and held his gaze for a minute, then looked away.

Hines walked on through the narrow gap between burned out cars and the beginnings of the cardboard slums. He felt the city heave a sigh of resignation and sadness. "It's not your fault," he whispered quietly.

Cleveport seemed to shrug.

Mary saw him coming and intercepted. "What are you doing here?"

"Nice to see you too."

She smiled, shook her head. She looked about forty, but he was convinced she was far older. Even in the rags and dirt of the street, trying to blend in, she radiated beauty and strength. Her auburn hair, like burnt copper, almost glowed under a twisted, dark paisley shawl. "I'm working here." She gestured around. "And there's a lot of work to be done."

"I see that. You're swimming against the tide."

She tipped her head to one side, forbearing expression. "And that's a reason to stop swimming, is it?"

Steven looked at the people, well beyond saving. "No," he said, resignedly. "I guess not."

"They're not all hopeless cases," Mary said, though her face had become sympathetic. "And besides, even if I can't save them, I can ease their burden. Their pain."

Hines nodded, gripped her shoulder. "You're a good

person."

"There are a few of us left."

"I need your help," Steven said. "It's something we need to keep a bit on the quiet, but I can't think of anyone else who has the skills I need. And it's paid work. It's a favor for me and a friend, I mean, but I'll pay you too."

Mary looked around, frowned. "Now?"

"Ideally, yeah. I've got a cab waiting."

"Just a minute." She walked back to a group around the braziers, who watched her curiously. They listened while she spoke, frowned and glared at Hines, eventually nodded reluctantly. Mary touched each of them in turn and they softened, relaxed into an almost soporific fugue state. Hines felt the magic swell in the air. He had never seen it as clearly before. He knew Mary was powerful, but hadn't seen her work so blatantly manifest before. It would only be visible to others with a talent, of course, but his ability was so slight it was rare that he could decipher much of anyone else's activity.

Mary came back over to him, grace and vitality in rags and dirt. She almost danced wherever she walked. "Come on then."

"Have you noticed anything recently?" he asked her.

"Like what?"

"Like with the talents. Do you feel it's stronger or something at the moment?"

Mary nodded, eyes distant. "The power is potent, certainly. It has been for a while, growing more so by the day. I've divined the stars and seen alignments I haven't noticed before. I would never have connected these alignments with the increase in the power, but it's there."

"Correlation isn't causation," Steven said.

"Oh, I agree. And it's unlikely too, but I can see no other reason. Of course, perhaps there is no other reason."

"There has to be a reason," Hines said, frustrated.

Mary smiled at him, one eyebrow raised. "Does there?"

15

Jerry Rundle sucked on a cigarette and grimaced at the stain on the asphalt. It rippled, its tiny neon pinpricks waving gently. The bells rang, distant and cajoling. He wanted to move closer, listen to that soul-salving music, but he kept the image of Blackford front and center of his mind, the poor bastard leaning over that patch in the apartment and the horror that ensued. And even then, the compulsion to go to that shimmering thing was almost unbearable.

The Blackford situation was going to see him investigated and thrown into a world of shit, but god bless the horribly understaffed police department. They were supposed to suspend him with pay – he'd shot and killed a fellow officer, for Christ's sake – but they simply couldn't spare the manpower. And after the briefing he'd just attended he wondered if they'd have enough cops on patrol even if they pulled in everyone and their cousins. And frankly, he was glad to keep working. The last thing he wanted was to sit at home and brood over what he'd done. What he'd had to do.

A van pulled up and two city maintenance crew jumped out. "You're Rundle?" one asked.

"Yeah. You got the stuff?" Rundle read Baker on the man's nametag, Jarrett on his partner's.

Baker nodded, pulled open the rear doors of the van. He hefted a large plastic tank onto his shoulder and wielded the long spray nozzle. "Where do you want it?"

"What's that music?" Jarrett said, head tipped to one side. He started down the alley.

Rundle grabbed his collar, hauled him back. "Don't go down there!"

"What the fuck?" Jarrett turned, face twisted in fury.

"How strong is that stuff?" Rundle asked, not letting go of the younger man's collar.

"Strip the tattoos off an angry biker, this would. And yeah, what is that music?"

Rundle shook his head. He couldn't hold them both back. "Spray there. From a distance, don't get near."

Baker looked at where he was pointing. "I don't see any graffiti… Oh, that glittering stuff. Man, that's beautiful." He started forward.

Rundle grunted in annoyance, flicked his cigarette away and snatched the spray nozzle from the worker's hand. Over the man's protests, he pumped the handle, blueish liquid bursting out to mix with the rain still falling. It spattered over the patch of nodding green domes and they buckled. All three men cried out in pain at the sudden, high-pitched squeal. Wincing, Rundle grabbed the nozzle from the ground where he'd dropped it and sprayed again, moving close to soak the patch point-blank. The squeal rose and wavered, then faded away. The oil stain on the asphalt broke up and drifted apart in the puddles of mixed chemicals and rain.

"Well, I'm glad this works," Rundle said, handing the nozzle back. He pulled a fresh cigarette from his pocket.

"What the hell was that?" Baker asked, leaning in for a closer look at the blackened, oily mess.

Rundle tensed momentarily as the worker got close, but nothing happened. "Whatever it is, it's messing people up. See how it sorta tempted you in?"

"I wanted to listen to it," Jarrett said wistfully.

Rundle turned to him, eyes hard. "And if you had," he said, punctuating his words with short thrusts of his cigarette, "it would have killed you. Spread the word to all your teams. Do not approach. Spray generously and kill this stuff wherever it's found. Can you do that? Isn't that what your superiors already told you to do? Keep your distance?"

Baker nodded, still looking at the mess on the road. He pulled a phone from his pocket.

"Make it very clear," Rundle said. "Make sure they understand that they'll be tempted to get close and listen. Don't let them." His eyes narrowed. "Say, can you tell your bosses to make sure everyone wears earmuffs? Or headphones with loud music playing? Tell them that." He didn't know if it would work, and the visual compulsion was almost as strong as the sound, but it had to be worth a try.

While Baker rang in to the city officials, Rundle called back to headquarters and made the same case. His lieutenant somewhat reluctantly accepted Rundle's suggestion and rang off to spread the word. Rundle had been hesitant to make the call, if he was honest. Nothing about any of this made any kind of sense. But if it worked, he'd advocate it. After seeing what happened to Blackford, how could he deny it? But what the hell had happened to that poor bastard?

According to the broken reports they were getting from elsewhere, and what he'd learned, and earlier dismissed, from the barkeeper, he'd been lucky to stop Blackford with his revolver. It had taken the barman several point-blank shots with a 12-gauge. And more reports were coming in all the time, people running around naked, assaulting strangers. The brass were already in serious damage control, suppressing news sources, telling people to stay home. They were fighting a losing battle if it kept spreading as fast as it had been.

"We got another one," Jarrett called out.

Rundle turned, dropped his cigarette and ground it out. "I'll ride with you."

It only took a few minutes to drive to the next location, a tall brown brick apartment block and a beat cop with a haunted expression and his fingers in his ears. The corner between the steps up to the building and the street was piled with garbage bags and the uniform stood with his back steadfastly to it. "Get away!" he yelled at someone walking down the steps. They leaned over to look into the shadows.

"I can hear something," the resident said.

Rundle ran up and brandished his badge. "Get inside."

The resident looked at him annoyed and Rundle grabbed his coat collar and hauled him through the doors. The man's eyes cleared when they entered the lobby.

"Stay here, please," Rundle said. "And don't let anyone else leave until I tell you. Won't be a minute."

The man nodded, brow creased.

Rundle returned to the street and saw Baker with iPod headphones in his ears, waving the uniform cop aside. He shouldered the chemical tank and approached the corner, eyes narrow in concentration. Rundle held his breath, but Baker looked around, spotted something and sprayed.

He sprayed again, nodded and pulled the earbuds out. "Done," he called out.

The uniform and Rundle joined Baker, looked at the slick black stain.

"The music's stopped," the uniform said. "Not listening to it helped. But I nearly gave in, I wanted so badly to look at it, then as soon as I remembered and blocked my ears, the temptation went away a little bit. What's happening here?"

"No idea," Rundle said honestly. "At least we've got some way to work against whatever the hell this is. Spread the word and keep searching the whole city. I doubt we'll get them all, but we have to try. My boss said they're drafting in help, whatever that means."

A van with a small oscillating satellite dish on top screeched to a halt and a woman in a tight business suit jumped out carrying a microphone. She was followed by a man carrying an umbrella to preserve her studio hair and another with a camera on his shoulder.

Rundle grimaced. "Oh, just great."

The woman went straight to business. "You're a detective with Cleveport PD, is that right?"

"I've got no comment for you," Rundle said, trying to walk away. He gestured to the maintenance boys and the uniform cop. "Go!"

They went, gladly.

"We're live, Detective. Can you please tell the people of Cleveport what's going on in their fine city? What did you just do there?" She pointed beside the steps where the black puddle was slowing rinsing away in the rain.

"We're working here, ma'am," Rundle said through gritted teeth. "Otherwise I have no comment for you." These news crews were supposed to have been called off, threatened with national security gags. There were always bloody superheroes among the reporters, grinning from their own moral high ground. The kind of assholes who triggered mass panic. He started away down the path, in the opposite direction to the uniform. The maintenance crew drove away, apologetic faces as they went by.

"The people have a right to know what's happening, Detective."

Rundle turned to her, his face angry. "Go to headquarters and wait for a statement there. I have nothing for you." He strode off along the sidewalk, refused to look back or respond to her repeated demands. Eventually she gave up and the news crew returned to their van. Rundle shook his head. Things were only going to get worse.

16

Sam Moore sits in deep meditation, preparing to draw the psychological strands of the population together. He's an expert and his skills have made him very rich. But he's been inexplicably putting this off for quite a few days and nerves rill through him like tiny fish darting through shallow water. Last time he made a batch of misery something had been different. It had never been easier, but a deep sensation, almost a pain, had scratched at him throughout the process. However, orders need filling and work must be done.

Moore clears his mind, retunes to the frequencies of pain. A large gauge needle hangs from his arm, clear tubing snakes to a small collecting jar beside him. Dave and Sally are watching, almost holding their breath as he works, thinking they're silent. They wait to work with him on whatever small amount he manages to produce, maybe a couple of hundred milliliters on a good day. Mix that with the sugar water suspension, mage the whole mix, refine it into a standing enchantment, coaxing pleasure from pain like deriving satisfaction from hard labor. Then they package it in tiny amounts, ampules waiting for a user to tickle it back to life with their own talent and ride the disquiet of the population like a rollercoaster.

But the presence of Dave and Sally is deafening, no matter how quiet they try to remain, their fears, their neuroses, their anxieties, hollering through the aether like the screams of frightened children in the dark. He will harvest from them first as he always does. And they won't know it, as they never do.

Moore's power leeches through the null space between

reality and thought, between actuality and wishdreams, between now and maybe. He gathers the most damaging and debilitating emotions of his two friends and weaves them into strands of intentions, physicalizes them in his mind and lets that essence flow through his body. Lets it become clear, liquid misery. His magic swells out, the deep itch burning as he directs that sweet fluid to the hole in his flesh, the needle within it, and a single drop emerges like a struggling newborn from an egg and trickles into the tube.

Moore smiles as his work begins, but an ache in his hindbrain, a noise in the base of his skull distracts him briefly. Annoyed, he pushes it aside, uses the discontentment of his friends to leapfrog from the derelict building they're in to the street outside. The poverty-stricken byways of the worst part of town. Cleveport's lowest paid, least considered populace. Their struggle is the hardest, their desperation the sweetest.

Sam Moore sails the astral winds through the roads and tenements of the struggling city and breathes in the misery of its population like smoke. He uses his unique skills to distill that essence, refine the emotion. Another drop squeezes free from the catheter, then another. He's rolling now, casually harvesting Cleveport's never-ending supply and the drips become a trickle, become a stream. Way too fast, way too easy.

Panic rises from Moore's groin, creeps up his spine like a questing predator, seeking his mind. His quarry has never come this effortlessly before, this quickly. The pain in his brain stem rises like a tide, electric shudders of agony through his head and body. He cries out, a weak, helpless sound, desperate for his eyes to open, but they stay closed as if glued together.

Dave and Sally are up, running uselessly left and right, yelling about what they should do. Sam astrally sees their eyes wide in horror at the misery flooding over the edges of the small collecting jar. The jar that usually takes two or three hours to fill maybe halfway. The half jar that is mixed and diluted a hundredfold to make even the strongest misery drug that sells for the highest price.

Moore flinches and shudders. One leg kicks out involuntarily and the jar skids across the floor and shatters against a wall, a glimmering, silvery trail of pure, high-grade misery making an arc across the filthy tiles. The needle hangs from Moore's arm and his blood pumps out with more and more of the distilled horror of the city, now a silvery pink mix of hatred and lifeblood.

The pain becomes a white noise in Moore's mind. All he knows is agony, all he hears are the cries of everyone in Cleveport, the desolation of those millions of souls, all channeling through him and pumping from his arm. Dave and Sally yell in a panic. Sally sobbing and retching as she shouts. The door bangs and they run, leave him to convulse across the floor. His face smashes and drags against the rough tiles, his skin flays off with the motion. His nose crashes down and bursts in fresh pain and blood, an eyebrow splits open. And all the while the misery draws the moisture from him, manifesting itself in his bodily fluids and Sam Moore is desiccating with the power of a process he can't stop. A process that has never been so strong, so vibrant, so total. His brain shrinks to a prune as his flesh draws tight and paper dry against his bones and still the arcane community's favorite vice pumps lurid, shining pink from his arm until his body has not a molecule of moisture left to give.

17

Hines's phone rang as the cab cruised along towards his apartment, Abby's name displayed across the screen. Good. He'd been wondering what to tell Mary if he didn't get the call by the time they reached his building. "Yo, you took your time."

Abby made a sound of disgust. "Fuck you, Hines, the city is in meltdown here. You won't believe what I just had a briefing about. Where are you?"

"Near my place. You?"

"On the way to the west side. I need you to meet me there."

"Okay."

Abby gave him the address and Mary raised an eyebrow as he hung up. He leaned forward, asked the driver to turn around. "You're giving me very good business today, sir," the happy Indian said.

"It's all on expenses, pal. Make the most of it."

He turned from the wobbling turban and flicked Mary an apologetic smile. "Sorry, we have to go west. I thought Abby would meet us here, but this is all a bit messed up."

"I don't honestly know if I can help you," Mary said. She'd told him as much before.

"I know, but I don't know anyone else who might either, so I'm happy for you to try."

They drove on in silence to a small industrial estate with row upon row of storage lock-ups, small garages with roller doors, each marked with a number. Hines watched the numerals. When they turned into the row with 167, he didn't need to count anymore. Two patrol cars with lights flashing blocked the way ahead and blue and white tape marked off a space beyond them. Hines tapped the driver's shoulder. "Here we go." He counted out the huge fare and handed it over. "Thanks for your patience."

"You don't want me to wait, sir? Maybe you need to go somewhere else?"

Steven grinned. Nice try. "No thanks, buddy. I think I've pushed expenses far enough for now."

The driver looked wistfully forward towards the police cars. "Shame, I've been enjoying this. You have interesting things going on!"

Steven patted the guy's shoulder. "Believe me, pal, you don't want anything to do with my kind of interesting."

He and Mary got out and the cab backed away. They walked to the tape and a uniform approached, hand up. "You can't come this way, folks."

"Abby Jones is here. She's expecting us."

The policeman frowned at them, then shrugged. "Wait a sec."

He turned back to the cars and called out. Abby's head appeared from the open door of unit 167. "Let 'em through," she said.

The policeman lifted the tape.

Steven nodded his thanks and they went under. There was a large station wagon parked in the lock-up unit. A man, clearly deceased, lay on the hood, reclining on the windshield. Abby and a couple of forensic officers were inside, one checking the back of the car, the other photographing the scene.

"This what your briefing was about?" Steven asked.

Abby shook her head. "I'll tell you about that in a minute. This is another death like the ones we talked about." She looked at Mary. "This our expert?"

Hines moved aside, gestured Mary through. "Yeah, sorry. Mary, this is Detective Sergeant Abby Jones."

"Hey, Mary." Abby reached out and the women shook.

Abby turned to the forensic officers. "You done?"

"Yeah, for here. No obvious cause of death, we'll have to get him back to the morgue."

"Okay, you two wait outside while I talk with these guys here. Send the patrols away, they have a lot of work to do in the city, get them onto that. And make sure they got the memo about blocking their fucking ears."

The man pulled back the plastic hood of his disposable overalls. "Yeah, what the hell is all that about?"

"Who knows? Send 'em on and wait outside. Once we're done here you can take this stiff with you and I'll seal up the scene. One of you can drive this car to the impound yard, yeah?"

The forensic officer nodded. "Sure, once the body's loaded I'll take it to the morgue and Geoff can take the car in."

"Great, thanks."

The men left and Hines heard their muffled conversation outside, the police officers' obvious reluctance to do whatever they were told to do. Abby waited patiently until the patrol cars drove off and checked to make sure the forensic boys were out of earshot. They stood chatting by their car a few yards away. "Okay," she said. "First off, check in the back of this station wagon."

Hines and Mary did as she asked. The trunk was packed full of polystyrene packing cases, each the size of a cigar box. Hines took one of the top packages and opened it. Five rows of a dozen small glass ampules were neatly tucked inside, each in its own indentation. "Sixty in a box, got to be a hundred boxes in here, at least. That's six thousand hits. That's worth a lot of moolah on the street, couple of hundred grand easy."

"So it's definitely misery?" Abby asked.

He shrugged. "Looks like it. Can I break one? I'll tell you for sure."

"Yeah, it's not cataloged yet. That's my job. Hardly in keeping with regulations to sample the evidence on the scene, but what the hell about this day is anything close to regulations?"

Hines pulled one small glass vial from the box. He snapped the top off and gingerly sniffed at it. "Smells like nothing at all." He held it away from his face, looking at Mary and Abby to stand back. They moved away and he crouched, put one hand to the concrete floor of the unit. *Hey, girl,* he whispered to the city, letting his skill flow through his fingertips. The connection to Cleveport was instant and stronger than he expected, the pulse and beat of the city, the massed life and its effect on the streets and buildings. The sensation of her mild distress had increased again. He winced at Jenny's presence, even though she was long gone. Her pattern was like an echo through his hand. He only ever felt that, saw her, through mirrors. Things were changing and he didn't like the way they were going.

The liquid in the ampule shifted as he focused on it with his talent manifest, turned to a swirling blueish gas and spiraled out of the glass. Hines broke his connection, tried to ignore the city's sigh of disappointment. He leaned further from the vial while the gas twisted up and away and dissipated. He wafted a hand around to make sure it was all dispersed. "Definitely misery," he said with a crooked smile.

He put the broken ampule into the polystyrene case and slipped it back into its place in the stack.

"What's going on here?" Mary asked.

"We got this report in and I happened to hear it. When they described the cargo in the car, I took it on straight away. There's other serious shit going down in this town, I'll tell you about it in a minute, but this is connected somehow, I'm sure. I convinced the Cap to let me stay on it. Mary, can you tell me how this guy died?"

Mary moved to look at the young man on the front of the car. "I don't know. I'll try." She put her hands on the dead man's face, one on each cheek, and closed her eyes. She winced almost immediately, shifted her grip. After a moment she pulled away. "His body is riddled with the effects of misery. It's like he overdosed on it, but I don't see how that's possible."

Abby pointed to the man's hand, one empty ampule with the top snapped off laying in his palm.

"Oh, I don't doubt he took some," Mary said. "But the extent of its influence is unlike anything I've ever seen. It can't kill, this stuff. Unless, perhaps, it's some new and extremely potent version. But even then, the very nature of it… I don't understand."

"Or the magic being stronger than ever is making normal misery deadly," Hines said.

Mary looked at him, face creased in a frown. "Is that possible?"

He laughed. "Who knows, I'm a useless conjuror. You're the expert. You agreed the magic in town is stronger than ever, right?"

Mary nodded, lips pursed. "I suppose it's possible, given that misery is made with the powers and activated with them too, that perhaps the increased vibrations through everything right now could be making the drug deadly." She shrugged. "It's possible, I suppose, but I'm really no expert."

"So we can expect a lot more ODs like this?" Abby asked.

Mary looked at her with sad eyes. "Sure, if we're right about this. Honestly, the stuff ruins so many lives."

"All drugs do that," Abby said. "For most people they're just a bit of good fun, but for a percentage of the population they're always going to be destructive. Same with booze and anything else. You'll always find people who take something too far. Or are so damaged they actively seek oblivion. But if this stuff starts killing everyone who uses it, we could see a massive increase in deaths. I don't need to tell you two how that's going to fuck things with the pen-pushers and the PD."

"This is attention our community really doesn't need," Mary said.

"So perhaps we need to figure out the source," Steven said. Both women looked at him quizzically. "If misery is like this now because the magic is getting stronger, we need to figure out why that's happening. The misery situation itself is a by-product. A symptom."

"And if we can't do anything about the magic?" Abby asked, wincing at the word.

Steven laughed. "Then I guess we're more fucked than ever."

Raised voices outside caught their attention. Three men in well-tailored suits appeared at the unit door. The forensic officers were behind them. "We told them they couldn't come in here," one of them said nervously.

"It's okay," Abby said. "Go back to your car, we're nearly done here." She looked at the three men, addressed the huge, thickly muscled one in the middle. "This is a crime scene, you can't be here."

The man craned his neck to see inside. His face flashed in annoyance when he spotted the body on the car, then he turned a smile to Abby. "What's happened here? Has there been an accident?"

Abby frowned. "Something like that."

The man opened his palms, supplicatory. "I hate to get involved with a police matter… You are the police, I assume?"

Abby flicked open her badge, pocketed it again without a word.

The big man smiled. "Yes, of course. Well, you see, the homeopathic remedies in that car are mine. I don't know who that person is, I can only assume he's the delivery driver. But I really need my product."

Abby smiled, but it was cold, like a shark. "Sorry, pal, this is a crime scene and that car and everything in it is impounded until we get a result on this situation. It's all evidence, I'm afraid."

The man's face darkened. "You can't do that! That's my merchandise. A lot of money is tied up in that."

"In homeopathic remedies?"

The man scowled. "You'd be surprised how much profit there is to be made in alternative medicines."

"Would I? You look like you've used a few alternative medicines yourself. You get all those muscles from supplements too?"

The big man ground his teeth. He looked like he was actually counting to ten. A thrill of adrenaline trickled through Hines's gut. Was this knucklehead dumb enough to actually attack a police officer? Abby slipped her hand inside her jacket to her shoulder holster. "I'll need your name and a contact number," she said affably.

The man growled in annoyance and turned away. His two friends followed. "I'll be contacting the department about this!" he said as he walked off, not looking back.

"I could really use your name," Abby called, but he got into a car and drove away.

Abby pulled out her phone and quick-dialed. "I need a name and address of the owner of a silver Mercedes C-Class." She gave the registration number. "Sure, call me back when you have anything. Thanks." She hung up and said to Hines and Mary, "Can we go to the morgue and double-check that the bodies there died the same way as this poor bastard?"

Mary nodded. "Sure, if you like. You're paying me."

"Am I?" Abby looked at Hines, one eyebrow raised.

He grinned like a mischievous kid. "If you're not, I have to pay her out of my earnings. Pal. Buddy."

Abby shook her head. "Come on, you can both ride with me. I've got a department car around the corner."

She stepped outside, waved the forensics boys back in. "Okay, get that body to the morgue and the car to impound."

She led Hines and Mary to her car and they waited while the forensic team did as she asked. When they were ready, she followed them to the precinct. "Just in case our musclebound friend decides to tail us," she said, by way of explanation. "Though I don't think he'll be that dumb."

She was right and the silver Mercedes was nowhere to be seen. Her phone rang as they crawled through traffic. "Hines," she said, pointing to a pad and pen on the dash, "write this down." She turned her attention back to the phone as she drove. "Yep. Yegor Koltsov." She spelled it out for Steven, then an address for *Yegor's Muscle and Fight*. She thanked the caller and hung up. "Given all the shit going down and the distinct lack of manpower right now, we might have to wait following that up, but good to know who it is."

"We?" Hines asked. He didn't relish ever seeing that huge, angry bastard ever again. Although he was glad his fruitless research into misery dealers was unlikely to be an issue now.

Abby glanced at him disdainfully. She pulled over to watch the station wagon full of misery pull through high gates into the police impound yard. As the lot was closed securely behind it, she said, "Let's get to the morgue and take a look at those bodies."

18

Yegor fumed and counted. He ignored the two behind him, asking questions about what they should do next, and the thin, nervous man beside him, who was smart enough to remain quiet. He held up a silencing finger and pulled out his phone, dialed. "Mr Crater," he said in Russian, hoping that would mollify the man. "I'm afraid I have some bad news."

"Not what I want to hear, Koltsov."

"No, sir, I know. But it seems our delivery driver got himself killed and the police found the car with our merchandise along with his body and have confiscated it."

Crater swore loudly down the line. "How did he die?"

"I don't know."

"The product is lost, you imbecile. Police impound in this city is a black fucking hole!"

"Yes, sir." Yegor ground his teeth. A black hole was his debt to this bastard now. How could it all have turned so much to shit? It should have been such an easy profit. He should kill the useless fucker who sat beside him, who put him onto this whole misery thing in the first place. He should have listened to his gut when the very concept made him feel uneasy from the outset. A magical drug, really? He was a fool! But the profit margin had been so high…

"You better have *some* good news for me!" Crater yelled at him.

"Well, I followed the police officer," Yegor said, trying to use his softest, most appeasing voice. "She had no idea I was behind her and she has two other people with her, clearly not cops. They were at the scene too. Something's going on. I don't know why she would have them with her unless perhaps they're experts on this misery stuff. Maybe, if they are, they might help us find some replacement merchandise."

There was silence on the other end while Crater mulled that over. "They were definitely not police?" he asked eventually.

"They can't have been. One looked like a tramp, she was dressed in rags. The other was too broken down and useless to be a policeman, but he was better dressed."

"There is no point in dealing directly with the PD in this town," Crater said. "It's too messy. But if you can isolate these two, bring them to me, they might help you pay off some of the debt you owe me." The line went dead.

Yegor slipped his phone back into a pocket. Perhaps he could pull himself out of this hole yet. He turned to the nervous man beside him. "This is all on you, Anthony, you realize that?"

"But, Yegor…"

"Shut up! You told me about this misery. You said you knew how to get a big score. You verified the merchandise with whatever that freaky trick was you did. All you needed was the capital. I got it for you. You *owe* me that capital, plus the profit I was promised."

Anthony scrunched up his thin face, wrung narrow hands. "Yegor, I have nothing like that kind of money!"

"And yet you owe it to me!" Yegor yelled. As the man shrank in his seat, Yegor said to the two in the back, "Get out and move around the building. I want to know when either of those two losers who were with the policewoman leave. I'll watch from here, you two cover the other streets. We must not lose them, you understand?" He turned to Anthony. "You too. Go and watch from across there, the entrance to the underground parking lot. If we lose them now, I will be taking what you owe me in either cash or skin. Got it?"

Anthony couldn't scramble from the car quickly enough.

One of the other men, hunched in the back half out of his seat, paused. "I told you he would be trouble," he said.

Yegor spun to face him. "Not now, Dmitri." His voice was dangerously low.

Dmitri shrugged and followed Anthony and the other thug across the road.

Yegor sat and counted while he watched.

19

Jerry Rundle patted the city worker on the shoulder. "Not your fault, Chuck."

Chuck sobbed, eyes wide in mystified horror in his dark-skinned face. "He just… he just went crazy. Screaming and he tore his clothes off and ran. Just ran away. I hid and he barreled right by me."

"Did he have his ears covered beforehand?"

Chuck shook his head. "Said it was all pointless, bureaucrats over-reacting. Then he went kinda still and tripped-out, like, you know? Leaned right forward over the thing and it…"

Rundle patted him again. "I know. I've seen it. Not your fault. You sprayed it, though?"

"Fucking-A! I drenched that thing."

"Can you carry on alone?"

Chuck rubbed a hand over his thick hair, seemed to pull himself slowly together. "Yeah, I guess so. What the hell is going on, man? This is some unnatural shit."

Rundle laughed without humor. "You are not wrong. Honestly, I have no idea what's going on, but we have to try to deal with it. Keep patrolling, keep your ears covered, spray anything you find."

Chuck grinned, gestured to the earphones around his neck. "I got Jimi's whole back catalog on here and more. Let that shit try to get past the greatest guitar player who ever lived!"

"Good work. Get to it. I'm sorry about your friend."

"Me too."

Rundle looked around. "Any idea where he went?"

Chuck pointed. "That way. Beyond that, who knows. I

was kinda stunned and could only think of spraying that shit away."

"Okay, thanks. Good luck."

Chuck climbed into his van and drove slowly off, scanning the footpaths and side streets as he went. Rundle watched him go, wondered how they were going to keep up with whatever the hell was happening. More reports were coming by the minute, and the majority were of people affected by the pools rather than spotting and calling them in. He pulled out his phone, dialed in to report Chuck's story. After the details were taken, Dispatch said, "Chief wants a word."

Without waiting for confirmation, Chief Watson blustered on. "Fucking mess we got here, Rundle. Big fucking mess."

Rundle nodded. *No shit*. "Yes, sir."

"I got civilians, cops and city workers all over falling victim to this unholy scourge. I got people saying they emptied clips into those affected and it made no difference. They just shoot chunks off the bastards and it doesn't even slow them down."

"What I heard too."

"So how come you took down Blackford with six bullets, Rundle?"

"Nearest I can figure is that I got him while he was still… changing. You know, not fully transformed or something. Must take a while to get through the system and I shot out the still human part of him."

"Big fucking mess," the Chief said again. "I got citizens making traffic jams on the roads out north, south and west, leaving town like rats. It's not helping."

"Maybe we need to close the roads," Rundle suggested. "Tell people to stay home?"

"Maybe we do. What the hell is happening here, Jerry?

We've got scientists working all over and they're all saying the same thing: This stuff is not possible."

"And yet here we are knee-deep in it. Chief, no offense, but why are you telling me all this?" Rundle had never heard his boss so unsettled and unfocused before. Watson was one of the most driven and direct men he had ever met.

"What? Oh, yeah, sorry, Jerry. Listen, we've got word from the mayor that the military are coming in. They're mobilizing a task force from Fort Carter as it's only an hour away. They're gonna work with us supposedly, but you know what that means."

"They're gonna come blundering in and screw all of us?"

"Pretty much, yeah. Still, hopefully they'll close up the roads and contain this shit. So I'm spreading the word and I want you to help pass it along. Keep everyone busy but try to pass control along to the army as quickly as possible. They want control, so let 'em have it. We got too many cops and workers dying out there. Let the army cop it. They're even suggesting curfews or military law."

"It won't come to that, surely?"

"Who knows, man? Who knows? Oh, and one other thing."

Jerry frowned. What the hell else was there? "Yeah?"

"Social media is going viral. We got civilians uploading smartphone videos and all kinds of shit. We got doomsday cults and alien invasion nutjobs having a field day. This has exploded beyond all control, but on no account are you to say anything to any media or talk to any civilians in case they're recording, you got that? We neither confirm nor deny *anything*."

"You got it, boss. I'm happy not talking to anyone at the best of times anyway."

"Good. I gotta go. Stay safe, Jerry."

The line went dead. Rundle stared at the phone for

moment. This morning had been just another wet day in Cleveport. Now military rule was on its way. He'd be glad to see the army take over, truth be told. Since he'd had to shoot Blackford in the head, all he wanted to do was hand this craziness on to someone else and occupy himself with something entirely different. Right now an early retirement and a long drive far away from Cleveport struck him as a fine option. But that wasn't a possibility just yet. People were being called in off vacation leave. Even those on sick leave had been called, asked if they were really too sick to come to work.

Screams shocked him from his reverie. A naked woman ran across the intersection fifty yards up the street, followed by a group of four or five men. As Rundle watched they pulled guns and pumped shot after shot into the woman's back. She staggered and stumbled but kept going. The men stopped halfway across the road, talked animatedly and decided they'd done enough. They ran back the way they'd come.

I just stood and watched a mob shoot a woman. And I'm not going to do a thing about it.

He called dispatch and reported the direction the woman had been heading and they assured the first available unit would go that way. He doubted anyone would get there anything like fast enough to find her. And what might she do in the meantime? He headed to the next item on his list: an apartment block that had reported an attack by a naked man.

20

Gina sat on the edge of a double bed in a musty motel room, lost in a daze of confusion. The sadache was passing, but it left her fatigued. Dreggy. Rufus had gone crazy. It scared her. She took her phone out, dialed home and again it rang through to the answering machine. Four tries over the course of an hour. Clearly, no one was home. Would anyone ever be there?

She fell back, stared at the dust-covered ceiling fan and the patches of water damage on the plasterboard above. They made Rorschach tests, that one a lion's head, that one a sea serpent. Her eye fell on a shape like a dog with its guts burst open and entrails lying across the ground in front of it and she broke. Great wracking sobs burst from her and she rolled facedown into the bedspread and let her grief and fear out. Trev was actually dead. She had watched him die. Her parents were dead too, right? What the fuck was that stuff she had seen in the kitchen? And Rufus, her big, beautiful bear who always lost his mind with joy to see her, had lost his mind in an entirely different and more permanent way. She was lost and scared.

Eventually the sobs receded and she hitched quiet, trembling breaths. She pulled off her clothes and showered, washed her hair, scrubbed herself clean to start again. But start where? Perhaps she was over-reacting. Maybe her parents were just in town or at a friend's and she would catch them eventually. They weren't answering their cells any more than the home phone, but maybe they were in company, phones turned off.

But she knew, deep inside she was certain, that the truth was far more sinister than simple social etiquette.

She pulled on underwear and flicked on the television. A newscast was underway, the reporter standing at an intersection in the heart of Cleveport. Gina dropped her jeans on the bed and went to find the remote, turn the TV up.

"… police are being very cagey in their responses. The majority of officials and police we've tried to talk to have been tight-lipped, simply repeating over and over that old mantra, 'No comment.' But it's clear that something is wrong in this city."

The screen cut to an image of a naked man, his genitals pixelated, running along the street. As he headed directly for the camera, the image began to shake, the cameraman obviously hurrying backward. The naked man's attention was suddenly diverted by something out of frame and he turned sharply to his left. The camera tracked and caught him disappearing into the doors of a 7-11 and screaming erupted from inside.

"More and more reports of people acting like this are coming in from all over the city and the suburbs," the reporter said over the images. "Particularly from the heart of Cleveport where the population is most dense. And the strange fungal growths cropping up everywhere are definitely connected."

The scene cut to an alleyway, shot from high above. The camera zoomed in and Gina gasped to see the oily black patch with speckles of glowing green across it. Exactly what she'd seen in her parents' kitchen. A woman entered the shot from one side, her head tilted as if listening.

The screen fuzzed into static for a moment, then cut to a studio. A well-dressed man behind a desk looked harried for a moment before composing himself. "Our apologies, we appear to have lost our outside broadcast signal there." He glanced off camera. "Can we..? Ah, right." He focused back to the world at large, smile plastered into place. "We can't return you to that footage, I'm afraid. Meanwhile, the police department has issued a statement that the poisonous chemical spill affecting the city is being contained, but the assistance of the military is being sought. Roads in and out of Cleveport are being closed and people are being asked to remain at home. Order will, apparently, be restored quickly. So please, don't panic, stay home and watch the news for updates." He paused, clearly listening. His brow creased. "And now we go to Gil for a weather update."

Gina sat on the end of the bed, clicked off the insane news report, one hand covering her mouth. A loud banging on her door made her jump and cry out. She looked over as the knocking repeated, louder and more frantic.

"Go away!" she yelled.

"You gotta let us in," a man's voice shouted. He sounded desperate.

"You're not coming in," Gina called back. "Go to the office!"

"We don't want a fucking room! We need to check you."

Gina mouthed words that wouldn't come out. "What?" she managed eventually.

The banging came again, heavy enough that she saw the door flex.

"Go away!" Gina screamed and the door burst inwards, the latch splintering from the frame.

A large man in jeans and checked shirt lowered his kicking leg and strode into the room, three more people behind him. Gina screamed, tried to run for the bathroom but the man was quick. He grabbed her arm and swung her around.

"We have to test you!" he growled.

The other three, two men and a woman, crowded in and grabbed Gina's arms and legs. She thrashed and screamed, tried to bite their hands and wrists, but they lifted her and used their body weight to hold her splayed on the bed. The big man who had kicked in the door pulled a shining bowie knife from his belt.

Gina fell silent and deathly still, ice closed over her gut. "What are you doing?" she whispered, her voice barely more than a croak.

"Gotta test ya! If we ain't allowed to leave, we have to protect ourselves!" The man leaned forward and drew the blade of the knife across the left-hand side of her belly.

Gina wailed, the pain red hot and exquisite. She craned her neck, tried to look up and see how much damage was done. Was he gutting her? Her blood flowed thick and free from the four-inch wound, ran across her stomach and over her hip, soaked into the waistband of her underwear. She cried and gasped, the cut burning furiously.

The four people stared for a moment at her blood, all of them frozen in an absurd tableau.

"She's clear," the big man said. "Stay here. Do not leave!"

The attackers turned and walked out, not sparing her a second glance. Gina staggered into the bathroom, pressed a towel against the cut and sobbed. She ground her teeth against the pain, finally chancing to look. The wound was quite deep, the side gaping open like an eye, but it seemed to only be through her modest layer of belly fat. She used her fingers to squeeze the sides together and pressed down on it. She gasped at the pain, but it was only surface discomfort, not any deep and life-threatening hurt that she could detect. What the fuck were those people doing? Testing her for what?

She kept the small towel against her body to staunch the blood and managed to drag on jeans and t-shirt one-handed. She went to the office, scanning for the knife-wielding lunatics. The whole place seemed strangely quiet. The office was deserted, but she was past caring. She searched around the desk and cupboards, went through to the small kitchenette behind. Under the sink she found a First Aid kit and pulled it open. With a noise of relief she found a packet of small stick-on butterfly stitches. She carefully wiped and washed the wound, then stuck it closed with a row of a dozen tiny patches like miniature dumbbells. She put a piece of gauze over that and stuck it down with strips of fabric sticking plaster to keep it all in place. The cut still burned enough to make tears stand in the corners of her eyes, but she felt at least mostly fixed for now.

Back in her room she quickly packed up the last of her things, pulled on her boots and jacket and went back outside. Fuck staying put. She needed to be with people she could trust, but the problem was she had no real friends. Her whole life had been not fitting in. Not happy at home, not happy at school. She'd finally met Trev and they understood each other, but now he was gone. None of her other friends were anything more than acquaintances she really didn't like much.

Except maybe Dave and Sally. Trev always got his gear from them and they were decent people. They seemed to get it, operated on her wavelength, at least in part. She got on really well with Sally. They lived in the inner city, their place a cool warehouse conversion on the western edge of the business district. They were probably the closest thing she had to friends and Sally had always been genuine. Maybe they were the help she needed.

A rumbling drew her attention and three army vehicles powered by, dark green and armored, covered in thick plates of metal. Their huge, deep-tread tires thrummed loudly against the asphalt.

A bus approached from the west, city-bound. Gina ran for the bus stop right outside the motel, waving frantically. The driver watched with his eyes narrowed but didn't stop.

As he shot by, *Not In Service* flashed across the front where the destination should be.

Gina stood forlorn, looked up and back along the strangely empty street. She pulled her phone free and dialed her mother again, knowing it would ring out. When it did, she rang Sally.

She thought that phone would ring out too, but after several seconds it was answered. "Yep."

"Sally, it's Gina."

"Hey there. Sorry, we got nothing right now. You'll have to try…"

"Sally, please, I just need some help."

"What kinda help? I've had a fucked up day, Gina, I'm not in a helpful mood."

"I need a friend." Gina cursed internally at the weakness in her voice.

"You okay, hon?" Sally barked a laugh. "Let's be honest, no one's really okay right now, huh?"

"What's going on?" Gina sounded plaintive now and she hated it.

"Go to Trev," Sally said. "You two just hole up together until this all passes, yeah? That's what me and Dave are doing after the shit we've seen today."

Gina drew a deep breath, chewed her lip. "Trev's dead," she managed, finally saying the truth out loud.

There was silence from the other end for a long while. As Gina drew breath to ask if Sally was still there, Sally said, "Where are you? I'll come and get you."

21

Pulling the car into the secure parking for the morgue, Abby finished filling in Hines and Mary on the city-wide panic.

"Clearly magical," Mary said.

Abby glanced back over the seat at her. "Really? Why?"

"You said yourself, the change rate is unnatural. As far as you guys have figured out, people get infected by this strange plant-like substance…"

"More like fungus, is the latest thinking," Abby interjected. "Kinda fungal spore pools or some shit."

"Right, okay. Fungus. So people get caught by these fungal spores and become almost entirely fibrous in less than an hour?"

"That's the best guess so far. The labs are all pulling overtime, but it's hard to get a track on what's really happening. The bodies of people affected, once they've gone mad and pinned everyone with as many of their needly things as possible, seem to just break down and disappear. If they're not stopped they eventually just seem to keel over and disintegrate."

"All in virtually no time at all," Mary said.

"Hours, yeah."

"So it's got to be magical. Can you think of any natural process that turns up out of nowhere and affects things that quickly? I mean, sure, there are drugs that can get into a bloodstream and have an almost instant effect on brain chemistry. That could explain the madness. But the physical changes? The production of those spines? No natural process on Earth works that fast."

"She has a point," Hines said. "And if the magic in the

city is becoming exponentially more potent by the minute, as it seems to be, then these things are only going to get more potent too. Perhaps that's even why they're here, because of the increased magic."

"Or is the magic increased because the fungal things are here?" Abby asked.

Steven shrugged. "Which came first, the chicken or the egg?"

Mary huffed. "The egg. I can't believe people still draw that ridiculous analogy."

Abby turned off the engine, twisted in her seat. "What?"

"Yeah," Hines said. "What?"

Mary looked from one to the other and back again. "Oh, you're serious? Goddess, whatever next? Birds evolved from reptiles, right? Chickens are birds?"

Steven frowned. "Yeah?"

"Well, reptiles had been laying eggs for eons before birds of any kind were around, so eggs came way before chickens."

Abby laughed. "I never really thought of that."

Mary lifted her palms. "Seems hardly anyone ever does. It mystifies me."

"Okay, haughty tramp lady," Steven said. "Keep your hair on." When Mary scowled at him he flashed her a winning smile and plunged on. "But anyway, surely the increased strength of misery, the fact it can kill people now, is because of the massive increase in magical power here. And these fungal things Abby's telling us about are either here because of that increased potency or at least extra strong because of it. Whether the greater magic caused them or they caused it is what we need to establish, yes? But either way, all this stuff has to be connected."

"Let's go see these bodies," Abby said. "Confirm they're misery ODs. That will help everything."

"It's moot now, isn't it?" Steven asked.

Abby shrugged. "I'm a completionist. It's good policing."

"You still insist on good policing in the face of all this?"

She glared at him. "What else is there?"

Hines pursed his lips, nodded resignedly. "Yeah. Point."

Abby led them through sterile, fluorescent-lit corridors. Several rooms were hives of activity. Bodies lay on tables surrounded by doctors and lab technicians. Some corpses were broken and blackened, fibrous, grassy tufts protruding where flesh and muscle should be. One room had techs in a panic as whatever they'd been working on liquefied and ran across the tables, dripped viscously to the floor. "Contain and analyze that shit!" someone yelled and rushed past them, face like a storm cloud.

It took about fifteen minutes for Mary to confirm that Abby's corpses had incredibly high concentrations of misery in their systems. She could find nothing else to suggest they'd died for any other reason.

"It's going to cause a lot more bodies to start turning up," Mary said, her face creased in pain. "There are a lot of people using misery out there."

"You think one hit is enough to kill someone now?" Abby asked.

Mary shrugged. "Maybe not. Recreational users may just experience incredibly powerful, unexpected highs and back off a little. But the broken people, the ones who use it for genuine escape rather than escapist fun, they'll take more. And they'll die."

"Way things are going, Cleveport won't have any residents left before long," Hines said.

Abby reached out, shook Mary's hand. "Thanks, really. I appreciate your time and expertise."

"No problem."

"We need to pay you. I guess you don't really invoice or

anything?"

Mary smiled. "Steven knows how to get funds to me. Whatever you think is the right amount, I'll leave that up to you."

"Really?" Abby had one eyebrow raised. "I really have no idea…"

Mary held up a hand. "Steven can decide. The celestial river flows. But maybe you could give me twenty dollars for a cab fare back to my work?"

Abby nodded, pulled her wallet from a jacket pocket. "Sure, sure. Here you go. And thanks again. I'm sorry if we've wasted your time. All this…" She gestured uselessly at the room, perhaps the world at large.

Mary took the money with a slight bow, tucked it in her dress. "I'm sorry I couldn't be more help. But anything like this must have a root cause. That should be your focus now. Look past this everyday stuff, the misery, even these pools of strange fungus." She smiled softly, kindly. "Look beyond policing. All rivers have a source."

"Perhaps we can call you again if we need something else?" Abby said. "I value your perspective."

"Of course. Again, Steven knows how."

"Thank you. And be careful out there. Don't go down any alleys or get close to naked people," she added with a wry smile.

Mary laughed. "The goddesses protect." She left, seeming to almost glide along the corridor back the way they'd come.

Abby looked at Hines, half a smile tugging at her lips. "Pretty smart lady, but a bit of a fucking hippy, right?"

Steven couldn't help smiling back. "Yeah, she's a bit airy. But she's brilliant at what she does and what she does is a hell of a lot of good for the broken people of Cleveport."

"Steven knows," Abby mocked in a surprisingly

convincing parody of Mary's soft tones. "You been there, Hines, huh? You hit that sweet hippy?"

His cheeks heated up even though he had nothing to be embarrassed about, except perhaps a strong desire to do exactly what Abby suggested. "Don't be so crass!"

Abby tipped her head back in a laugh. "Oh, he doth protest too much! You have, you dog. Who can blame you? She's smoking hot in a pale, red-headed, wafty kinda way."

"I have not."

Abby's eyes narrowed. "Oh, but you want to, yeah? Well, like I said. Can't blame you for that. She seems a bit older than you, though. She's gotta be around forty."

"That's only a few years more than me. Anyway, I think she's actually way past that and just looks about forty." Hines grinned at Abby's sudden discomfort. "Ha! Even now you balk at the magic talk!"

Abby shook her head, chewed at a thumbnail. "Dude, I've known you so long, all the weird shit you did when we were kids. You've helped with weird shit I've investigated before, but it's been peripheral, you know? Sorta edges here and there I could mostly avoid."

"But real."

"Sure, of course real. But easy to dismiss. This stuff today? It's getting out of control, Steven. No one can ignore this madness."

Hines drew in a deep breath, sighed. "Don't underestimate the human ability to ignore the fantastical. If the city somehow gets a handle on this and gets it under control, it'll be reduced to internet sites of conspiracy theorists and whack jobs inside a month. The government will see to that."

"And if the city doesn't get a handle on it?"

"Well, then I think we're all done for so it doesn't really matter."

Abby's phone rang. She looked at Steven a moment longer, then answered. "Jones. No, I understand, but I am working on that. What? No, I'm sure the bodies and the fungus stuff are connected. It's hard to explain. Listen, I have an expert with me and we're running some scenarios. I think I might be able to figure out the connections to help with bringing this thing under control. Yeah, quick as I can. Okay, leave it with me." She hung up, pocketed the phone.

"Did you just call me an expert?" Hines asked.

Abby snorted. "Yeah. But you know what an expert is, right? An ex is a has-been and a spurt is a drip under pressure."

"You want my damn help or not, Jones?"

She blew him a kiss. "You know I do. So what do you suggest? They want me on the street tracking these fungal pools and helping eradicate them. The fucking army are coming in, Steven. This stuff is getting heavy. If I'm going to avoid being seconded to fucking foot patrol, I need to come up with answers. Strategies."

Hines nodded, tapped his fingers together while he thought. "We're pretty convinced these fungal things are connected to everything that's going on magically, but they just popped up out of nowhere, right?"

"Yeah."

"So some of your people are working on patterns? Trying to figure out where stuff is happening?"

"I guess so."

"Then maybe let's start by asking them. See if we can spot where these things might have originated. Then maybe I can ask Cleveport for her help."

Abby frowned at him, shook her head when he gave her the look. "You can't do that now?" she asked.

"Communing with the city is not like talking to a regular person, Abby. The more information I have, the easier it is to understand her."

"Okay," Abby said. "There's a central task force. Let's ask the lab boys what they know, then get upstairs."

She led him out of the morgue and back towards the labs.

22

Mary walked down the front steps of the police building and looked up and down the street. This was a quiet part of town, not a great deal of foot traffic. She was unlikely to score a passing cab. With a sigh of resignation, bracing for the walk ahead, she turned towards the business district, figuring a few blocks in that direction would bring her within a far better chance of a ride back to the underpass. Assuming the city hadn't entirely shut down yet. She briefly considered beseeching the goddesses for help. It would work, of course, but using the powers for something so mundane as getting a cab seemed frivolous. Petty. And given the strength of those powers right now, perhaps even a little dangerous. The energies were buzzing in Cleveport and she was not comfortable with that development. She also doubted that her planetary alignment theory held much water after all. Something altogether more insidious and earthbound was happening. She didn't think it would end well.

She turned her face to the rain as she walked, enjoyed the cool patter on her cheeks, and didn't notice the man step in front of her until he spoke.

"Need a word, please." His voice was heavily accented, Russian or some other Eastern European country. The word *Slavic* slipped ridiculously through Mary's mind as he grabbed her arm.

"Let go of me!" she cried, awash with adrenaline and fear.

The man pulled out a phone, thumbed a button. As Mary fought against him, he waited a moment before saying, "I have tramp woman. East side."

Mary stilled herself, intelligence taking over from outrage. "I am not some wide-eyed little girl you can manhandle," she said quietly. She gathered the powers, let the celestial river flow through her and wished heat into the man's hand.

He screamed, high and terrified, staggered back holding his wrist as his palm blistered and bubbled. Mary's mouth fell open in shock at the damage she'd caused, far in excess of anything she'd intended.

The man turned furious eyes on her. "The fuck did you do?" he demanded and started towards her again.

Scared for her safety and his, Mary froze for a moment in mental turmoil. She could surely not risk further magic of that degree. Could she control anything anymore? As he reached for her, self-preservation won out over concern for spilling blood in the river of the goddesses. She thrust one hand forward, cried out, "Away!"

The man lifted from the ground and flew backward. He hit the sidewalk with a grunt some ten feet from her and writhed in pain. Mary turned to run and another man was hammering along the path towards her. She flicked her fingers, as if to deliver a backhanded slap, even though the man was still several yards distant. He grunted as his face whipped to one side and his feet came out from underneath him. He hit the ground, scrambled back up with fury in his eyes. Mary raised her hand again and something clamped her arms to her sides. The first man had her in a bear hug, his horribly burned palm stuck out as he locked his grip on its wrist with his good hand.

Mary slammed her head back, felt the crunch of his nose along with his howl of pain, but he didn't let go. The second man got to them and slapped Mary across the cheek, hard enough for her vision to cross and her ears to whine. She gathered power again, determined to escape these violent attackers and tires screeched up beside the mêlée. A hand with a gun appeared through the side window.

"I won't shoot you dead in the street," the huge man in the silver car said. "But I will destroy your knees and you will never walk again."

The fight stilled, Mary locked in the one man's arms as his friend backed away a pace or two. The one holding Mary twisted her to face the gun's promise, its dark barrel pointing at her legs.

The man in the car said something in Russian and the second man stepped forward and cracked a fist across Mary's chin. Everything went black.

23

Jerry Rundle stood outside the apartment building and listened. Distant sirens and gunshots drifted to him through the downpour. The rain itself sang a soft hissing melody against the bricks and asphalt. He turned his face to it. How easy it would be to just stand here in the rain and let the city go to shit. He closed his eyes, let the drops patter across his face. He saw Andrew Blackford, leaning forward, mesmerized by the glittering thing. The spores burst up and Blackford raged, Rundle fired, Blackford kept coming until the sixth shot finally dropped him.

Rundle gasped, snapped his eyes open. Fuck this day, really.

He pushed open the front doors of the apartment building and went inside. He knocked at the first apartment and got no response. Nor to the second or third. He stood outside the fourth with his ear pressed to the wood and clearly heard a television or radio inside, reporting the news. He caught snatches of warnings not to panic and how it was best to stay indoors.

He banged again. "I can hear you in there. Open up, it's the police." No response and the TV clicked off. Silence reigned. Rundle shook his head. "Shit on me."

He went up to the second floor and tried knocking up there. The third one someone yelled, "Fuck off!"

"It's the police," Jerry shouted back. "Open up, I need to talk to you."

"Talk to someone else, man. I am not opening that door."

Rundle took a deep breath, steadied his anger. "I got a report there was an attack here, by a naked man. I'm here to investigate."

"Then you know damn fucking well why I ain't opening that door. Fuck off!"

Annoyed as he was, Jerry really couldn't fault the man's logic. He started to turn away when the resident called out again.

"It wasn't here anyway. The screams came from upstairs."

"Thanks."

The third floor was the penultimate one, the building old and small, the brickwork crumbling, the facades broken down. The paint inside was peeling and half the doors looked like they'd been salvaged from a tip. This end of town was yet to gentrify and remained a bolthole for the poor. Soon enough they'd probably be sequestered by the elite, repaired, redecorated and rebranded as boutique and quaint, then sold for ten times their current value. A hundred times their actual value, if Rundle's opinion was ever consulted, but of course, it never was.

He hammered at the first residence, impatient. "Police, here about the attack that was reported."

"Down the hall." The voice was elderly, female, cracked and tremulous.

"Open up, please, ma'am. Talk to me a moment."

There were shuffling footsteps, the clunk of several bolts and the door opened on three inches of security chain. The scent of lavender wafted past a tiny woman who must have been a hundred years old. Her skin was ash pale and striated with deep wrinkles so developed they were probably better described as folds. Her eyes were blue and still bright. "Hello, dear," she said, her smile toothless but warm.

"Sorry to bother you," Rundle said, too tired to return her smile. "Did you call in the attack, ma'am?"

"No, sir, but I heard the banging and screaming." She nodded to the end of the corridor. "Down there."

"Why didn't you call it in?"

"Because I knew plenty of people would and I figure your poor switchboard gal is rushed off her feet today."

Rundle smiled despite himself. "Yes, you're probably right. Thank you."

She nodded and the door clicked closed. Bolts slid and thunked back into place.

Jerry took another deep breath, steeled his nerves and walked along the hallway. The apartment at the end stood open. He slipped his gun out, reloaded and ready, held it two-handed before himself as he crept forward. Furniture was broken and scattered in the tiny hallway. A picture frame lay smashed on the floor, glass-like transparent fangs scattered across a dark, floral carpet.

A soft moaning came to him from a room to one side. Rundle stood motionless, refusing to acknowledge the trembling in his hands. Eventually he stepped forward and swung his gun into the doorway, looked over it with narrowed eyes.

Bile shot into his throat and he gagged, staggered backward. With an involuntary cry he gasped in a breath and stepped forward again, wishing he'd been mistaken. But he wasn't.

A man, maybe twenty-five, occupied the floor beside a single bed. He beseeched Rundle with eyes full of pain and fear. He reached out arms that bristled with dark, thick spines. Similar needles were stippled across one side of his face. There were hundreds of tiny red pinprick marks on his skin where he'd been stuck with more spines. As Rundle watched, several of the spines vibrated and sunk into the flesh, out of sight. They left similar red spots behind. The man's torso was skinny and bony, scattered with black spikes and spots too, but only as far as his lower ribs. Below that, his body was gone, melted into the carpet of his room. The pool he was creating was black and shimmering and from it rose tiny stalks with rounded tops. Some of those miniature domes began to flicker the merest hint of green.

The man's mouth opened and he moaned again, a deep, plaintive sound of longing and desperate need. His jaw worked, his lips rippling as he tried to form words, but nothing more than that hurt lowing escaped.

Rundle shook his head. "No, no, no, not again." And he pulled the trigger, the back of the man's head bursting across the bed and the pale wallpaper behind him. His body arched backward and lay still, the fingers of both hands clutched once, twice, at empty air and stilled. Slowly, almost too slow to see but not quite, his torso continued to sink into the pool of black ichor and tiny fungal blooms. More stalks shiveringly rose, like a nervous snail's eyes remerging from a child's touch. As Rundle stared a gentle ringing began at the edge of his hearing and he cried out, slammed the heels of his hands over his ears.

He backed away, pulled earplugs he'd bought at a pharmacy from his pocket and jammed them in deep. He used his phone to snap half a dozen pictures of the poor melting bastard, then slammed the bedroom door shut.

Rundle turned and ran out of the home, puked noisily into the hallway. After a moment he spat, gasped for breath. Looking up, two other apartments slammed quickly shut. He couldn't blame anyone. If there was no fucking cactus person or shimmering black pool in your home, keep all the doors and windows shut and locked and stay there. It was the only safe bet. But how long would that be the case? People would have to venture out for food eventually. His anger at the other residents for not opening to him seemed ridiculous now.

Rundle paused as a realization hit him. That poor bastard in there was turning into one of those pools of spores. All he'd seen so far were people affected by the explosion of particles.

That guy melting away in his bedroom must have been a victim of a naked attacker, but one bullet to the brainpan had ended him. If people had reported an attack in this building, it must have been one of those fibrous, unkillable victims of the spores. In which case, when they attacked and injected those spines into their victims, it must cause that hideous melting to happen. Then that person, attacked and injected with all those shivering needles, became a pool, only to infect someone else with a burst of spores. Was that the infernal lifecycle of these unnatural things? If so, the attacker could still be here somewhere.

Rundle steadied his hand, stalked back into the apartment. He stopped in the hallway, by the closed bedroom door with that rancid horror sealed behind it, pulled out one earplug and listened. He heard the music. With a cry of fear, he rammed the earplug back in even as his hand with the gun reached for the door handle. With his hearing blocked again, the compulsion passed. But for a moment, while he'd heard that magnetic music, he'd noticed something else. A whimpering. An animal whine.

He moved slowly through the small apartment until he reached the end and a kitchen. He groaned at the sight of a body lying face down on the dirty linoleum, black like a three-dimensional shadow. Cowering in a corner was a dog, a rust-colored mongrel with its eyes wide in fear, and black, shimmering bristles all around its mouth. Rundle watched it warily as he moved to the corpse. It was what remained of a man, but like a man made of blackened grass, flattened out. Like a bulky scarecrow with all the clothes removed, left to rot. As he watched, it broke down further, slowly sinking under its own weight, thin white filaments threaded throughout. The barman had described something similar. Seemed like those affected by the pools ran amok in madness, grabbing at anyone they could to get those spines into them.

Eventually, the attacker turned so far to vegetation that they dropped and rotted away, preternaturally fast. But all those they had touched, infected with the spines, melted into those horrible glimmering, singing pools and drew in more victims. Could he possibly have that right? It was a lifecycle that seemed fast and pointless, other than to simply consume humanity.

But maybe that was its point.

Rundle shivered in disgust.

He turned to face the dog and crouched. There was Labrador in its heritage, and maybe something bigger, like Mastiff. He was one scrambled mix of ancestors, that was certain, but he was a handsome hound and strong-looking. And scared. "Hey, buddy." Rundle held out one hand, palm up. He'd always liked dogs, always considered them far better than people. Society could learn a lot from dogs.

The hound shied back, whimpering, its distress clear even through the earplugs. Rundle shuffled closer. "Hey, buddy," he said again. "It's okay."

The attacking man had obviously tried to infect the dog. Spines bristled in its fur and were stuck around its lips like a parody of a beard. But the dog seemed unaffected. The spines weren't burrowing in like he'd seen in the man in the bedroom. So were dogs immune? Were humans the only victims?

Rundle had some leather gloves for the cold Cleveport nights in his jacket pocket. He slipped one on his right hand and reached out again. Carefully, as the dog tried to press itself into the wall, he plucked a few spines from it mouth, dropped them to the floor. The dog sniffed his hand, frowned, whined. Rundle lifted its collar tag, saw *Barkley* in swirling script. "Hey, Barkley. That your name?"

The dog whined and sniffed again.

Rundle gently pulled more spines free. The dog began to

relax. In a few minutes Rundle had pulled away all the black bristles he could see and he coaxed the dog from the kitchen down the hall. It stopped and whined and scratched at the bedroom. Rundle pulled on its collar, dragged it into the corridor outside the apartment and pulled the front door shut.

He crouched, gently stroked the dog's wide, smooth head. "Sorry, Barkley. You had a pretty bad day, huh? Don't worry, I'll take care of you."

Barkley was a fairly big dog, well-muscled with a wide head and deep mouth. He was a complete teddy bear, that much was obvious, but he'd definitely gone on the attack with the spiny bastard who'd killed his master. Rundle imagined the dog as companion, helping to protect him in case a mad attacker confronted him. The hound seemed immune, after all. With everything else that had gone on this day, taking a stray dog on as a partner seemed completely normal.

"Stick with me, Barkley, yeah? We'll look out for each other."

A nervous voice drifted down the hallway. "That's Barry's dog."

Rundle turned, saw a pale face in a crack of doorway looking over a security chain. The old lady he had spoken to before. "This Barry's place?" he asked.

"Yes, sir. He's dead, isn't he?"

"Yes, ma'am, I'm afraid he is."

"You gonna take care of Barkley?"

Rundle looked down at the dog. It leaned against his leg and panted nervously up at him. "Yes, I do plan to."

The old woman nodded. "Good. That's good. He's a good dog. Barry was a good man. Worked at the leather factory on Yarrington."

Rundle made notes with his stub of pencil. "I know that

place. You know Barry's surname?"

"Kale." She spelled it out for him.

Rundle wrote it down, along with the woman's apartment number. What the hell was the point, really? But procedure was safe, familiar. "What's your name, ma'am?"

"Edna Jervis." She spelled that out, too.

"Thank you very much. Now you stay inside and only open for the police, in case they need to ask you more questions, you understand?"

"Yes, sir." Edna closed her door quietly without another word.

Rundle crouched and patted Barkley again. He drew great comfort from the soft, warm feel of the dog under his hand. Barkley licked his stubbly cheek once and Rundle made a noise of disgust that couldn't mask his short laugh. "Ah, get offa me." He pulled his phone from his pocket and dialed in. "Better report this sorry state of affairs, eh boy? And I think I need to get me a meeting with some lab boys."

24

Hines held the door open for Abby and she tipped him a sarcastic smile of thanks. The lab beyond was huge and bustling with activity. A tall, balding man spotted them and pushed his way through the crowd of technicians. A fat man in a heavy overcoat was hot on his heels.

"That's Chief Watson," Abby said to Hines. "And a city Detective Sergeant with him, name of Rundle."

She said no more as the men reached them. "Jones, big fucking mess we got here," Chief Watson said. "You know Jerry Rundle?" He pointed at Hines. "Who the fuck is this?"

Steven bristled at the rudeness but held his tongue.

"This is Steven Hines. Good friend of mine and the nearest thing I've found yet to an expert on what's happening."

Watson grunted, reached out a hand. Hines shook. "Good to know ya," Watson said.

"The lab sent us up here," Abby said. "I think we need to centralize our information."

"No shit. Rundle here just came in with some interesting news. Jerry, you wanna fill 'em in?"

Rundle nodded, dragged a hand over his face. Before he opened his mouth to speak, a dog had slunk up alongside and sat right by the overweight detective, leaning against the man's leg. Rundle followed Steven's gaze, grinned crookedly. "Where to start, eh? I'll give you the short version." He pointed at the dog. "This is Barkley, my new best friend, and I'm going nowhere without him. Don't ask. But I've discovered dogs are unaffected by this fungus that's got the city going bananas. He can hear the song of it much sooner than I can too, and he starts growling and carrying on. Basically, he's an early warning system. Means I don't have to go everywhere with earplugs in. Also means the army are about to start using their own canine division in a very quick retraining program to start detecting these things." Rundle paused for breath, grinned crookedly again. "Sorry, I promised you the quick version.

"So we've got martial law, unofficial until the mayor makes a statement at a press conference in one hour. He'll also tell the populace that there is an indefinite curfew while the outbreak of a deadly poison in Cleveport is dealt with. They're going with a chemical spill scenario and I have no idea how they plan to pull that off, but it's not our problem. People will be told to avoid anything unusual.

"Our problem is figuring out what else we can do. I've been talking with these eggheads here after a couple of interesting encounters of my own and we've figured out that the pools of fungus are there to propagate themselves. They infect someone, then that person very quickly turns into a mass of currently unidentified vegetable matter. But until that transformation is complete, said person is driven agonizingly insane and attacks anyone they see. Their victims are stabbed fulla nasty, painful spines and they melt down and become a singing pool of fungus stuff waiting to attract some other poor schmuck and I honestly can't believe I'm telling you all this like it's a fact but it is and there you go." Rundle stopped, gasped in a breath and dragged a hand over his face again.

"That's the whole lifecycle?" Hines asked with a frown. "Seems kinda pointless."

"Simple life is exactly that," Abby said quietly. "Simple. Humanity and its supposed greater purpose is the natural aberration. Most life just propagates itself and dies. Born, eat, fuck, die, repeat."

Hines turned his frown to her. "You're a cheery bastard, aren't you?"

She grinned, but her mockery was tinged with a fear that matched the dread in his own gut. Things were really bad in Cleveport and showed no signs of getting better.

"So this thing is an epidemic and it doesn't affect dogs?" Hines asked Rundle. "That's basically all we know?"

Rundle shrugged. "Not quite. It seems to only affect people, like it's coded purely to wipe us out, but it's not that tough. It's vulnerable to basic fungicides, insecticides and industrial cleaning agents. You know, like the stuff they use to strip graffiti off the walls? It's not robust, chemically speaking, and we have crews out everywhere spraying like crazy. The army are getting in on that too. But it's replicating itself so damned fast, it's hard to keep up, and it's hard to find. But you're the expert on this stuff, apparently, so why don't you tell us what you know?"

Hines looked to Abby, one eyebrow raised. How much should he tell him? She made a face that eloquently conveyed, *Fucked if I know.*

"I'm not so much an expert on this particular stuff," Hines said, "as on unnatural phenomena *like* this." He ignored Abby's small sound of surprised approval. "I'm hoping I can track down the source of this problem if I learn more about it."

"Any other day I'd tell you to get the hell out of my station," Chief Watson said. "But this is not a normal day. I have no idea who the fuck you are, but if you can help us you have free rein in Cleveport with my blessing." He looked around the group. "You three work together. You're excused from foot patrols from now on. We're pretty much going to be reduced to enforcing curfew in an hour anyway. You have my permission to do whatever you think necessary to stop this madness. Now I have to go or the mayor is gonna throw me in one of those fucking awful pools of jelly or whatever the hell it is." He swept away without a backward glance.

"Ever seen him so untogether?" Rundle asked.

Abby turned from the retreating Chief to look directly at the detective, her eyes dark. "No, I have not. He's pretty much lost it, huh?"

"Yeah, I think so. No one's saying for certain, but there's a rumor going that his wife fell victim to the fungus stuff early today, one of the first."

"Gwendolyn, really?"

"You know her?"

"Not well, just met at some bullshit meet and greet dinners, you know? But she seemed lovely."

Rundle nodded, one lip curled. "Yeah. Well, apparently he got the call early and before he could do anything about it, the city descended into hell. So he's stayed here and tried to focus on what's happening. But he's not holding up well, as you can see."

"We're all going to be fairly irrelevant soon anyway if the army are taking over," Abby said.

Hines didn't like that idea. "The army will fight the enemy they can see," he said. At their questioning looks he went on. "You know, even if they eradicate the fungus and all that, it won't help in the long run. Where did it come from? Why is the magic so strong? How much more will spring up for every patch they get rid of? It's clearly the arcane increase that's made these things so virulent, it has to be. They're not a natural phenomena no matter how much anyone wants to talk about poisons or chemical spills or whatever the hell else. And they'll just keep popping up, right?"

Rundle waved a hand between them. "Wait, did you say magic?"

Abby chewed her bottom lip for a moment, fixing the detective with her gaze. "You've seen some weird shit today, right?" she asked. He nodded. "Okay, so how open are you to believing some even weirder shit? Honestly, you think there's anything natural about any of this stuff?"

"But some kind of damned magic?" Rundle asked.

Hines sighed. They had little time and needed help. "Come here." He took Rundle's elbow and led him out of the lab. Abby and the dog followed. When Rundle opened his mouth to speak, Hines held up a hand. "Give me a moment." He took them downstairs, along the corridor and out a fire exit at the back of the station into a rain-soaked alley, the downpour reduced momentarily to a cold, gusting drizzle.

"This damned weather, really," Rundle muttered.

Hines crouched, looked up at them. "I'm a citymage. I have a very limited and specialized skill set. I'm a weak and fairly irrelevant mage, but my talent is a deep and esoteric connection with the city. I won't explain it more than that, so don't ask me to. But I have magic. Watch."

He put his hand to the wet asphalt at his feet and closed his eyes. He felt her immediately, Cleveport, thrumming in his nerves. Their link had never been stronger. She exulted in his touch, almost preened at his total attention. But she wasn't well. She manifested discomfort in his mind again, even a fear of why she felt the way she did. But she reveled in his presence nonetheless. *Missed me, have you?* he asked the city, ignoring, for now, her malaise. He enjoyed their closeness and knew his obsession with her was as unhealthy as her obsession with him. But he couldn't help it. *I need your cooperation, if you don't mind. A little bit of a show to get this guy on side.* He let his energies relax and flow through his hand, let his mind and body become one and take the city in as a third part of himself. He let the bond they shared become momentarily physical. The asphalt yielded to him and his hand sank into it as if it were water.

Abby and Rundle gasped. Hines shifted his hand and

made a ripple through the road surface. Picturing his intent in his mind's eye, he scooped up a handful of the asphalt-like sand and swirled it between two palms before letting it pour back into the hole. He pressed it up into a wave and let it stand free. "I can ask the substance of Cleveport to respond to my will," he said, voice quiet with concentration. "I can manipulate her, communicate with her, much more. It's hard to explain, but this is the clearest visual example I can give you." He ran a hand over the road to smooth it down, seamless like nothing had moved.

Thank you, sweetness.

He opened his eyes, looked up into Abby and Rundle's uncomfortable faces.

He staggered slightly as he stood, the sensation of connection dragging a moment before it disengaged. That little display had been far easier than he'd expected and far stronger. Abby's face became hard, accepting but refusing to condone or think too deeply on it. Rundle was unashamedly wide-mouthed in shock.

"What the hell did I just witness?" the detective asked.

"There is magic in the world," Hines said. "And at least here in Cleveport it's getting stronger than it's ever been. Stronger than it should be. Have there been reports of any of this stuff anywhere else, other cities?"

Rundle snapped his mouth closed, shook his head. "No, not that I know of. Everywhere else sure is reporting about Cleveport though, and the outbreak we got here. But officials are shutting down news reporters and anything else. They're in major damage control, though they have no idea what's happening."

Hines nodded, his suspicions more confirmed. "This is local. But honestly, the way things are going, it's not gonna stay local for long, right?"

"There's magic?" Rundle said, shaking his head. "I don't

… I mean …"

"It's all connected," Abby said. "That's our point."

Hines held up a hand, counted off on his fingers. "There's a horrible fungal infection all over Cleveport. There's a massive increase in the strength of magic throughout the city. Dozens, maybe hundreds of people are dying from ODs on an arcane drug that's been physiologically harmless until now. The authorities are concentrating on the outbreak, but they're dealing with the symptoms, not the cause. Without knowledge of the magical, they've got nothing. We have to track down *why* the magic in Cleveport has increased. That's why the drug is killing people. That's why the fungal outbreak is so virulent. In fact, I'm convinced the fungus stuff is only happening because of the magic. It's not stronger because of it, but actually exists because of it. I've no proof of that, but I think that if the magic hadn't increased like this, that fungus would never have gone as rampant. But who knows? Chicken and egg, right? We have to trace the source, like Mary said."

"And if the army are busy dealing with the symptoms," Abby interjected, "and the Chief is at a loss for what to do, I reckon it falls to us to seek out the real problem."

Rundle nodded, rubbed at his chin. "How many others are going to believe anything you just told me? Hell, I don't know if I believe you and I just watched you stir up a road like it was pudding."

Hines grinned. "And I can hardly go around showing off to everyone trying to get people on side." He looked down at Barkley, who returned his gaze suspiciously. The dog huddled closer to Rundle's leg. "Your dog actually gives me an idea though."

"Yeah?" Rundle absently scratched Barkley's head.

"I need you to keep believing weird shit for me, okay? There's a bunch I know, call themselves Cyberdawn. They combine cutting-edge technology with magic and biology. I learned recently they've been working on something that could help us."

Rundle frowned. "That right?"

Hines raised his hands, supplicating. "I don't pretend to understand their reasoning, but I know they've been combining sensory tech and transmitters with dogs and birds and other animals, and then maging that stuff to make the animals into super-sensitive biological drone servants. They control them like robots, but they're not clumsy and slow like robots. They're dogs or whatever, with all the agility and everything else a dog has, and all of its senses, only under the control of the magetechs at Cyberdawn."

"That fucking Johnson guy gave me the creeps," Abby said, disgust plain on her face.

Hines gave her an apologetic look. "Yeah. He thinks he's humanity advanced. He's fucked up. But this stuff they're doing with dogs and birds and whatever could help us, right?"

"They're doing nothing of the sort to Barkley!" Rundle said.

"No, no! But you said animals aren't affected by the fungus. Only humans. If you can convince Cyberdawn to send their animal army out into the streets of Cleveport, perhaps they can track down these fungal pools and start to make us a map of the outbreak. If we can trace that back, add to it data you can access about places already cleaned up, and data about new outbreaks, perhaps we can trace the source of all this. We need to start getting a bigger picture of it."

They were quiet for a moment as Hines's plan sank in.

"And what do we do?" Abby asked. "No offense to Jerry, but why send him to Johnson? The guy is a prick, but at least you already know him."

"Yeah, I hear ya," Hines said. "But you and I need to go

see an even bigger prick. We're going to need someone to help us make sense of anything these guys find out and for that we're going to need a more powerful mage than me and a more esoteric specialist than Johnson."

"So who do we go and see?"

Hines drew a deep breath, sighed. "My father."

25

Mary refused to let her fear show. She was groggy from the earlier knockout, a sick headache throbbing behind her eyes. But she was strong. The goddesses would protect, as they always do.

The large, bald Russian paced back and forth in front of her, hands behind his back. The chair she sat on was hard and cold, like the room. Concrete walls and floor, one large reinforced door and nothing else except her and this man, who had said, "My name is Crater and you will answer my questions!" in his heavily accented voice.

Mary had told him she would happily tell him nothing at all and another beating wouldn't change her mind. And so he paced. The men who had brought her in were nowhere to be seen. She gave a wistful sigh. Hines. Just what had he had entangled her in?

"I will ask the questions anyway," Crater said. "And you will hopefully have the sense to answer."

Mary smiled, laid her hands together gently in her lap. "Ask anything you want," she said mildly.

"Good."

"But I won't answer."

Crater scowled, stepped forward, raising one hand as he came. Mary held her breath against the wave of panic that flooded her and lifted her chin, inviting the blow. Crater stared, hand halfway up, then slowly lowered it.

"What were you doing with the police today?" he asked.

Mary smiled, though she felt her lips tremble.

"You accompanied a policewoman and another man to a … a crime scene today. A dead man and a car. I'm not asking this, I know it."

Realization dawned. The men who'd appeared at the garage earlier were the same ones who'd abducted her off the street. She hadn't really paid attention to them at the time, yet now it was so obvious. But it made little difference really. At least she saw the connections clearly. This man was probably the true owner of all that misery in the car. Which only made her less likely to tell him anything. She worked every day with the damage caused by substance abuse. Mostly alcohol and drugs in the mundane community, but she'd dealt with many talented people and their misery addiction, misery-triggered psychosis and schizophrenia and manic-depression. The community more deeply touched by the flow of the celestial river was no less prone to being broken by the world and its temptations.

"Now," Crater said, interrupting her thoughts, "here is the stuff I do not know. Why are you helping the police with this?" When she said nothing, he nodded. "My people tell me there was one policewoman, another man who looked nothing like a policeman, and you. Who was this other man?"

Mary looked up at him, defiant. She held his eye and prayed to the goddesses for help.

Crater nodded again. He pulled a large cigar from his jacket's top pocket, made a big deal of trimming the end with an elaborate sliding blade device clearly made for the job. He took his time lighting it, puffing it to a glowing coal, and fragrant smoke filled the small room. "Why did you then go with this strange man and the policewoman to the morgue?"

Mary kept her lips tightly pressed together. Crater nodded over her head this time, towards the door at her back, and she jumped as hands clamped her arms to her sides. A rope was whipped quickly around her and the chair several times and pulled tight. Crater stepped forward and pressed the burning end of his cigar to her cheek. The pain was instant and incandescent. She screamed, high and shrill, adrenaline flooding through her as her bladder let go.

The hugely muscled man from the car and his two friends stepped around the chair to face her, all with questioning eyes at Crater. They were more than happy to beat her again. She was convinced they would happily kill her. The goddesses protect those who protect themselves and though she had vowed to never do harm, she was going to break her vow. The flow of the river was high, a flood about to break its banks anyway, and she drew on it.

She directed the pain in her cheek into her arms, used it to empower her muscles along with a heavy dose of the celestial flow and burst apart the coils of rope like they were nothing more than twisted tissue paper. She stood, her face a mask of righteous fury as her auburn hair swam around her head in a static halo of rage. The wrath of the goddesses surged through her like never before. Whatever was happening in the world, it was potent and hard to contain. "You do not have power over me!" she screamed, and thrust one hand forward.

Crater shot back across the small room, crashed into the wall with a rush of breath and a crack of the back of his head against the concrete. He slumped to the ground like a sack of butter. Mary turned to the others. The big man moved quickly away as the other two converged on her. She opened her arms like she was welcoming them both into a group hug, then slammed her palms together. The men's forward motion became fast sideways staggers and they crashed into each other, grunting, shoulders popping, and one man's forehead cracked into the other man's chin. Without waiting for them to fall, she flung her hands apart again and each man flew out to the walls and cried out in pain.

Mary froze, the huge man in the over-tight suit stood in one corner, a gun leveled at her face. "What the fuck are you?"

Light and thunder exploded from the barrel.

Yegor trembled, his pistol hanging at his thigh. The crazy woman lay half out the door of the small storage room, most of her face and all of the back of her head spread across the workshop behind her inert form. What the fuck was she? He knew about the misery thing, had recently learned there was something more than natural in the world. He had come to accept that, especially as there was such a profit to be made from it. But this? And all the other crazy shit going on the city right now?

He turned and crouched by Crater, who groaned weakly. He lifted the boss into a sitting position, noted the blood on the back of the old man's head. Not too much. He gently tapped one jowly cheek, brought the man around.

There was another groan and one of his boys, Anthony, dragged himself to his hands and knees, head hanging groggily. He had some questions for that bastard, the one who had led him along this path. The one who assured him there was real magic in the world. Yegor glanced at Dmitri, but the strong Russian lay perfectly still, eyes staring blankly at the door. Had that bitch actually killed him? He ground his teeth. Dmitri was a good man and a long time friend. What a fucking mess. He turned his attention back to Crater.

The boss blinked at him, brow creased in a frown. "What the fuck?" he said, his voice slurred. He reached up, pressed one hand to the back of his skull and winced.

Yegor said, "Anthony, get over here, you fuck. Explain."

Anthony sat back on his heels, narrow face a picture of pain. "I'm so dizzy," he murmured.

"Fuck your dizzy," Crater said, holding up a bloody palm. He pressed it back in place. "Talk."

Anthony nodded, winced and stopped. He drew a deep breath, opened his mouth to speak, then held up a hand and staggered to the door. He made a sound of dismay at the corpse of the woman and leaned out the door to vomit noisily.

"Fuck me," Crater said, eyes closed against his own hurt.

"It's concussion," Yegor said, feeling some sympathy. Anthony was not a physically strong person. "Give him a minute."

Anthony returned, dragging one sleeve across his mouth. "Sorry. Sorry, I … Sorry." He sank down to sit cross-legged. "There's really not much I can explain. The merchandise you were buying is a drug, used by magical people."

Crater's eyes popped open, his face an angry question.

Anthony flapped one hand weakly. "I apologize, you'll just have to accept it. The magical population live in the world, among normal society. Hell, they are normal society too, they just have various talents. Some more than others. I don't know why, but it seems like everyone's ability is increasing at a furious rate." He gestured towards the door. "That woman was a witch, white witch probably, a healer. Her ability read to me was strong but narrow, you know? Great at what she does, but no super mage. And you saw the power she wielded just then."

"No match for this power," Yegor said, waving his gun between them.

"Lucky for you," Anthony said. "Any slower and she'd have smashed you too."

"You keep your hocus pocus," Yegor said. "It's no match for a good handcannon like this at my side."

Anthony shrugged, gave a reluctant nod. "If you have time to fire it, sure. Luckily you did. On your own, against her, with the talents potent like they suddenly are, my money would have gone to the witch every time. Not normally," he added quickly. "But recently."

Crater had listened to their exchange in silence. He lifted a hand. "All of this matters not to us. She is dead, and just as well. But what does matter to us is our profit. *My* profit. Perhaps it's time to find this man who was with the policewoman, yes? And the policewoman, too. I want them both."

Yegor stared at the floor, shook his head. "Right now? I don't think so. It's all too crazy out there. We should write this whole thing off as a loss and keep our heads down until the city settles again."

Crater fixed him with a steely gaze. "I do not accept loss. You think I got to where I am today but *accepting loss* when things got difficult? I got tough when things got difficult, I fought on, I persevered and that's why I'm the King of Cleveport now. Believe me, there are things about me you can't imagine. Either of you."

He stared, daring Yegor to contradict him. Yegor frowned. Crater was hardly the King of anything. The Italian mob had more power and were always fucking with Crater's operations. The Jamaicans had far more money. Shit, even half the biker gangs were more organized and profitable and wielded greater power than Crater's operation. But Crater managed to mostly avoid or pay off the majority of their attention and he honestly believed his own bullshit.

Crater could see Yegor mulling it over. "You owe me. You have the kind of money you owe me? Hmm? Because I can take it from you. Take your gym, maybe? Or burn it down and take your insurance money. Leave you with nothing, eh? You want to accept that loss, Koltsov?"

Yegor thought about counting to ten. Then he thought about maybe not counting at all and finishing this fat bastard off here in his empty storage room. Where were his men anyway? The idiot was alone and if Crater went away, Yegor's debt went away too. And whatever slice of the pie

Crater really controlled would be up for grabs. Yegor would be in a prime position to help himself before anyone else even knew the "King" was dead.

A grin spread across Crater's face. "You start to finally think like a man!" He shot one hand out and Yegor lifted off the floor and flew up and away. His back slammed into the ceiling of the small room, his legs hung over the door and he stayed there, locked into place with invisible bonds. Something began to constrict his breathing.

"My god," Anthony muttered. "You've been masking your talent all this time."

"You think I've never heard of misery?" Crater yelled. "You think I built this empire with muscle and forged fucking bank notes?" One hand still extended, remotely holding Yegor in place, Crater stood. A gesture from his other hand and the concrete floor in the doorway burst as if a mine had gone off. Mary's body flipped and ragdolled out across the workshop. Crater brought his hand down slamming Yegor into the new hole in the ground, the breath exploding from his lungs.

Yegor rolled, struggled to hands and knees, gagging as he gasped for breath.

"You know fucking nothing," Crater said in a dangerously quiet voice. "I want either my merchandise or my money. But on top of that, I want my reputation intact. You think people aren't watching me? Waiting to feed off my corpse like fucking vultures? Like you were just considering only moments ago?" He switched to Russian for the first time that afternoon. "Go out and get me this man and this policewoman. Understand? This outbreak in the city is the perfect cover, the police are stretched thin, the populace in a panic. Have you not seen the roads blocked with people trying to flee? The army are stretched thin too, trying to prevent that. Everyone is being turned back. Soon enough this place will be shut down and quiet. Avoid the army patrols and bring me the people I need."

Yegor pulled himself to his feet, nodding emphatically, every bone in his body singing with pain. He was having trouble comprehending the sudden turn of events and just wanted to get out. He would have to supply what Crater wanted, but then he'd be gone. Perhaps before he found those two if he could figure out a way. It was well past time he left Cleveport behind. This city had been nothing but a curse on him since the day he was born in it.

"You know, the powers really are deliciously strong at the moment," Crater said, juggling electric sparks between his fingers.

The man was full of unpleasant surprises. Yegor dragged Anthony up by his shoulder. Was everyone in this godsforsaken town magical except him? He thought Crater's name was an exaggeration, an allegory, not a literal truth. "Come on, let's do as the boss says."

He towed Anthony out through the workshop and into the rain.

26

For once the rain had almost stopped and the clouds parted here and there. A ruddy sun sank behind the mountains, casting fingers of molten gold along the strangely quiet streets. But thunderheads stood out like sentinels to the east, more rain coming even while the current downpour had reduced to gusts and drizzle.

Gina stared into the light reflecting off the wet asphalt, one hand pressed against her throbbing side. She jumped as a car emerged through the brightness, then smiled to see Sally behind the wheel of the beaten up old Ford. Sally looked anything but pleased. The front end had a dent Gina didn't remember seeing before and the windshield was cracked.

As the car pulled up to the curb, Sally leaned over and popped the lock. Gina got in. "Thanks so much for picking me up."

Sally nodded, her face set. "Lock your door."

Shouting caught their attention. They twisted in their seats to see behind as a crowd of people came blundering from the back of the motel. Two were naked, one a big, strong man Gina recognized.

"That's the fucker who cut me!"

"Cut you?" Sally roared away from the curb, gunned the car hard towards the city. "We gotta beat the cordons," she said, frowning at the road ahead.

Gina watched the mob become smaller behind them. The last thing she saw was the crowd turn and start pumping bullets into the two naked runners. The man who'd cut her staggered and jerked against shots, but didn't go down. She heard distant screams as he embraced one shooter before Sally slewed around a turn and put buildings between them.

"What's going on, Sal?"

"You think I know? This fucking town has gone crazy."

"People keep saying that lately and you'll get no argument from me. I mean it, thanks for coming out for me."

"I nearly didn't make it. There's an enforced curfew, the army are blocking off streets turning people back whichever way they're going. It's a quiet chaos out there, but honestly, hardly anyone is trying to travel anyway. Loads fled before, then the roads were closed. Now they're dividing the city into closed sections. Only the naked crazies are still running around."

"The hell is happening?" Gina whispered.

"Cleveport is quickly becoming a ghost town, folks locking their doors and hunkering down." Sally gestured at the windshield. "Talking of naked crazies, one of 'em bounced off right there, didn't even slow him down. Went right up over the roof and I saw him in the rearview mirror jump up and keep running. Came out of nowhere, I must have been doing forty miles an hour when I hit him."

Gina felt tears rising. "Jesus."

Sally looked over at her, eyes dark and haunted. "Don't you live somewhere out this way? Why don't you go home, lock yourself in?"

"That's what I tried. But I think my parents are dead. And my dog is crazy." The tears breached, but Gina was all sobbed out. She let the tears flow, telling Sally the whole story, including the recent attack at the motel and the bus that wouldn't stop.

Sally was silent for a long while after Gina stopped talking. Eventually, she said, "Fuck. And Trev's dead?"

Gina nodded, feeling numb inside. "I watched him die. He huffed up a mis-hit, glazed over and dropped dead. I nearly died too, it knocked me out cold."

"Something is seriously fucked up in Cleveport, G."

Sally plucked at a silver stud through her bottom lip. Several earrings and a nose ring glinted as they caught the last light of the setting sun. Her long, platinum-bleached hair glowed. "Our supplier had a really bad time today too." She told Gina about Sam Moore's horrible demise, pure misery pumping out of him in gouts as she and Dave ran for their lives. "Seriously, G, I ain't ever seen anything like that. And we're getting loads of calls about people ODing on the mis. You can't fucking OD on misery, man, but you saw it happen to Trev."

Gina frowned. "I've never seen you take a hit."

Sally barked a short laugh. "Honey, you've only ever been to our place about three times. It's ain't like we're BFFs."

Gina looked down at her lap, stung. "Sorry."

Sally reached out, squeezed her knee. "No, I'm sorry. That was unnecessary. I do think of you as a friend, G. We've been to Trev's, we've been out. I seen you a lot more than three times." At Gina's grateful smile, she went on. "But I don't have a talent. I can't do misery. I like a joint and a few drinks, that's my game." She turned the car hard, tires screeching as they rounded the bend at a dangerous speed.

Gina tensed, gripped the side of her seat. "What about Dave?"

"Yeah, he's got a bit of magic. Nothing real special, he's like a bit psychic or something, you know. Untrained and proud of it. But enough to spark up a hit of mis and enjoy it. When he does that I smoke weed and it's all pretty compatible. He ain't touching the misery now though." Sally looked over, eyes narrow. "Say, what's your talent, anyway?"

"I can conjure illusions," Gina said. "I'm untrained too, but Trev was teaching me stuff. I'm not very good."

"Illusions? Like what?"

Gina thought about it. Always easier to show than explain. She concentrated on the street ahead, imagined a sleek, strong unicorn with glistening white flanks and a long silver horn galloping out of the side street and towards the car. Before she'd even finished the preparation, her image was real, pounding along the tarmac, its hooves ringing even over the roar of the engine, the last of the sun's rays reflecting brightly.

Sally cried out, stamped on the brake. They slewed sideways and she hauled it back in line.

Gina waved her hands, shook her head, willed the illusion to vanish and it shattered into a million pieces like glass all around the car right before it ran over the old Ford.

"Fuck's sake," Sally said, taking back control and hitting the gas again. "You scared the shit out of me!"

"Me too," Gina said. "Sorry! That was easier and clearer than anything I've ever done before. It almost happened without me trying."

Sally nodded, her expression grim. "That's what Dave was saying. The magic's getting lethal around here."

"Why's it happening?"

"If we knew that, honey, maybe we could stop it. Because I don't think for a minute that any good will come of it. Now keep an eye out for the army. We're getting close to where they were setting up cordons. I've come across a few blocks, hopefully I'm ahead of them."

"If they're enforcing some curfew, we just tell them we're going home," Gina said. "Your home, I mean. Surely that's what they want?"

"I don't think even they know what they want. I saw them turning people back in both directions from the same barrier on the way here. I told you, it's fucking chaos."

"So what do we do?"

Sally shrugged. "If we see army, we change direction and try to go around them. If we do get stopped, we tell them we're going home and hopefully they let us through. But I'll try to avoid them first." She looked pointedly at Gina. "I really hope I can get back in. Back to Dave."

"I'm sorry," Gina said weakly. "I hope so too. I'm really sorry."

"Stop apologizing for everything. It'll be okay. I couldn't leave you out there on your own. Maybe I should have, but just because this town has gone crazy, doesn't mean I have to join them."

"Thanks, Sal."

They drove on, Sally cranked the stereo and old school Pantera amply filled the silence. The sound system was as flash as the car was fucked, probably worth more than the vehicle it was mounted in. They nodded to the music, lips pressed tight. Gina sensed the taut concentration in Sally. They scanned for naked crazy people and army cordons as they went. Even without all the bus stops, it was a long drive back towards the heart of Cleveport, but the nearly empty streets gave them a clear run and Sally paid no mind to urban speed limits.

Gina caught sight of a group of people wrestling down a side street. She jumped as more shots rang out and Sally said, "Here we go."

Gina was about to say it was no problem, the group was a block away and occupied, when the car slowed for a large armored vehicle ahead. Soldiers milled around a heavy-looking yellow and black barrier, pulling it across the street from sidewalk to sidewalk. Sally shook her head, made a right turn.

"We'll try Prince Street, if I can get there."

Tension built. Gina couldn't help feeling it was all a big mistake. She should never have called Sally, never should have put her in this position. She opened her mouth to say so, to apologize yet again, when Sal swore. At the junction with Prince Street was another barrier across the road a couple of blocks down.

Sally turned left, gunned the Ford for half a block, then turned right into a narrow alleyway. Emerging into the next street across, she turned left again, back towards the city. "No cordons I can see yet," she muttered, and floored it.

Gina gripped the edges of her seat, pressed her feet into the floor pan. She'd never been a great passenger, especially at high speed. But Sally was relatively relaxed, albeit in a highly focused way. Gina would have to trust the other woman's driving skills. The speedometer crept up and up, the tall buildings and parked cars whipping by in a blur of colors and architectural straight lines, bent by speed.

"If they're still setting up, maybe they haven't got this far yet," Sally said. "I came up two blocks the other side of Prince Street to get to you, which was already a long detour. If they've cut off stuff as far as the river and the bridges, we're fucked to get back."

A blue car heading across town a couple of blocks away passed in front of them. It disappeared between buildings to the left of their street and Sally pushed the Ford on.

"That's the first moving vehicle we've seen since the suburbs, isn't it?" Gina asked as they approached the junction the blue car had crossed, heading straight on.

"Yeah. I think we've done it, we're back inside the army cordon now." Sally floored it. "Or we're ahead of them setting up. Either way, if that…"

Her words were cut off in a maelstrom of screaming metal and raining glass. Intense motion tore at them, the buildings spun around and around, tires howled against the asphalt. Pain flared in Gina's head as it cracked against the passenger side window. Her vision crossed, pain and disorientation clawed at her mind and blackness swam in her eyes.

Sally said, "Oh fuck oh fuck oh fuck," and they spun

again then jerked to a halt, the car bouncing up the curb before slamming back onto four wheels and rocking on its suspension. The engine revved furiously but the car went nowhere. A high-pitched whine curled through Gina's hearing.

She scrabbled at the door, found the handle and popped it open. She had visions of leaking petrol, sparks, massive explosions, but some half-numb part of her brain knew that was movie bullshit. Wasn't it? "Sally! We've got to get out," she said anyway. "Sally, you okay?"

"Yeah, I think so." Sally's voice was slurred, like she was suddenly staggeringly drunk. "Something fucking hit us." She got her door open and fell into the street.

Gina stumbled out her side, ran around to see to Sally. Dizzy, she forced herself to move. This was her fault. All of it. Everything was her fault. In the gathering dark of the evening she saw the back end of Sally's Ford was pretty much gone, just a tangle of torn and crumpled metal from the shattered rear window back. Spirals of rubber across the tarmac marked where they'd spun three or four three-sixties before catching up against the curb and taking out a mailbox.

Rain began again in earnest. She looked along the street. Twenty yards away, its front end pretty much torn off, engine parts strewn along the asphalt, was a very expensive looking silver Mercedes. A giant of a man, bulging muscles forced into a tight designer suit, strode towards them, his face twisted in fury.

Gina's stomach fell. She pulled Sally to her feet. "Sal, we gotta go. Seriously, we gotta go!"

Sally stepped drunkenly left and right, muttered, "Wha…? Waitaminute."

A white panel van pulled up behind the ruined Mercedes and a thin man hopped out, ran after the muscular giant, calling something.

"Please, Sally, run!" Gina said, her voice cracking. Her head throbbed, her vision crossed and all she wanted to do was flee, but she couldn't leave Sally behind.

"The fuck are you doing?" the behemoth roared. He backhanded Gina across one cheek and she spun, stars burst all around and something grazed her face. She realized it was the road she was lying on.

Gina pulled herself to hands and knees. Sally cried out, her friend kicking and thrashing in the big man's grasp. The other one reached them.

"Yegor, leave them, the others are getting away."

The giant, Yegor, dragged Sally along the street, back towards the van. "This day is getting more and more fucked up," he said. "Something will go my way, even if it's only this. I will not leave them. Bring that one, put them in the van."

"What for?"

"Just do it!" Yegor yelled.

Gina was too dazed to resist. Her feet were a mile away from her body, her boots skipping and bouncing along the road as the thin man dragged her along. The door of the van slid open and the air *whoomphed* out of her again as she was thrown in and hit the floor. Yegor and Sally were already there, the big man wrapping rope around Sally's wrists, then pulling it taut and tying more around her ankles.

Sally spat curses and semi-coherent demands. Yegor cuffed her into silence. "Drive!" he yelled as the other man climbed into the front seat. "Catch up to that cop bitch!"

He wrapped duct tape across Sally's mouth and turned to Gina. The van swerved around the wrecked Mercedes and accelerated away. Yegor taped her mouth too, then set about binding her arms and legs.

27

"Was that an accident behind us?" Hines asked, squinting in the darkening distance in the side mirror.

Abby shrugged, glanced at her rearview. "Maybe. Not really our concern, is it?"

Hines winced as the presence of Jenny drifted into the corner of his view, pale arms reaching for him, her face a mask of longing. He looked away with a small noise of pain. "Guess not," he said. "Funny state of affairs when a cop ignores an accident."

"Bigger fish to fry. You okay?"

"Sure."

Abby slowed the car, looked at him. Her face was mottled with color from the dashboard. "Seriously, Steve, you okay?"

He gestured at the side mirror vaguely. "I looked too long."

"Why do you see her like that?"

"No idea. It's an aberration of the situation." He grinned, their old catchphrase coming easily to his lips, but he knew how hollow it sounded.

"It's not really her, is it?" Abby asked. She turned her attention back to the road, but continued to drive very slowly through the empty streets. The army roadblocks were proving effective. Lights were on in buildings, but no vehicles or people could be seen. Her window wipers swiped rhythmically at the rain, increasing again after a brief lull.

"Just my fevered mind, you think?" Hines said. "Manifestation of my grief?"

"Isn't it?"

He picked at his nails in his lap, not wanting to look up, to meet her sad eyes. Hopefully she was watching the road anyway. "I don't know. You know as well as I do that things exist well beyond our everyday experience. Whether there's life after death, or ghosts or any of that shit, who knows? There's some stuff that will always be a mystery, right? I've seen her this way ever since Cleveport took her. Whether I really see her or just imagine it doesn't really matter to me. It happens."

"Just like you still believe the city took her?" Abby asked. She spoke carefully, trepidation in her tone.

Hines didn't blame her. He was prone to anger when the subject came up. "Cleveport is a covetous bitch, Abs. We've been through this before. When Jenny and I got too close, she got too jealous."

"And threw a building down on you both."

Steven looked up, defiant now. "Yes. I've been intrinsically tied to this city since birth and she didn't like me getting close to another woman." He rubbed absently at his knee, throbbing with renewed vigor. "She crushed us both, killed Jenny and gave me a nice painful reminder of her ownership. I've accepted that, so you'll have to accept it as well."

"Steve…"

"It's not something I need fucking therapy about, Abby. It's not a delusion. It's real. The magic is real. I'm a citymage and my partner, whether I like it or not, is Cleveport. And right now that connection is more powerful than ever. It's just how things are."

They crawled along the road in silence for a while. Eventually Abby said, "I'm sorry, man. I know how hard this stuff is for you. I try to understand."

"Yeah."

"Really, I do. It's just so far outside my… experience. My

grasp."

"Which is why you just have to accept things as I explain them to you."

Abby drew a deep breath. She was about to probe deeper, he could tell. "How come the covetous bitch let you and Jenny get so close for so long? You guys were engaged."

"That's exactly the point," Hines said. "I'd had plenty of girlfriends before, fooled around, had a few short relationships that were never going anywhere. When I seriously committed myself to Jenny, that's when Cleveport needed to make her point."

Another moment of quiet crept by before Abby asked, "Why are you so tied to her?"

Hines laughed softly, shook his head. "You really want to know this stuff now? After all the years we've been buddies, all the different ways you've ignored it?"

"Well, given recent events, it's pretty impossible to deny this crazy shit."

"So you're finally ready to actually *know* me, your best friend."

He caught Abby's wince out of the corner of his eye, felt momentarily bad for her. But really, he had good reason for his disdain.

"We've been really good friends for a long time, Steve," she said. "This stuff didn't matter before."

"It's *always* mattered to me!"

She pulled to a stop at the curb. "I'm really sorry. I've spent so long refusing to focus too hard on the esoteric shit that I've just enjoyed our friendship on a different level."

"Your level. Not mine."

"I get that. Sorry."

He looked up, finally met her eye. Pain was evident there. He reached out, put a hand against her cheek for a moment. "Our friendship has always been the most important thing to me, regardless," he told her. "Even when Jenny and I fell in love, you were still there and just as important. Jen loved you too."

Abby smiled, put her hand over his. "I know. I miss her too. But tell me, what's with you and Cleveport?"

"We really have time for this now?"

"Steve, you said we're going to see your father. You told me your parents were dead. You were born an orphan, you said, whatever that means."

"Okay, okay." He was glad she'd finally asked, finally opened herself enough to accept the knowledge, but her timing was ridiculous. "I'll give you the quick version. We can talk about it more later, yeah?"

"Sure."

"Okay. My mother died in childbirth. I was born in an alley, right out onto the cold road. I was found squawling in a pool of blood, still connected by the umbilical to my dead mama."

Abby covered her mouth with one hand. "Steve, Jesus…"

"You wanted to know. People with magical talent are born with it, it's coded into us. We can cultivate it or not, in some people it can be very strong, not so much in others. I've never had a great talent, but I was born with what little I have. When I entered this world, my mother left it and there was nothing but me and that cold, dark alley. The city felt me, she took a liking to me and connected with me. We've been linked ever since. I grew up feeling her, feeling her emotions and thoughts and desires. Cities are living entities, Abby, never think otherwise. All cities are, but especially Cleveport for some reason. Only most people, even the talented, can't communicate with them, can't resonate on their frequency. But some folks can, citymages. And that's *my* talent. We're rare. Even though my skill is slight, it's there. I knew from an early age that leaving Cleveport hurt too much. I'd told Jenny all about everything and she was cool with it, but I had no idea the city wasn't. Typical guy, huh? No idea how the other woman feels about anything?"

Abby half-frowned, half-smiled. She shook her head, saying nothing.

"So yeah, I discovered just how jealous she was when I asked Jenny to marry me. And she left me a reminder in case I ever forgot again." He rubbed at his aching right knee.

"So I get that you're an orphan," Abby said. "Fuck, Hines, you're an orphan in the most terrible way! But you said we're going to see your father. You're not orphaned if you have a dad around."

Hines pursed his lips, old anger rising. "When I was a teenager, maybe fifteen or something, I finally got to thinking about who my dad might be."

Abby's eyes went wide. "We'd known each other a long time by then, Steve! You did this and I knew nothing about it?"

"You were never good at hearing this stuff. I decided to track down the man who found me. The city helped me find him. I remember his exact words when I told him who I was: 'You lying there, born fresh from your mama, and her lying there half in darkness like she'd been born from the alley. Like a Russian doll set of life and death.' I've never forgotten those words, that image. I thanked him for finding me and calling an ambulance and the police. I went into care, obviously. But after I talked to that guy, I also tried to track down my biological father. I used my talent again, asked Cleveport for help. It's when I first got the idea about how I could use my skill to make a living, find missing people in the big city and all that. Anyway, Cleveport made it easy for me. She already knew who he was."

Abby looked out the window at the tall buildings all

around, the railway track on pylons passing over the road half a block away. "I'm getting a little creeped out by this sentient city thing. Is she listening now?"

Hines laughed, patted Abby's knee. "It's not like that. I mean, yes, she is listening, she's aware of everything I'm aware of, but the sentience is different. She's not a person, doesn't think like a person. It's all emotion and massive overlapping thought processes. She's a city, Abs, you can't imagine what kind of a being she is. She hosts a population of multiple millions right out through the suburbs, she's built of cement and glass and electricity and gas and happiness and sadness. She's like a man-made god, gone rogue. That's what all cities are."

"And she told you who your dad was?"

"Yeah. Because he's a rare one like me, a citymage. His talent is far stronger than mine, but he's messed up. He can't really handle it and hides in drink and drugs and lives on benefits and is a total loser. So she knows him well, but he does all he can to ignore her. That's his thing, hiding from shit. He abandoned my mother when he found out she was pregnant, left her with nothing. That's why she died giving birth in a goddamned alleyway, alone. I met him once, quickly realized all this and never saw him again. So I'm an orphan because he's dead to me. But his talent is strong."

"Fuck, Steve, I'm sorry. I didn't know any of this…"

"Because it's the magical stuff. It's been in your blind spot all these years."

"So why are we going to see him now, your dad? If he's such a fucking loser?"

Hines raised his hands, exasperated. "Because there is mad shit happening in Cleveport right now, even she feels… I dunno, almost scared. I've never sensed anything like it before. And as much of a fuck up as he may be, my dad is the strongest citymage I know. He's the only other one I know! If we can drag him up out of whatever wasted funk he's in, maybe between us we can commune with Cleveport and figure out what to do."

"He's not a misery user, is he?" Abby asked.

"No. That's one thing he won't touch. It's made from an intrinsic part of the city. Too close to our talent. Truth is, that's why I don't like it either."

"Then he's hopefully not OD'd somewhere."

"I've haven't seen him since that first time when I was a teen, but I know where he is. Cleveport always knows where he is. She's always disappointed that he won't be more of a part of her. But I'm sensing a change here. Something… I don't know. Something different."

"So the city doesn't hold itself to the same monogamous standards she expects of you, then?"

Hines grinned crookedly. "It's not like that. It's… hard to explain."

"Sounds a lot like an abusive relationship."

Hines lifted his stiff and aching knee a little, gestured at it. "You think?"

"But your dad won't play along?"

"No. And he suffers for that. But I can feel him out there, he's not dead. She's letting me know where he is and her attitude to him is softened somehow. I just hope that between us we can come up with something."

Abby nodded, lips pursed. "Right. Okay." She looked over at him again, eyes glittering in the dim dashboard glow. "I'm not going to ignore any of this stuff anymore. You're more than a brother to me, Steve, and I don't want to deny any part of you."

Hines rolled his eyes. "Yeah, sure, sure. I'm glad, really, but let's leave the D and M bullshit for later. We've got work to do, Jones."

She grinned, leaned over and kissed his cheek. As she sat

up and reached to put the car in gear again a white van screeched to a halt across the front of them. Abby's hand disappeared into her jacket, but before she could pull her gun, the side door of the van flew open and a huge man with an automatic weapon stepped out, stood framed by their windshield. He gestured at Abby with the gun barrel, and shook his head.

"What the hell is this?" Hines said, raising his palms to either side of his head.

Abby slid her hand slowly free, empty, and copied his gesture. "I have no idea. But that's the big fucker from the crime scene earlier. Remember the dead misery courier?"

"Is this really about a load of drugs?" Hines asked, incredulous. "With everything else that's going on?"

"Never underestimate the criminal mindset," Abby said bitterly.

"Get out of the car!" Yegor yelled. "Slowly and no tricks. I fucking mean it. I am done with counting to ten."

"I have no idea what that means," Hines said. "But I suggest we do as he says."

"Yeah. I think you're right."

They cautiously popped open their doors and stepped from the vehicle. Yegor kept the gun trained on Abby, but watched Hines as well, his eyes flicking from one to the other. "You," he flipped his chin at Steven, "come around this side."

"Yegor," the driver shouted. "Crater's calling."

"Then answer the fucking phone, Anthony, do I have to babysit you? Tell him we're coming in now, with the people he wants."

The big man's jaw twitched and he ground his teeth together. A deep rage threatened to burst from him at any moment and Hines wondered how little coercion it would take for that trigger to be pulled, for bullets to spray like the incessant rain across them all. Abby was tense beside him.

She'd be looking for an angle to make an escape. If she went for her gun, hell would erupt.

He slipped his mind to the city to ask her help. It was always easier with skin contact for some reason, like his bare baby ass that first moment he entered this shithole of a world. Even his shoe leather interrupted his link usually. But the magic in Cleveport this day was disturbingly strong. As soon as he put his will to her, Cleveport responded. But her ripples of fear and sickness had intensified again. He quailed inside. Like the first time you see your mother cry, he imagined, and understand your parents aren't gods, only normal people. Even a hint of Cleveport's frailty made his bowel turn to water.

"You're making a mistake," Abby said.

"Shut your bitch mouth," Yegor said.

Hines bristled at the insult, but even without a gun this guy could turn him into paste in an instant. Steven was no hero, not in a flying fists and bravado way at least. And anything he might be able to work with his meager talent would need time. More time than it would take Muscles here to pull a trigger.

Yegor stepped forward and reached inside Abby's jacket, pulled out her gun. He slipped it into his pocket and rummaged again, retrieved her phone. He dropped that to the asphalt and smashed it under one heel, then turned to Hines.

"Got a gun?"

Hines shook his head.

"Cell?"

Steven grimaced, took his phone out and offered it. All his work contacts and lots of other important stuff was on there. Yegor nodded at the ground and Hines sighed. He dropped it and the man stomped on it. He gestured them into the van with the automatic. They had no choice but to comply.

On the floor of the vehicle, pressed up against the back doors, were two girls. Trussed and gagged with tape, groggy and terrified, eyes wet and swimming. Abby moved towards them, one hand out.

"Sit the fuck down!" Yegor yelled, and booted Abby in the backside. She stumbled and fell, crying out as her head bounced against a hard metal wheel arch. With no effort at all, Yegor slung Hines in and they made a heap of four entangled bodies. Yegor slid the side door closed with a clang and climbed over into the front seat without taking his eyes off them. He sat leaning over the back of the seat, his weapon panning slowly left and right. "Drive!" he said to the thin man beside him. "Get us back to Crater's."

28

The journey across town had done nothing to ease Rundle's discomfort. In one messed up day he had seen people turned into straw, he'd shot a guy dead, and a policeman at that. He'd watched, and ignored, a mob gunning down strangers and now he had to accept it was all the result of some magical influence. Magic, really? How was a grown man supposed to parse that?

He wasted a bit of time after Jones and Hines had left, searching for background on this Cyberdawn and Johnson, but had come up empty. He had nothing to go on except the word of Jones's friend. But given the way this day was going, it was unlikely to be the end of the weirdness. His gut roiled. The weirdness might be only just beginning.

He pulled up at the address Hines had given him and killed the engine. The streets were deathly quiet, pretty much everyone obeying the enforced curfew. The army were aggressively ensuring that compliance. Twice he'd had to flash his police ID to get past a cordon and even then the guards were reluctant. How long until even the police weren't allowed to move freely? Fortunately the city center was largely ignored, the military presence a huge ring circling through the inner-city suburbs, the only open side the port and the ocean beyond.

Night had settled over Cleveport like a wet blanket, everything glistened, damp and still. The rain beat a soothing tattoo on the roof as Jerry finished the sandwich he'd grabbed from a 7-11 that had been abandoned and left open. He'd got one for Barkley too, and the hound was grateful, wolfing it down in two bites. Rundle lit a cigarette and drew deeply. He flicked an apologetic look at Barkley, sitting erect and attentive on the passenger seat. "Sorry, buddy." He put the passenger side window down a few inches and the dog turned his nose to the fresh, cool night air. A few spatters of rain found their way inside and Barkley licked at them.

Rundle let his own window down a little and watched cigarette smoke curl out to be beaten apart by the falling drops. All he wanted to do was take his new pal home, cook up a proper feed and collapse in front of the TV. This day could take a hike. But there was no getting away from it and his job was to face it.

He drew deeply on the cigarette a few more times, then flicked the butt into the rain. He dialed the number from Hines. It rang several times and just as he thought it was going to cut or go to voicemail, a voice answered.

"Yeah."

"Is that Mr Johnson?"

"Who's this?"

"I'm a friend of Steven Hines, wondered if I might talk to you for a moment."

There was a moment of silence on the other end before, "Hines's friends are usually cops, in my experience."

"I am that, sir, yes. My name is Jerry Rundle, Cleveport PD. But we're all in a hell of a mess here and Hines thinks you might be able to help us."

The silence was longer this time and Rundle suspected Johnson had hung up on him. As he drew breath to check, Johnson said, "This is an unusual day, Mr Rundle, I'll give you that."

"It surely is. So you mind if I have a word with you?"

"You're doing that right now. What do you need?"

"Thought we might chat face to face if that's okay? I'm outside your place now."

There was a sigh down the line, then, "Wait."

This time Rundle heard the distinct click of the line going

dead. He looked at the display confirming the call had ended. "Well, that was a little abrupt, don't you think?" he asked Barkley.

The dog wuffed softly.

Rundle was halfway through another cigarette when a man, early twenties maybe, with an umbrella approached the car.

"You want to see Mr Johnson?"

Rundle wound up the windows, stepped into the rain. "Yes, I do. Thanks. Mind if I bring my dog?"

The young man shrugged. "I guess not."

"Don't really want to leave him in the car on a day like this, you know?"

"Fair enough."

His escort offered Rundle the umbrella, but he waved it away. He let Barkley out, locked the car and turned up his collar. "I've been wet for weeks on end. Getting kinda used to it. Lead on."

He followed the bobbing umbrella around a corner and in through a side door, then grinned apologetically when Barkley paused and shook vigorously, spraying the small office with a fine mist of water.

"You'll need to leave your weapon here," the young man said as he closed up his umbrella. "Don't worry, you'll come back this way and it'll still be here. Those are our rules."

Rundle shrugged. Why should anything about this day be normal? He left his piece on the desk and they moved on through the building and eventually reached an ornate door. Beyond it was a huge office. Rundle marveled for a moment at the glass display cases before Barkley's growls distracted him.

The dog was hunched low, teeth bared, as he looked across the room at another hound. The black and tan mongrel sat impassively, watching Barkley. Johnson stepped around the desk and stood between them. He made a small gesture towards his pet and it lay down and closed its eyes, as if it had fallen instantly asleep. A hawk on a perch swiveled its head.

"Regular dogs don't much like ours," Johnson said, extending a hand.

Rundle shook. "Hope you don't mind my bringing him. We're new friends and he's had a rough time. And I really don't want to leave him outside right now."

"Understandable. It's no problem." Johnson crouched and gave Barkley a few gentle strokes. He spoke softly and Barkley settled, turning his attention from Johnson's dog for the first time.

"You're good with animals," Rundle said.

"You could say that. I understand them, especially canines. I've worked with them a lot." He gestured towards his desk.

Rundle took a seat and Barkley lay at his feet, curled up in contentment. "That's actually kinda why I'm here. Hines told me that maybe some stuff you've been doing with animals could help us out."

Johnson sat in his voluminous leather chair, facing Rundle across the expanse of his expensive desk. "Is that right?"

"Well, it seems that whatever this infection is that's spreading through the city, dogs aren't bothered by it."

"You think it's an infection, Mr Rundle?"

Rundle paused, sensing information behind that question. In his experience, the less you claimed to know, the more you could find out. "It's not?" he asked.

Johnson smiled crookedly. "Most news channels are calling it an outbreak. You think that's more accurate?"

"Well, it certainly seems to have broken out in a very short time, but honestly, Mr Johnson, I have no idea what the hell is going on in Cleveport today."

Johnson stood and paced behind his desk. "It's spreading like a virulent infection, that much is certain. The replication rate is unbelievable and you're right, it seems to only affect humans. I say 'seems to' because it's actually primates. We exposed a chimpanzee to it and he was turned instantly."

"Jesus H…"

Johnson held up a hand. "Let me finish. I'm giving you all I know because we're very busy and I'm sure you are too. So far we've learned that the spores from those fungal pools will only trigger in the presence of a primate. Why? We have no idea. But we've tried several other animals and nothing else, thus far, causes that reaction. Even though we're trying to figure out why the thing only affects primates, I don't know that we ever will. Given our time restraints, it's less important than stopping it. Well, we're actually more interested in containing it. I'm not sure we can stop it. Not entirely. Pesticides, industrial cleaning agents and the like destroy it, but there's no time. It replicates faster than we can kill it, even with the civil servants and army on the case. So I'm open to suggestions."

"Just who are you people?" Rundle asked.

"Let's just say," Johnson replied slowly, "that we have distinct vested interests in Cleveport and our ability to work autonomously of the authorities. But we're on your side right now, so don't worry."

"Right now?"

"Let's not be so naïve as to think that sides can't change, Mr Rundle."

Rundle shook his head, shrugged. "Okay, sure. What else can you tell me?"

"How about you tell me something now? Why have you come here?"

"Hines said your animals might be able to track…"

Johnson nodded, sat back down. "We're way ahead of him. We've been using our non-human agents to search for a pattern. We have birds above, dogs tracking through the streets. But Cleveport is a very big place, Detective, and it takes a lot of time to cover it all."

Rundle glanced over at the sleeping dog again, at the hawk on its perch watching impassively. "You control animals?"

"Yes, with technology and magic. Please don't ask for more explanation as I can't be bothered and it really doesn't matter. Come with me."

Johnson stood abruptly and led the way through a side door into another, smaller office. Rundle followed, thinking what an arrogant prick this Johnson was. Barkley hauled himself up and padded along behind them.

Five people lay on recliner chairs tipped almost flat, seemingly asleep. Others sat at desks, watching screens and tapping at keyboards. "Ignore them, they're busy," Johnson said, and walked to the far end of the space.

He indicated a wall taken up almost entirely by a map of Cleveport, an enormous screen with incredibly high resolution. Johnson tapped something and a satellite image covered the screen.

"This is the Cleveport you're used to seeing," he said. He tapped something else. Scarlet points erupted like a deathly case of measles all across the map. "Notice all the red dots?"

"Hard to miss," Rundle said. "That's a lot of dots."

Johnson slid away the satellite image to reveal the high-scale street map again. The dots remained. "Every one of those is a fungal pool, either dealt with by us, the clean-up crews or the army, or recently found by our people and their charges."

"Their dogs and birds and what-have-you?"

"Precisely." Johnson tapped again. Hundreds of blue

dots appeared. "These are all reports of attacks."

Rundle stared hard. After a moment he moved away, examining the pattern from further back. The mass of red and the mass of blue overlapped almost completely, but from a distance it was clear that the red began nearer the mountains to the west of the city and progressed eastwards in a narrow band before spreading out. Attacks were thickest through the most densely populated areas, which made sense. But the red swelled out to the north and south, spreading along the coastline like an infection through healthy flesh. As the red smeared outwards, the blue followed. "It started in the hills?" Rundle asked.

"Looks like it," Johnson said. "It seems to have headed directly into the city and begun its outward progress from there."

"You make it sound… deliberate."

"You don't think it is?"

Rundle's eyes narrowed. "What the hell is this, Mr Johnson? I mean, really, do you know?"

Johnson looked away from the map for the first time. "What is it, Detective? Intelligent, is what it is."

Johnson's eyes glittered and there was something in that gaze that put Rundle on edge. Here was a man absolutely convinced of his own authority. A man who seemed to look down on pretty much everyone and everything. Rundle had tagged that personality trait almost instantly. Being a detective for as long as he had meant a person developed the ability to read people. He'd read Johnson like a book on meeting the man and now he read something else. He read fear. And fear in a man like Johnson was something of which to take notice.

Rundle reached down, absently scratched at Barkley's head. The dog pushed up into the his palm. "Intelligent?" Rundle asked eventually.

Johnson gestured expansively at the map. "You don't think so?"

"Surely we're just seeing the spread of something aggressive like a cancer is aggressive. It's just moving into territory that gives it the best chance of replication. That's no more intelligent than a mold."

Johnson pointed to the hills and mountains behind the city. The red dots were clustered around one particular section of foothills and from there snaked directly to the city where they spread widely and the blue dots were far thicker. "Look here. Where these red markers emerge from the hills is all suburbs, yes? Cleveport itself has grown like a cancer. There was a time when this was a harbor town and nothing lay between the city and these hills except wide open country. Oh, a few farms, of course, which grew as the population grew, but it was mostly open land. Then, as the city grew, it spread away from its ports like a stain, consuming that land as it went. It ate up the farms and the countryside alike and washed up against the foothills. Like water will spread and fill whatever container it's poured into, Cleveport, albeit very slowly over decades, has filled all the available space between the ocean and the mountains. Otherwise, it's just roads and highways leading in, either from other cities and towns to the north and south or over the mountains to the inland habitations, yes?"

Rundle nodded, not really sure where Johnson was going with this. "So what's your point?"

"My point is, Detective, that all the Cleveport suburbs to the north and south of where this 'infection' emerged are just as densely populated as this area here through which it traveled so quickly. But see how it heads directly downtown? Its spread to the north and south is minimal. It made a beeline directly for the city itself, the absolutely most densely populated parts first. Why do you think that is?"

Rundle pursed his lips, finally seeing the relevance. "So it could infect as many people as possible in the shortest possible time. To prevent us getting the jump on it."

Johnson turned to face him again. "Indeed. It didn't spend time slowly traveling through the veins and muscles. It went directly for the heart and then began its attack in earnest."

Shivers of a deeper fear than ever rippled through Rundle's gut. Everything about this day's events had the hallmark of the weird, the unexplainable. But it had been a dumb, vegetable attack up until this point. While horrible and virulent, it had felt like nothing more vindictive than a common cold, albeit far more deadly. But this, a targeted, intelligent assault, was altogether more terrifying. And it implied a likelihood to fight back. "So what the hell do we do now?" Rundle asked. "Can you and your animals help?"

"I hope so." Johnson gestured to the people lying along one wall on their reclined chairs. "These five are all focused on one thing, directing their animus talents at tracing the source of the outbreak. We've stopped trying to track the dispersion. If this infection, Detective, is smart enough to go straight for our heart, we must be smart enough to go straight for its brain."

"And what do we do when we get there?"

Johnson smiled coldly. "Well, isn't that the question? I was rather hoping you might have an idea."

"I think Hines has some skills and contacts that might help." Rundle barked a laugh. "Jesus, I'm thinking things I would've considered insanity just a few hours ago."

"Having your eyes forcibly opened to the world can do that to you."

Rundle realized Johnson was completely serious. "I can report back to my superiors and they can report to the army. We can send in troops and whatever else if you give us whatever locations you find…"

Johnson cocked an eyebrow. "But?"

"But I think they're not the kind of people we need. Are they?"

"Oh, they'll have their uses," Johnson said. "But we need to bring other skillsets to bear initially."

"I'll get back in touch with Hines and Jones," Rundle said. "If you can call me right away with a location when you find one, I can get them there. And maybe your people can get there too?"

"We will send in animus units, but we'll stay remote, if that's all the same to you. I suggest you work on getting Hines in there first. People who have a better idea of the bigger picture."

"Bigger picture?"

"The less mundane picture, Detective. You understand?"

Rundle nodded. He didn't want to say magic, but that's what Johnson meant. "You think they'll be able to fix things?"

"Who knows?" Johnson said with a shrug. "But people like Hines are eminently expendable and we can learn a lot from their experience. Hold the military back and they can mop up whatever fallout there might be. Once we learn more from Hines, perhaps we can formulate a plan where my skills can be better deployed."

Rundle frowned, shocked by the casual nature of Johnson's assessment. "That's damn cold, man."

"I prefer the term *pragmatic*, Detective. After all, the entirety of Cleveport and very quickly the rest of the country is at stake."

"I suppose so."

"Incidentally," Johnson said, pointing at the harbor on the map screen. "I assume the ports are closed? And the airport?"

Rundle's eyebrows rose. "Shit on me! I've got calls to

make."

Johnson gestured towards the door. "And I'll be sure to give you any updates as I get them."

Rundle hurried from the office, dialing as he went. Barkley trotted behind, sandy brows knotted in concern.

29

During the long, quiet drive back across town Hines had tried to ignore the muffled sobbing of the girls while his mind worked in overdrive. There had to be a way out of this. But locked in a van with a gun barrel staring into his brain, it seemed unlikely. The man with the gun was a bag of personified rage, muscles twitching in his face incessantly. The driver kept quiet, eyes on the road.

"We'll pick our moment," Abby whispered, head turned towards the girls so Yegor wouldn't see her lips moving. "Not in the van, but wherever we're going."

"Okay," Hines said. If there ever was a moment.

He glanced towards the girls. One was blonde, long hair tied back, dried blood in a trickle from her nose. Dozens of earrings and a nose ring glittered in the dark from the flickering light of passing streetlights. Her eyes were wet, but subdued. She looked drunk. Concussed. The other girl was all fuck-you, with short dark hair and hard eyes. She was equal parts fear and anger, and she stared at Hines like everything that had happened to her was his fault. Maybe she was right, he honestly had no idea what had brought them all together. Could it really be greed for drugs?

The van bounced and pulled into sudden fluorescent light. A large roller door rattled down behind them and the engine was loud in the big warehouse before it cut and silence descended like a cloud. Hines shifted to see through the windshield. Not a warehouse. A huge mechanics workshop, a few cars suspended on hydraulic lifts, machinery and tools all around, car parts piled on benches. But no people.

Yegor climbed from the van and pulled open the side door. The gun didn't waver as he stepped back. "Out. Each of you, help one of them." He nodded towards the two girls.

"Their feet are tied," Abby said. "How can we help them?"

Yegor winced like he had a migraine. "Fuck. Anthony, cut their feet free."

The thin man maneuvered between Yegor and the van, leaned in with a pocket knife and cut the ropes. Steven took the arm of the angry dark-haired girl. The four of them stumbled from the van and stood under harsh light.

"I'm a police officer," Abby said, her voice low and quiet. "You are making a big mistake."

"You think I give a fuck?" Yegor spat. "Shut the fuck up and move." He pointed to a door leading out the back of the workshop.

Anthony ran ahead, opened the door and called something. Yegor walked behind, jabbing them randomly in the back with his weapon. Was there any chance of surviving this encounter? Fear squirmed through Hines. He didn't want to die, he didn't want Abby to die. He didn't want any further trauma to befall the young girls, whatever their story might be. He needed to be out there, doing something to save his city. The injustice of it all, the powerlessness, chewed holes through his gut.

"Throw these two in the cooler for later," Yegor said. Anthony dragged the girls aside.

Hines felt a pang of panic for them. He held onto the dark-haired girl's jacket sleeve a moment too long and it was dragged from his grip, leaving scores from his nails in the leather. As they were pushed into a concrete room with a heavy metal door, she looked back, her face a mask of desperation. Her mouth was a straight black line of tape but her eyes spoke volumes. *You're the only hope we have. No one else knows we're here. Don't let us die.*

He might have been projecting all that and she was

simply conveying an unformed animal fear, but it amounted to the same thing. What the hell could he do? He felt paralyzed. Perhaps Abby was thinking more clearly. He hoped she was.

Anthony slammed the door on the frightened women and locked it, handed Yegor the key, who dropped it into his pants pocket. Abby watched closely, frowning in annoyance. Trying to get that key would be an exercise in suicide.

They were pushed further along, past another room with a hole in the concrete floor like a small bomb had gone off. A dark brown stain covered the ground by the door and Hines's blood ran to ice. A scrap of auburn hair was stuck in it. A thin silver chain glittered against the wall, one of Mary's bracelets. He staggered, knees momentarily jelly at the shock. Abby glanced at him and he nodded to the proof. "Mary," he managed in a choked voice.

Abby's eyes widened. "Fuck!"

"Shut up and move!" Yegor barked, jabbing them again. They climbed a flight of stairs and went through to an office. The walls were wood-paneled and red leather was striking throughout. Behind a huge mahogany desk sat a powerful-looking man smoking a cigar. His face was thunderclouds and pain. Magic rippled about him, unchecked. Most people concealed it, but this man reveled in it. He was a mage, and far more powerful than Hines.

"He's magic," Hines whispered to Abby and arched from the steel barrel jammed into his spine.

"Shut the fuck up and get inside," Yegor said and shoved them both. "Mr Crater, these are the two you wanted."

"Finally done something right," Crater said, letting tendrils of blue smoke curl from his lips like snakes. He indicated two red leather chairs in front of his desk and Yegor forced Hines and Abby into them.

The presence of the hulking man right behind him made

the hairs on Hines's neck tremble and itch. Anthony remained by the door, looking frightened. Yegor twisted Steven's head forward as Crater sat up, planted his elbows on the desk.

"So," the boss said. "You're the two who fucked up my shipment. You owe me a lot."

Abby snorted. "You know what's happening in this city right now?"

Crater leaned back, laughed. "Yes. Opportunity. Unbridled opportunity. But that is not the point nor your concern."

"Opportunity? The place is falling apart, you fucking lunatic! There are bigger things than your drugs…"

Crater exploded around his desk and cracked the back of his hand across Abby's cheek. She cried out as her head whipped to one side, blood spattered across Steven's knee. He rose, animal instinct, wanting only to hurt this barbarian who had hurt Abby, but Yegor's iron grip pinched agony into his neck and forced him down. The feeling of impotence became liquid in his chest.

Abby sagged forward in her chair, almost unconscious, but hauled herself upright. She looked groggily left and right until her eyes fell on Crater. Hines marveled at her strength. "You enjoy that?" she slurred. "You like to hit women?" She spat blood onto his expensive shoes.

Crater looked down at the mess across his feet, back up to Abby and laughed heartily. "Oh, you have a fire. I like that, I really do. I respect that kind of passion. But spit at me or talk out of turn again and I will kill *him*." Without taking his eyes from Abby, he jabbed one thick finger at Hines. There was no doubt he meant it. "Yours is not the power here," Crater went on. "You are absolutely ineffectual. You will answer my questions and nothing else. Understand?"

Abby stared at him, defiant but not pushing.

Crater leaned close, too close, almost touching Abby's nose with his own. "The last woman who tried to withhold information from me met with a very sudden and violent end. Understand?" he roared.

"Yes," Abby said through gritted teeth.

Hines sucked breath deep, trying to slow his hammering heart. Mary. Poor, innocent, beautiful Mary was dead because he'd dragged her into this. All she ever did was help people. How could he ever live with this guilt?

Crater returned to his opulent chair, puffed on his cigar. The end glowed briefly then flared into life, bright orange. He let thick, pungent smoke curl in the air between them. The fact that he enjoyed his authority so belligerently only made it harder for Hines to bear.

"There is something going on in this city," the boss said eventually, "and it is most intriguing. The police are so busy with the army and whatever else is happening that I'm getting away with murder. Quite literally. I wish I had more men at my disposal as there are so many opportunities out there right now. And my own personal *magiya* is like nothing I have ever known." He turned his gaze to Hines for the first time. "You know something of this, yes?"

"Don't you think it's a little odd?"

Crater grinned, smoke curling through his teeth like he was some pale, corpulent dragon. "Of course, but I concentrate on my business and let others focus on theirs. Someone else will be learning all about what happens here and I will find out when I choose to. Meanwhile, I worry about my own concerns. As you should be. But no, you had to get involved in *my* affairs."

"Actually, impounding illegal drugs is kinda *my* business," Abby said. She gave a crooked smile, one side of her mouth already swollen to double its normal size.

Crater frowned. "Honestly, do I have to kill him to shut

you the fuck up? And you seem to be under the mistaken impression that misery is illegal. You have simply impounded my homeopathic remedies without reason. In effect, you have stolen from me. I could sue."

Abby stared hard, her lips closed.

"Or is there a reason?" Crater asked.

"Oh, I can talk now? The dead body lying on top of your 'remedies' is reason enough. They are legally impounded until that investigation is complete."

"A tenuous reason to hold my merchandise, Detective Jones. Yes, I know who you are."

"Given that your courier died of a misery overdose, I'd say it's not tenuous at all."

Crater's eyebrows popped up. "Misery overdose? You know, this swollen fool here," he indicated Yegor, "thought I was unaware of the stuff. He thought he could take me for a ride and skim the greater profit."

Yegor blustered. "Not at all, I was upfront with you about costs and profits…"

"Shut the fuck up. You think I don't know what you were planning? Regardless, he underestimated my abilities and my knowledge and so do you, Detective Jones. A person cannot overdose on misery."

"Up until very recently, that was true. But things are changing. Changing dangerously." Abby lifted her hands in appeal. "Our stumbling across your product was coincidental. We're actually investigating what's happening in Cleveport. We're the people that will find out what you will at some point choose to know. Let us go and we'll get on with it."

Crater shook his head, a frown creasing his brow. "It can kill now?"

"What? Yes! It's another symptom of the increased potency of everything magical in Cleveport."

Crater turned to Hines. "She's bullshitting me?"

"Nope."

Crater leaned back, puffed on his cigar again. After a moment he opened a drawer and pulled out a small walnut cigar box. It had an intricate mother-of-pearl inlay of twisting serpents. "Anthony, come here."

The man's voice from the back of the room was small, weak. "What?"

"Come here."

"I don't do drugs, Mr…"

"Come here or I will turn you into a stain on the wall."

There was a moment's pause. Hines assumed Anthony was weighing up whether it was better to be killed or face Crater's curiosity. When the boss tipped his head to one side and raised a hand, Anthony hurried forward.

Crater stood and pressed the small man into his chair. He took a small glass ampule from his walnut box and snapped off the top.

Anthony's eyes were wide, his skin milk white. "Mr Crater, please, I don't want…"

"What you want is irrelevant." Crater gestured, magic swelling in the air as he directed his talent at the drug. The liquid in the ampule swirled and curled out of the top in an oil rainbow twist of shimmering smoke. Crater held Anthony's head in one huge hand and jammed the ampule into the poor man's nostril. The glass cut the septum and blood trickled over Anthony's lips as he moaned in fear. His moan blurred into a sigh of intoxication, the drug spiraling up his nasal passage. His eyes rolled back. He sank bonelessly into the chair, breathing in short gasps.

Crater turned to Abby and Hines. "He appears to be alive. Just a lightweight. I suppose the effect is far stronger now, but that's all."

"You ever seen someone go out that fast from misery

before?" Hines asked. "It's never that strong, you know that. Even for a lightweight."

"I do know that. The *magiya* is increased. But he is not dead."

"Probably not enough," Yegor said.

Crater looked up, grinned. "You don't want to save your friend?"

"He's an asset, but not an irreplaceable one. Honestly, he's the one who started all this bullshit with magic fucking drugs. I was happily ignorant of it all until he came to me for money."

"And you came to me?"

"And now look where we are."

Crater laughed heartily. He took out another ampule and snapped off the top.

"Don't!" Abby said. "Please, just believe us."

Crater held her eye while he magicked the misery alive and jammed the small glass bottle up Anthony's other nostril. The thin man shuddered and cried out. He arched in the chair, "Ah! Ah! Ah!" escaping his lips, then fell still.

Crater turned his attention to his victim, felt at his neck and wrist. He stood back with pursed lips. "Hmm. Dead."

Hines looked away.

"Jesus," Abby whispered.

The office was silent for several moments, the smell of Crater's smoldering cigar strong.

He took Anthony by one arm and hauled him out of the chair and dumped him on the ground. "Yegor?"

The big man moved around, hefted Anthony's corpse over one shoulder and carried him away. Hines heard the door open and close.

"This is all very interesting," Crater said, resuming his seat. "And I want my merchandise more than ever."

"You know what?" Abby said. "You can have it! You can

all kill each other. It'd be doing this city a service."

Crater chuckled, and Hines said, "Except he'd sell it to talented kids only just exploring their new skills. To innocent mages who do no harm and just enjoy getting wasted like you and I do with a good scotch."

Crater gestured to Hines and nodded, smiling.

Abby shook her head, looked away. "Ah, fuck you."

"But I will have my product, Detective Jones. You will get it for me from the police impound yard. You can do this without question or warrant, especially now with the police in such disarray, yes?"

Abby sighed. "Yes, I suppose I can."

"Good. Then you will go with Yegor and do exactly that. I will hold your friend here as insurance of a safe delivery. Easy, no?"

The door opened and closed again. "So what now?" Yegor asked.

"I saw on the CCTV the two girls you brought in," Crater said. "Why?"

"They messed up my car. They're for me to deal with. I'll take them with me when all this is done."

Crater stared, a deep rage coloring his cheeks. Eventually he said, "Very well. In the meantime, you will be going with Detective Jones here to recover our merchandise, while I hold Mr Hines as surety."

"Okay."

"But we need more men. So before you go, I want you to make some calls and pick up some people."

"What?" Yegor sounded insulted. "I'm a messenger boy now? I have more important things to do."

Crater shook his head, puffed his cigar. "You forget your place and to whom you speak. You will show me the respect I'm due or I'll replace you as easily as you plan to replace Anthony. Don't forget who you are."

Hines saw muscles twitch in Yegor's cheeks, watched his lips move like he was counting. "Yes, Mr Crater," he said after a few seconds.

"Good man. Now, put these two in the cooler with your bitches and they can all make friends together while you gather our forces. Then you take Jones and get our stuff. When you return, take your girls and do whatever you please. Assuming the misery is returned to me, we will call everything even, yes?"

"All of it? But I'm out a lot of money, Mr Crater. You only partly bankrolled this caper…" His voice petered out in the face of Crater's stare.

"My profit margin, remember? We call everything even, yes?" Crater repeated.

Yegor nodded, lips moving silently again.

"Good."

Yegor grabbed Hines and Abby by their elbows and pulled them up. He thrust them towards the office door, swinging his gun up from his hip again. As he was pushed along the corridor, Hines wondered if there would be any point at which an opportunity would present itself. He had one slim hope that these delays might afford them a possibility. Crater wouldn't let either of them live once he had what he wanted. Yegor unlocked the concrete room and pushed them inside where they fell next to the girls huddled together in one corner. As the door slammed and locked again, Hines scanned the space. His eye fell on a tiny camera behind a bubble of smoky plastic near the ceiling above the door and the last of his hope slipped away like cigar smoke in a strong breeze.

30

Jerry Rundle hung up his call to the aviation authority and leaned back in the driver's seat to light another cigarette. Barkley sat on the passenger seat watching rain streak the windshield. "So that's that, fella," Rundle said. "Cleveport is cut off from the world. The military were way ahead of me. Apparently nothing's been allowed in or out for hours."

Barkley huffed softly.

"Gotta wonder if any of that stuff got through before the shutdown though, eh?"

Barkley huffed again. Rundle reached over and ruffled the dog's damp neck. He lifted his phone, dialed Abby's number for the tenth time, shook his head when it went straight to voicemail.

"Why would she turn her phone off? It's not even ringing out. It's unlikely she's got no reception anywhere in this town."

He sat quietly and enjoyed his Lucky, smoke curling lazily out of the inch gap at the top of the window. When the cigarette was down to the butt, he flicked it out and drew a breath. Saliva caught in his throat and he coughed violently, hunched forward as he hacked and wheezed. Barkley whined while his coughing eased and Rundle gasped.

"Man, I gotta give up, I really do." He looked at the dog. "I know, buddy. I really gotta give up. I will." He paused, the weight of existence suddenly descending on him. Barkley's open, honest, brown eyes glittered in the light from the dash in the otherwise dark car. The engine ran so the heater could keep them warm and its purr was muffled by Rundle's pounding heart.

He turned in his seat, took Barkley's chin in one palm. "I

make a pledge to you now, my new friend. This day has woken me up to all kinds of shit I'd been willfully ignoring. Once all this is dealt with, I'm taking the early retirement I'm entitled to. You and me, Barkley, we're gonna retire. We'll move somewhere warm and dry and inland, far from the ocean, okay? I promise. There's more to life than all this. Well, less, actually. I want less from life. I want some peace and quiet. And when we move, I'm going to give up the smokes." He paused, frowned. "Did I just sign my death warrant? I sound like that 'only two days from retirement' extra who always dies in cop movies. Well, shit on me."

He scratched Barkley's chest and sat straight again. "Nothing else to do but get on with it for now, eh?" He put the car in gear and pulled away. "We'll head west and wait for word from that Johnson freak. And with any luck, Abigail damn Jones will turn her phone back on in the meantime and I'll get her to meet us. And hopefully her friend Hines can do something about it. Hines! Talk about freaks. Jesus."

He drove off into the dark and the rain.

31

Abby kneeled beside the girl with the short dark hair and took hold of the tape at her mouth. "This'll probably hurt a bit."

The girl nodded, narrowed her eyes. Abby peeled gently. As soon as it started to move, the girl whipped her head to one side, the tape stripping away, leaving a red mark. The girl swore in pain, shook her head.

Abby grinned. "Hardass. I'm Abby."

"Gina. Help Sally, willya?"

Hines moved over to the blonde. "I got it."

He gently pulled away the tape from her mouth and started in on the ropes around her wrists. Abby freed Gina's hands. The girls rubbed where the bindings had left their skin sore. Sally pressed a palm to the side of her head.

"You okay?" Abby asked her.

"I guess. Still a bit groggy."

"We were in a crash," Gina said. "Sal took a big hit. Then that big fucker hit me. I've got such a headache." She rubbed her side. "And my cut is burning."

"A car crash with Yegor there?"

"That big muscly fucker, that's his name? His car was totaled, so was Sal's. But he grabbed us and threw us in the van. You know the rest. Who are you guys?"

"I'm police," Abby said. She gestured to Hines. "Steven here is my pal. He's been helping with an investigation that's overlapped with some of Mr Muscles's interests. We're in the same boat as you."

"We have to get out of here," Sally said. "They'll kill us for sure. Probably after raping us. Probably all of us," she added, with a pointed look at Hines.

He winced. "Yeah, well let's all try to avoid that, shall we?" He looked more closely at Gina. "You're a talent."

"Yeah. So are you."

Sally said, "So is there a way out of here?"

Hines gestured with his head. "There's a camera up there. I'm not sure how we can do anything without the big boss knowing. Maybe when they come to get us we can fight free or something."

"They'll have guns," Gina said. "And I'm no fighter. Are you?"

"Hardly. Abby can kick butt like a pro, but probably not against several armed men."

"Don't you fucking discount the possibility," Abby said, eyes hard. "But I'd much rather a different plan. Let's call me kicking everyone's butt a last resort."

Gina stared at the camera, brow creased in thought. All eyes were drawn to her. "You're thinking deeply," Hines said.

"If this big boss couldn't see us," Gina said quietly, "is there a way out?"

Sally shook her head. "A solid concrete room with a steel door? Hardly. I bet even Abby isn't that kickass."

"Don't fucking discount the possibility!" Abby said with a laugh. Smiles flickered around the tight space, then died.

Hines's attention was still on Gina. "Why?" he asked.

"Why what?"

"Why do you ask that?"

Gina looked away from the camera finally, met his gaze. "*Is* there a way out, if we were unobserved."

Hines nodded, hope kindling in the cellar of his mind. "Yeah, there might be."

"My talent is illusion," Gina said. "It'll take some doing, but I can potentially fool that camera. The way my power is right now, I think I could pull it off. No way would I have dreamed of anything so complicated before, but these days my skills are kinda ramped up."

"That's true for all of us," Hines said. "Everything's heightened in Cleveport lately."

"Why?"

"We're not entirely sure. That's what we're trying to find out."

Gina's eyes drifted back to the camera. "So how long do you need to get us out of here if I can fool that?"

"Not too long. Assuming she works with me."

"She?"

"Cleveport." He waved a hand absently. "It's complicated."

Shouts erupted outside and the door clanged open. Yegor stood there, his expression dark, angry. "Right, you and I are taking a drive to the impound yard." He grabbed Abby's shoulder and hauled her up.

Hines cursed inside, wished they had more time. He looked beseechingly at his friend.

"England for the gold," she said, and Yegor pulled her away. The door slammed and locked behind them.

"We have to move fast," Hines said.

"What did she mean just then?" Gina asked.

Hines smiled. "An in-joke. We have very little time. We have to get out of here. How do you plan to fool that camera?"

"Well, if I can concentrate, get a good mental image of us here, sitting like this, I can project that image in front of us. Like holding up a picture in front of the lens, you know? Then you can do whatever you do behind the cover of it."

"How long can you maintain that?"

"I can hold it indefinitely. It's more whether it's a convincing enough illusion. At least, until I have to move. Then it'll be harder to keep in place."

"Okay. Will it take you long to set up?"

"Few minutes to really get a clear picture if the three of us sit still."

Hines turned, sat with his back to the wall opposite the door, the three of them slumped in a resigned line. "Let's act like we've given up then, that we're just waiting. You can recreate this?"

Gina nodded. "I think so."

She looked left and right, closed her eyes. Her magic swelled. She looked around again, used her talent once more.

While she worked, Hines pressed one palm to the cold stone floor. He relaxed, let his mind sink into his city. She ached, sickened and demoralized. The whole of Cleveport, from the mountains to the sea, was melancholy and discomforted. It pained him to feel her this way.

I'm trying to help. I'll do all I can. But you need to work with me. Show me where to go.

Cleveport's love and obsession smothered him, needier than ever.

Hines winced inside. *I'll help!* He told her. *But you have to help me too. Where?*

Images rose in his mind, the ground beneath the room that was their prison, thick rock leading to a dark, hollow place. A dripping tunnel, dank and fetid, water traveling in a brick channel at its base. Hines sighed. Well, it was unpleasant, but it was a way out.

"How are you doing?" he asked Gina as he opened his eyes again.

"Pretty much ready. But what are *you* going to do?"

Hines patted the concrete floor. "I'm going to make a hole right here, big enough for us to go down. I'll go first. Sally, you follow me. Gina, you follow Sally and hold that illusion as long as you can. I'll try to seal the hole again before your illusion drops. To anyone watching, it'll looked like we simply blinked out of existence."

Gina turned a skeptical gaze to him. "You're going to make a hole? In solid concrete?"

"This city and I have an understanding."

"Okay."

He smiled, tried his best to reassure her. "Honestly, it'll be fine." He hoped he wasn't lying. He'd never manipulated the substance of Cleveport on such a scale before. Desperate times though, they called for equally desperate measures. And the way he was feeling, the magic coursing through him more and more by the hour, he was sure he could do pretty much anything if he needed to. And he needed to get them out of here fast. And he needed guns. Or at least, a gun. One thing at a time though. "The illusion up?" he asked.

Gina's expression was serious, eyes slightly narrowed in concentration. "Yep. That camera is looking at a moving painting of us, but you can't go anywhere beyond my feet or you'll break through it."

Hines looked at her legs straight out before her, toes pointing up. "Okay, that's plenty of room. You sure they can't see if I start now?"

"Sure as I can be."

"Okay." He turned onto his hands and knees, pressed both palms to the cold concrete floor. Cleveport ached into him, her desperation clawed at him. She was like a child who had no idea why they felt so awful and just needed to be held, soothed.

I'll do all I can, he promised. *Work with me.*

He let his talent out, linked with her as thoroughly as he was able, and gently opened her rocky flesh. As he eased his hands apart, the hard floor rippled and folded back, like a stony gray eye-opening. Sally gasped, Gina flicked a look over. "Keep your illusion strong," Hines said.

The girl grinned. "I got it, no problem. That's quite

impressive what you're doing there."

"Thanks." He concentrated, let the eye turn into a throat and opened it down at an angle of about forty-five degrees, sloping away under the back wall of their prison. He eased it further and further apart until the hole in the floor was three feet wide and the slope gave onto a rushing darkness. Water lapping and foul smells swept up into the room.

"What the hell?" Sally whispered.

"Sewers." Gina's nose wrinkled in disgust.

Hines ignored the complaints. "When you slide down the chute here, there's a drop at the bottom of about seven or eight feet into the sewer, so brace for that. Try not to go face down. I'll go first and hold it open. Listen for me, Sally, and follow as soon as I say."

Without waiting for a reply, he turned his legs under him, sat on the edge of the hole and slipped in. The swift ride along the smooth rock was frightening in the dark and he popped out, freefalling for a second, before his feet hit water, then bricks. He gasped, slipped and staggered, but managed to avoid a collapse. His injured right knee whined with pain and he grabbed it, hissing. He was nearly up to his thighs in shit and piss and who knew what the hell else? But he was out.

"Sally, go!"

He heard her muffled cry of fright, then she blocked the weak light coming from the room above and was suddenly crashing into him. He staggered again, went down to one knee to save her falling. The sewage swept briefly up to his waist before he regained his feet. Sally stood next him, hands up near her shoulders, face twisted in disgust. She thankfully chose not to complain.

"Okay," Hines called up. "Gina, come down. Please hold that illusion if you can. Sally, you'll have to catch her, and it's going to get dark."

Sally gave him a look of concern, then turned to face the hole above them. It darkened again as Gina filled it. "Here I come!"

She yelped at the sudden acceleration and Hines put his mind to the floor above, slammed it shut behind her. Darkness was instant and total. He let the tunnel close in Gina's wake, ensuring it didn't catch up to her, then there was crashing and splashing and cries of disgust. He was knocked and sat back into the sewage. It made it halfway up his chest this time and there were more shouts and curses as they struggled to stand.

"Fucking gross!" That was Gina. A least she was unhurt.

"Did you keep your illusion up?" Hines asked her.

"Yes, right until I hit Sally and we went in the drink. Now I'm fucking soaked and freezing and literally covered with shit!"

Hines breathed a sigh of relief. To anyone watching, they would simply have vanished. They had some time, at least, until anyone looking might track them down. "We have to move," he said. "Anyone got a light?"

Gina's magic swelled again and a ball of luminescence popped into existence. They all winced at its brightness, covering their eyes.

"Dial it down a little?"

Gina laughed. "Sorry about that!"

The light dimmed and they looked around. Sally squealed, frantically brushing a wad of soaked and shit-stained paper from her chest, then she squealed again as she looked at her hand. She bent to the water at her knees to rinse her hand and Gina's light revealed all manner of floating horror. Sally deflated, beaten, arms falling to her sides.

"Everything is just fucked," she said in a weak voice.

Hines nodded. "It really is."

The light shimmered off damp bricks, furred with a pale

lichen. The channel of sewage had edges either side about a foot wide that ran above the effluent. They climbed from the stream and carefully moved forward, glad to be standing on dry ground even if they were soaked through. "We need to find a ladder to a manhole," Hines said, limping heavily. "When we get out of here, I have to get to the impound yard and help Abby."

"What did she mean by 'England for the gold'?" Gina asked.

Hines grinned. "It was her way of letting me know when she's planning to make her move. A couple of years ago, cold winter time, she and I were working a case and we had to check an impounded vehicle. It was late, like ten at night or something." Rats scurried past, dropped into the sewage with squeaks of fear. All three studiously ignored them. "The guy on duty in the impound office at the time was called Harry. Nice guy. He was moaning about the weather, about working late, about everything! Me and Abby chatted with him a bit, tried to cheer him up. So then Harry pulls out a bottle of bourbon, says to Abby, 'You're not going to report me, are ya?' And Abby says no, and one thing leads to another and an hour later we're all rolling drunk having a great time, watching the winter Olympics on Harry's little TV set. Anyway, England were in this one event – mind your heads here, the brickwork is low – and they were dead last, the athlete was so bad. I can't even remember the sport. But old Harry, he's drunk as a skunk and he keeps saying, 'England for the gold! England for the gold!' We were drunk too and it was about the funniest thing ever. But then Harry overbalances on his chair, he's laughing so hard and grabs for the edge of his desk. There's an almighty bang and smoke and a hole in the wall and electrics sparking and all kinds of shit. Turns out he'd grabbed for the desk, but caught the trigger of a shotgun he keeps taped under it, in case anyone comes threatening in the night. Sobered us up very quickly, that did."

They moved on in silence for a moment, then Gina said, "So Abby is planning to use that shotgun."

"Bingo." Hines pictured the situation, her leading Yegor into the office to get the keys, going to the desk, grabbing the shotgun instead. He hoped she didn't mess it up. "She's gonna need some backup."

"No way will we get there in time," Sally said.

Hines knew she was right. Him getting a gun would only delay them further and they were already too late. Yegor had left with Abby in a car ages ago, they would be at the yard by now. If Abby's plan had worked, Yegor would be riddled with buckshot and bleeding.

Or Abby would.

"Yeah. I guess she was just telling me the plan, and where to meet her. Hopefully she'll wait for me, at least for a little while."

"How long?"

"Let's hope long enough. Here's a ladder."

Rusted loops of metal ran up the wall, disappearing into a darkened tube of brick. Gina pushed her ball of light upwards until it reflected back off a dark cover, inscribed with city insignia. After a slippery climb and a little coaxing of the city from Hines to help shift the heavy manhole cover, they emerged on a dark, deserted street.

"Thank fuck it's still raining!" Sally said, arms out to her side as she turned in a slow circle.

The rain was heavy and insistent, a beautifully clean and cold balm after the stinking, dank sewers. It slowly sluiced the worst of the sewage from them, but the rank odors remained. Hines rubbed at his aching knee and looked around.

"Anyone know where we are?" he asked. The area was

familiar to him, but he couldn't get his bearings.

"That's Arlington Street." Sally pointed. "There's a hardcore club just down there that Dave likes."

Hines found his bearings. "Ah yes, of course. We were driven a long way by those psychos."

"The impound yard is that way," Sally said. "I know because I had a car in there once. Long story. But it's a fair way, we'll need a vehicle."

"We?" Hines asked. She was right about the direction and distance, but he wondered at their safety in sticking with him. "You guys are welcome to head off now. Thanks for your help getting me out of there, but you don't have to stick around. Just get a long way away from those Russians."

Sally laughed. "No shit, buddy. My place is on the way, so you can drop me off." She glanced at Gina. "You wanna stay with us?" she asked. "Or him?"

Gina looked a little lost. "Today has been so messed up. I don't know what to do."

"I want to get back to Dave," Sally said. "That's all I want, to be home with Dave. You need to decide what you want."

"There could be any number of those crazies around," Gina said.

"And we don't know if the army has contained the fungus yet," Hines said.

The girls turned to look at him, spoke simultaneously. "Fungus?"

A burst of automatic gunfire shattered the night, bounced back and forth off buildings. They looked around, unsure where the sound had come from. Another burst, then again, rapid short bursts echoing around the streets.

"That getting nearer?" Hines asked.

"Let's stick together for now," Gina said. "It's safer. We'll find a car, you and me get dropped off at yours, Sal, and

Steven can get back to Abby. You sure you're okay with that? I can hang with you?"

Sally gave Gina a quick hug. "Of course. Either way, let's get the fuck away from that lunatic's dungeon and whoever is shooting out here."

Hines was happy to agree with those sentiments. "This way." His stomach rumbled. "Damn, I'm starving." The beer he'd had for lunch was hours ago. "Wish I'd eaten when I had a chance."

"Actually, me too," Gina said. Sal nodded.

They scanned the street. "Won't be any shops open now," Hines observed.

A dull roar rose in the distance, growing quickly louder. The three of them spun, checking the skies. A dark airplane flew low over the buildings and a thick spray burst from somewhere beneath it, trailing a cloud that fell with the rain.

"Cropdusting the stuff," Hines mused. Thankfully it was a block or two away.

Gina and Sal turned to look at him. "What?" Sal asked.

"Never mind. We have to keep moving. We'll look out for a chance to eat on the way."

Another hum of airborne engines drifted to them from further away. Hines hoped they didn't get caught in any clouds of poison. They moved on through the pouring rain. Occasional shouts echoed along the strangely empty streets. Sometimes a shot or a burst of automatic fire made them jump and look nervously around. Aircraft near and far buzzed in the darkness. But no cars moved, no people were anywhere to be seen. Hines pulled his jacket collar up, the dark, cold and wet starting to get to him. If only he had a phone, he could call… who? Abby's phone had been taken too. Could he call the police station and ask for help? Call a friend. Well, a professional colleague, maybe. Beyond Abby he really didn't have anyone he would place in the category of friend. He still planned to make sure his father got off his ass and helped them, though. He just needed to get back to Abby first.

"Up there." Gina pointed right, towards the next intersection. Traffic lights, blurred by rain, changed from red to green. A car sitting at the junction stayed put. "The driver's door is open, isn't it?"

They stood still for several moments, watching. The lights turned amber, red. Still they watched. The lights went to green again. The car didn't move.

"Let's see," Hines said. He led the way up the street, cautious of every gap, every alley or doorway. "The city is never this still," he muttered. "It's unnatural."

They drew nearer. The car's engine running. Exhaust curled from the pipe into the cold air. Hines went to the back and peered in through the rear window. He moved cautiously, checked the wells in front of the back seat. No one. "Looks like we got lucky. Wonder where the owner went." He slipped into the driver's seat, sighing as he was finally able to take the weight off his throbbing knee. He revved the engine and it roared healthily. The fuel indicator read half full. "Get in, let's go."

With noises of relief the girls jumped in, Gina in the front passenger seat, Sally in the back. As they slammed their doors, Hines gunned the engine, pulled a tight U-turn and drove hard for the impound yard.

32

From the warmth of the car, one hand absently massaging the back of Barkley's neck, Rundle watched the group of twenty or so people in the street ahead. Barkley huffed. "They come this way, I'll gun it," Rundle said softly. The car's engine hummed.

The group argued and gesticulated, knives waved in the air, occasionally catching the glint off a streetlight. One man swung a rifle side to side but was clearly as frightened of the gun as he was of the situation.

"Nothing so damned dangerous as an armed populace, Barkley, you remember that."

Barkley huffed again. The radio crackled with empty static, the car's efficient heater droned, the windshield wipers flicked lazily across the glass.

Rundle had turned a corner to see the mob in the road ahead, about a block away, and had stopped. He was about to back up and take another block around when their activity caught his attention. They were clearly circling something, but it was obscured. Wincing against the cold and rain coming in, Rundle wound down his window to hear better.

"I'm not one of them!" A woman's voice, high and terrified, laced with sobs. "Neither of us are. We're just trying to get somewhere safe!"

As the crowd milled, Rundle caught a glimpse. Two women on their knees, hands clasped at their chests, looking frantically around, like wild animals desperate for an exit.

"Just cut them and prove it!" a gruff voice barked.

More muffled shouting and commotion ensued. Just more mob justice. Rundle shook his head. Nothing he could do against those numbers without getting in a firefight, and then what? The crowd surged, women screamed. "It's blood!" someone shouted.

"I told you!" the woman yelled. "Now get the fuck offa me!"

Rundle put the car in reverse. Maniacal laughter broke through the shouting. Howls of surprise and horror erupted as three naked men burst from an alley across the street. They grabbed members of the crowd in bear hugs and the held people screamed in agony. The rifle went off and its bullet pinged the tarmac not two feet from Rundle's car.

A deep rumbling grew and three army personnel carriers turned into the street on the far side of the mob. Soldiers with automatic weapons took aim, fired short controlled bursts into the mob.

Jerry hammered in reverse, swung a bootlegger turn and powered across the intersection away from the crowd. More shouting and gunshots rang out. He wound up his window against the weather and gave Barkley a reassuring pat. "We really should just drive the hell out of town and keep driving, hey, buddy? I tell you what, if I don't hear from Abby soon, that's what we'll do."

Another army vehicle came the other way, moving slowly. An armored car with an open top and a soldier holding a thick hose. They came to a stop and the soldier pulled a lever to jet something bright blue from the nozzle into a darkened alleyway.

Rundle turned away from them at an intersection as a loudspeaker hollered, "Citizen, get off the streets or you will be shot!"

He had no idea if they were talking to him or someone else. He pulled his phone out, dialed Abby again. Straight to voicemail once more. He shook his head. This whole thing was getting too crazy. He'd keep heading west, but if he wasn't able to reach Abby by the time he got to the mountains, he wasn't stopping. He would drive over those bastards and keep heading inland until the wheels fell off his damned car.

33

"This is my building," Sally said.

Hines pulled over to the curb in the quiet street. He exchanged a look with Gina. "Reckon you'll be okay?" she asked him.

"Yeah, sure. You guys just stay safe. Lock up and stay inside."

Sally looked out of the window, eyes narrowed to stare through the still falling rain. "Lights are on in our apartment."

"Pretty sure he'd have waited up, right?"

Sally frowned, blinked away tears. One hand rubbed absently at her bruised and swollen head. "Fuck this night, really. He expected me home hours ago. You can imagine how worried he is."

"Did you think he might have gone looking for you?" Hines asked.

She didn't answer for a moment. Eventually Hines said, "I'm in a hurry here, but I won't leave you guys if you don't want me to. Go on up and see what you find. Then come and let me know if you're going to stay here or you want to stick with me. Honestly, I don't know how much protection I can offer you, but better the devil you know, maybe?"

"Wait here," Sally said. "I'll be back in a minute."

Without waiting for a response, she jumped from the car and ran for the building.

"We can't let her go alone!" Gina burst out. "What if there are crazies in there?"

Hines killed the engine. "Let's go."

They got out and he remotely locked the car as they chased after Sally. No one was likely to steal their stolen car that way. They entered the apartment block, the slapping of footsteps disappearing up the stairs.

"Elevator's been broken for years," Gina said and ran through a swing door.

Hines followed, cursing his knee and the broken elevator equally. He came to the eighth floor breathless and hot. Gina moved slowly along the hallway beyond the stairwell. At the second apartment, Sally stood in the open doorway with both hands to her mouth. Hines could tell she was holding in a scream.

He and Gina stepped either side of Sally. Inside, blood smeared the walls and floor. Photographs were broken across the carpet. A man in his twenties lay in a twisted heap, his body rent with holes from a shotgun, delivered at close range. Beyond him, at the end of the short hall, another man slumped with his back against the wall, hands limp either side of his legs, his throat open with a frozen scarlet waterfall down his chest. Sally sobbed.

Gina wrapped arms around her and made unintelligible noises of comfort, tears streaking her cheeks. Hines could only assume one was Dave. He stepped back, looked to the other doors. Some apartments were open, others closed. He caught movement and briefly saw someone's eyes widen in shock before locks clicked into place.

"We should get out of here," Hines said quietly. "I'm so sorry, really I am, but this violence is city-wide. People are going crazy and we don't know who might still be here."

Sally turned, buried her face in Gina's shoulder. Gina held her tight, looked at Hines with wet eyes. "What now?" she asked.

A loud, metallic voice rang out, made them all jump. "Citizens of Cleveport, remain in your homes. Lock the doors and stay inside until further notice. This situation will be contained soon. For your own safety, stay indoors and await further instructions."

Hines moved to a window at the end of the landing. "Military," he said. "This is serious business."

"I can't..." Sally started. "I can't stay here. In there. What do we...?"

Gina held her tight. "We don't have to stay here."

The army announcement began again, further away and fading.

Hines put a hand on Sally's shoulder. "Let's get to Abby. I have to go, regardless of what the army are saying. I'll just have to do my best to avoid them. We'll be safer together, at least. Abby can help us to arm ourselves and we can try to sort this out."

Sally allowed herself to be led down the stairs. Gina helped her into the back seat of the car and moved to the front passenger door.

"Do you know them both?" Hines asked.

"The guy all shot up was Dave. The one with his," her voice caught and she swallowed. "With his throat cut was a friend of theirs. I've seen him around. I think he was a friend-client kinda guy, you know?"

Hines shook his head. "Damn. Let's go." He wondered what the hell had happened in Sally's apartment, but it was enough to know that deep violence had occurred and anyone who survived in that block was in lockdown. And he couldn't blame them. It seemed like whatever mob or monsters had come that way had already moved on, but who could be sure? Cleveport had always been a crazy place, but now the lunatics had truly taken over the asylum. He drove away slowly, watching where the military vehicles had gone. When he was sure they were out of sight, he accelerated hard for the impound yard, hoping Abby was okay.

"What if it was me?" Sally's voice from the back was small and soaked with grief.

Gina twisted in her seat, hooked one arm over the back. "What if what was you?"

"What if Dave was beside himself with worry, wondering where I was? What if he opened the door to… whoever that was without checking, thinking it was me finally back?"

Gina's face twisted. "Then it's really me. The only reason you came out was to look for me, so it's all my fault."

"Enough!" Hines snapped. The girls jumped. "Don't go looking for blame. This whole day, this whole town, is completely messed up. Looking for who did what is pointless. It's the fault of whoever attacked them and no one else."

"I suppose so," Gina said quietly, but she didn't look convinced.

Hines stared at the dark, wet road ahead. "I know it's no solace and you'd do anything to change the fact that he's gone, but blame is useless. Believe me, I know. I've lived with it for a long time and it gets you nowhere. People are always telling me it's not my fault and I never believe them. But I hear you guys now and it's true. It's not your fault." He was rambling but couldn't stop. Perhaps he was talking to himself more than them. "You know that kind of violence wasn't committed by a creature, by some natural force. That was premeditated. This might not make you feel better, but you need to know it. The crazies in this town right now are of two types. One is affected by some fungal poison bullshit and they're out of their minds and not in control of their actions. But they aren't using guns and knives.

"The other type of crazy out there is the opportunist. The fucking mercenary, looking for any excuse to wipe away the veneer of civilization and go on a rampage. Society as we know it is a thin and weak fucking veil, nothing more, barely held in check by majority will. When people break it, the murderers, the rapists, the pedophiles, we're shocked and it makes the news and we smash them with the law to preserve our patina of so-called society. But when the walls start breaking down you quickly realize how many lunatics are barely held in check at all. Usually only the most extreme give in to their base nature, but remove the controls and it's anarchy. But it is *never* the fault of the good folk out there, like you two. The only person to blame for a killing is the killer. It doesn't matter what happened that drove that person to want to take a life, that person chose to kill. Just like the only person to blame for a rape is the rapist. A girl could be drunk and naked on a table and that still doesn't make it right to fuck her. If someone does, it's because they decided to commit rape. Simple as that."

He drew a shuddering breath, caught Sally's wide eyes in the mirror. He looked away before he saw anyone else in there.

"I haven't known you long," Gina said quietly, "but I've never heard you talk like that."

"Sorry, I'm angry," he said. "And more than a little frayed. Please, excuse my language. But whatever is happening in this town right now, some people are poisoned and not in control and others are choosing their path of action, and only they are to blame for their choices. At no point does any of that become your fault."

Gina stared at Hines, slowly shook her head. "Fuck, man."

Sally pulled herself up in the seat, caught Hines's eye in the rearview mirror again The wisp of Jenny's shadow, reaching for him in the glass, as well as Sally's despairing gaze, and he looked away. He loved his city and he hated her too, but it had been the choice of Cleveport to collapse that night. To crush Jenny and pin him down so he couldn't help. He'd had no idea of her jealousy, not really, until then. Of all the things he'd done that led to Jenny's death, it was Cleveport who made the choice. He knew that to be true. But no matter how much his logical mind knew it, he still burned with guilt. He was guilty of loving Jenny and that had killed her. Who the hell was he to try to tell these two they bore no guilt? It was certainly easier to believe for them than it was for himself. But whatever he really believed, Gina and Sally needed to hear something to give them strength back.

He braked as an armored personnel carrier passed at a junction half a block away. "They'll come back." He turned hard into an alley and cut between buildings, rubbish and bottles crunching and shattering under the tires. The last thing he needed now was a flat. As he turned left at the end of the alley, a vehicle flew down the road behind them. "I was right," he said.

"Did they see us again?" Gina asked.

"Who knows?" He accelerated and powered straight through the next junction before turning a hard left again. "We're nearly there anyway."

They drove on for another couple of minutes, trying to check all directions at once, then Hines swerved through a junction and pulled up alongside a chainlink fence topped with rolls of razor wire. "Here we are."

The rolling gate of the yard stood wide open. Hines inched forward and turned in. A white van was parked just inside the gate, obscuring the office. The rest of the large lot was a wide asphalt parking lot, all manner of vehicles parked in neat rows. Mostly sedans and station wagons, but among them were big SUVs and trucks of various sizes, a few motorcycles. They all glistened with rain and the harsh glare of halogen lights high above like a sports stadium, causing glitters in the dark.

Hines parked alongside the van and his heart double-skipped. A large wet, gray lump lay on the ground, bright scarlet sluicing from its abdomen.

"That's Yegor," Gina said, awe in her voice. "She got him."

Hines slumped in relief, then wondered if Yegor had got Abby too. Half the office doorframe was splintered and broken. Two metal steps led up to the pre-fab building itself and a dim yellow glow leaked out into the night.

"But where's Abby?" Sally asked, echoing Hines's fear. She let slip a sob. "Too many people dead!" Her one sob turned into another and she was suddenly crumpled in a heap of grief on the back seat. Gina scrambled between the front seats and gathered her friend into a hug, murmuring to her.

"Take care of her," Hines said. "I'll go check."

He climbed from the car, his knee stiff and the ache bone deep. He flexed it once, twice, then stepped forward, limped cautiously to the office door. He climbed the steps and peered inside.

"Took your sweet fucking time, Hines."

Nothing had ever sounded as good as Abby's voice at that moment. He hurried inside, found her on the floor behind a desk. The front of it was blown away and the room stank of cordite and gunpowder. Blood spattered the flecked gray linoleum floor. Abby's left leg was propped up on a swivel chair, one eye was swollen and blackened, her lower lip red and sticking out.

"Abby! Are you okay?"

He pulled the desk away.

"We had a bit of a tussle, Yegor and I." She grinned, then winced and put a hand to her lip. "Strong and angry fucker he is, but thankfully I got to the gun. Just." She pointed to the shotgun lying beside her. "He's dead, right?"

"Yeah, well dead. You did good, Abs."

She struggled to sit up straighter, pressed a hand to her

raised knee with a gasp. "I was lying here feeling sorry for myself. Must have blacked out for a while. I'd pretty much decided you hadn't managed to get free and was wondering what to do next. I'm glad you came." She looked up as Gina and Sally entered, holding tightly to each other. "You two still here?"

"They decided to stick with me," Hines said. "I couldn't have escaped without them. I'll explain later. How bad is it?" He nodded to her leg.

"Pretty fucked up. I wanted to be more like you."

"You did the wrong leg then, you dick."

"Gotta retain some of my own flavor."

Their grins spread into soft laughter and Abby pressed a hand to her lip again. "Cut it out."

Hines crouched and felt along her leg, carefully helped her straighten it.

"It hurts like hell," she said. "I've been too scared to even try moving it again after the pain of putting it up there." She hissed as he moved it. "Damn, Hines, you smell like shit. Like, literally."

"I'll explain that later too, it's all part of the same sorry tale. What happened here?"

"I had to do this crazy leap over the desk but landed on the fucking swivel chair. I was only interested in getting to the gun. Thankfully I could reach it from where I fell, but the pain was blacking me out. Once Yegor went flying ass backwards I decided to have a little nap."

"Lightweight." Hines pressed along and she winced and slapped his hand when he touched the side of her knee. "I don't think it's broken," he said. "Reckon you might have twisted up your ligaments here something bad, though."

"You'll have to help me get around. Gina, there's a first aid box in the next room behind me. Can you get it? Maybe I can find something to strap up my leg. Steve, go see if Yegor has a working phone on him. We can use the desk phone here, but we'll need a cell when we leave. Then we can get some weapons from the lockup next door and get back on the trail."

"You going to be okay to move on?" Hines asked.

Abby sneered. "Do I have any choice?"

34

Jerry Rundle watched the rain course down the windshield as he scratched Barkley's ear with one hand and smoked a cigarette with the other. Seemed like sitting in his car, patting a dog and smoking, had become his new job. He was pretty okay with that. He'd parked at the junction to the mountains highway that led from Cleveport over the craggy peaks and off inland. Off to his retirement. He was past the desirable suburbs, then the sprawling tracts of affordable housing. Everything that made Cleveport was behind him, with the exception of the one road out over the hills. And the last military cordon had only let him through with the promise that even city officials would be in lockdown any time. No chance to get back in, according to them, and that was just fine with him.

He took a last draw on his cigarette, savored the smoke as it filled his lungs. "Well, boy. Looks like the city has gone to hell in a handbasket and no one is going to…" His phone rang, vibrating against the plastic of the central console. He stared daggers at it. "Well, shit. What did I expect, eh?" He didn't recognize the number, but that was no real comfort.

He pressed the answer button. "Rundle."

"Hey, it's Abby Jones."

Rundle tipped his head back against the headrest and sighed. "I'd pretty much given up on you."

"Yeah, we ran into some trouble. Sorry about that. What have you got?"

"That Johnson guy you sent me to? He's a freak, but he's got it going on. Got this whole animal army out there tracking shit down and whatnot. Dogs and birds mostly. He's found a pattern. Whatever is happening, it's originating in the mountains west of town. I'm at the highway now. Last text I got from him said they'd almost traced the source and were homing in on it. I can call him and find out what they've learned since."

"The source is in the mountains?" Abby asked.

"Yeah. And Johnson reckons we're going to need people with skills like your friend Hines to fix it. Or to learn more anyway." He chose not to mention Johnson's cold assessment of Hines's expendability.

"Okay. He's with me. We're going to get someone else who can help and then we'll meet you. Contact Johnson and see if you can get us a final location. Call me on this number, yes?"

Rundle pinched the flesh between his eyebrows. "Yep, no problem. I'll get back to you." He hung up. He'd almost allowed himself to imagine being done with everything. Had been moments away from letting everything fall behind. But he had a duty and would do his job to the best of his ability.

And then he was most definitely going to drive off and never look back.

He dialed Johnson's number.

"Hello, Detective Rundle. I wondered when you'd call. I thought maybe the fungus had got you."

"Nothing so simple. You could have called me."

"I've been busy."

Rundle bit down a retort. "What do you have?" he asked instead.

"There's a small community on a rambling farm in the foothills, on Galley Road. The one leading towards the Perpendicular Point Lookout. You know it?"

Rundle sniffed, lit another smoke. "Sure, I've taken visitors up there. Hell of a view on a clear day."

"Well, as far as we can tell, our current outbreak started there."

"At a farm?"

"Well, it's a commune, bunch of hippies living off the grid, you know the sort of thing. There's nothing further west, and nothing in particular north or south of it, but there's strong evidence of the outbreak originating there. We're still searching to make sure, checking there aren't multiple sources, that sort of thing. But I suggest you get your people to the location. I feel you'll find what we're all looking for."

Rundle nodded, face wreathed in smoke. With everything going on, the burn in his lungs and the trails curling around his eyes felt like the most normal thing in the world and he intended to hang on to it. "Right. I'll let them know. You want updates? Only fair to share information, right?"

"No need. We have airborne animus there, so we'll know what's happening. I'll text you the address."

The phone went dead. Rundle stared at the screen. "Pompous ass." He jumped as a message arrived with a Galley Road address.

He forwarded it to the phone Abby had called from and added, *I'll wait on Galley Road, 1km east of the property, until you get there.*

He put the phone down in the center console and leaned back to enjoy his cigarette, staring out at the pouring rain. Barkley lay on the passenger seat and put his smooth, tan head in Rundle's lap. Jerry stroked it gently. "Once more into the breach, eh, dog? I'm not going to enjoy this, I don't think. Might be best if you wait in the car when we get there."

Barkley whined softly.

"Yeah, whatever. We'll see."

35

Abby leaned into the crutches and moved experimentally forward. Her leg, heavily bandaged around the knee, took her weight.

"Anything this lockup doesn't have?" Hines asked, gesturing at the crutches.

She grinned. "You'd be surprised what gets left in the cars we impound. Found a dead body once."

"Nice. How's that feel?"

"Cold and stiff by the time we got to it." She grinned.

Hines shook his head, nodded to her leg.

She took another couple of steps, curled one lip. "Actually not that bad. I'm not going to be running and jumping any time soon, but I can get around."

"Here." Gina passed her a glass of water and a couple of painkillers.

"Thanks." Abby swallowed the pills and pocketed the packet with the rest. "What about weapons?"

Hines pointed to a desk. "There's an automatic each there, 9mm for the most part. And I found a pump-action shotgun. Think we should take that?"

"I dunno, Steve Rambo. Reckon you can kill someone else with it rather than yourself? I certainly can't use it. I'll have trouble enough with one-handed weapons."

Hines shrugged. "I'll take it anyway."

"Hey, there's a vending machine here!" Sally called from the back of the large space. "Who's got some coins?"

"Try that desk," Abby said.

Within a couple of minutes they'd gathered enough dollars to get several bags of chips, cookies and chocolate bars. They sat on the floor, devouring their haul like kids at

Halloween.

"Not much of a healthy meal," Hines said eventually. "But damn, I needed that." He felt a little sick, but his body sucked up the energy.

"It'll keep us going," Abby agreed. "Good find, Sal."

Hines stood, handed a pistol to Abby then held out one each for Gina and Sally. They looked at the guns as if they might bite. "You don't have to use them, but might be better to have them just in case, yeah?"

Gina took one, turned it over in her hands. "Heavy."

"Yeah." Hines pointed. "That's the safety. It's on now. If you do need to fire it, flick that up then just point and pull the trigger. It'll have some kick, so brace for that."

"If you've never used a gun before, you probably won't be able to hit a barn at point blank range," Abby said. "But you might be able to scare people off with it if nothing else."

"Not those mindless crazies," Sally said, taking a weapon. "I hit one with my fucking car and it didn't stop him. They won't be scared of bullets."

There was silence for a moment, then Hines said, "Well, no. But better to be armed than not today, I reckon."

They all tucked a pistol into belts or pockets and Hines hefted the shotgun. "Time to move on then?"

"To your dad's?" Abby asked.

He nodded. "See if he's in any mood to help us. It's not far from here."

They climbed into the car Hines had liberated, Abby in the front passenger seat, Gina and Sally in the back. Hines drove cautiously at first, checking all the junctions carefully.

"City's dead quiet," he muttered. "It's unnatural. But then random army patrols just go sailing by."

Abby watched out her side window, nodded. "It's amazing how quickly they shut everything down. They obviously ran scenarios like this somehow, in preparation."

"Preparation for this?" Hines asked.

"For something. Anything. Zombie fucking apocalypse, who knows. Whatever, the cordons are obviously working. I wonder how far this enforced peace spreads, how far the infection has traveled. No way are there enough personnel to contain everything if they didn't get a lid on it here."

"You don't think they did?"

"You heard what Rundle said. It started way up in the hills. Could've got anywhere by now."

"Then let's hope there's something we can do at the source."

Another plane flew low a few blocks over, spray falling widely in its wake.

Hines drove on for several minutes, then pulled over. "Just a sec."

He opened the door, leaned out to put his palm flat against the road. Cleveport gusted into him, anxious and breathless. It disturbed him deeply that his confident, powerful city was so disrupted. She psychically wheezed, like an old woman with emphysema.

My dad? he whispered mentally.

His eye was drawn to a row of houses, long since converted into shops and offices. They were back near the ports, in the oldest parts of Cleveport. Above the converted houses were apartments, and below were basement flats. Several had lights on, a couple of curtains twitched here and there. A distant scream drifted from the direction of the ocean, followed by the subtle pop of gunfire. Hines looked towards the basement flat at the end of the row.

"Thought so." He sat back up into the car. "We're here."

They made their way across the street like a party of war wounded. Hines limped on his gimpy knee, Abby stumped along with crutches. Sally had one hand pressed to her head and Hines wondered how bad her concussion was. Gina kept pressing one hand to her side, so she clearly wasn't unscathed.

"You girls could wait in the car if you want," Hines said. "This guy we're going to see is a wasted, unpleasant son of a bitch."

"No way I'm sitting out there on my own," Gina said.

"We might be a ragtag bunch of losers," Sally said, "but we'll stick together."

At an expensive-looking nail salon at street level they made their way down worn stone steps into shadows. The front door of the basement apartment was black and peeling, the leadlight window beside it grimy and cracked.

"Nice place," Abby said.

"Probably even worse inside."

"He wasn't here when you last visited?"

Hines knocked on the door. "That was years ago, Abs. He wasn't far from here, actually, in a converted warehouse on the north side of the docks. Probably got too expensive for his benefit payments and he had to downgrade."

They waited for a moment and nothing happened, no sounds from inside. Hines knocked again. Still nothing.

"Sure he's in there?" Abby asked.

"Cleveport is."

"So what do we do?"

Hines scanned the group and laughed. "None of us are really up for kicking a door in, are we? Not like the movies, is it?"

Sally stepped forward. "Well, I probably can't kick it down, but get out of the way." She crouched and dug around in her jacket pocket for something. She stopped, looked up at Abby with narrow eyes. "You're not going to be a cop about this, are you?"

Abby shook her head. "Not sure what you mean, but no. I don't think so anyway."

Sally pulled a rolled-up leather strip from her pocket and opened it up to reveal a series of thin metal tools with twisted and notched ends. She raised an eyebrow.

Abby grinned. "Ah, I see. I think we have extenuating circumstances right now."

Sally worked her tools into the lock. "If it's dead-bolted inside, there's nothing I can do about that."

A heavy click sounded and Sally turned the picks. The lock turned with them and the door popped open. She smiled. "Not dead-bolted."

Hines patted her shoulder. "Well done, little thief. Thanks."

"That never happened," Sally said, pocketing her tools again. "It's a hobby and I never do it to real houses. Okay?"

"Sure," Abby said, with an exaggerated wink.

"Let me go first." Hines stepped into the gloomy apartment. No lights were on, no sound came to them. An odor of waste and rot rose to meet him. He winced and pushed on. Maybe he'd find nothing but the alcohol-soaked corpse of his father. The shotgun hung in his grip, tapped gently against his bad knee. He moved cautiously on. Pale light came from a door at the end of the short hallway. He raised the weapon as he turned into the room and gasped.

His father lay naked on the floor, carpets torn up, furniture pushed aside to reveal the cold stone beneath. The glow, a soft, radiating blue, rose from his father's pasty, graybrown skin, rippled along xylophone ribs and scrawny limbs. Where the man's body met the floor, the flesh and stone merged, a seamless joining of human and city as if he was half-melted into the ground. His eyes flickered, bulging and bloodshot, the same blue light drifting up from the whites. His lips parted, dry and cracked. "Hey, son," he said in a rasping whisper.

Hines took a couple of tentative steps forward. "Jesus,

Arthur, what the hell?"

"Wondered when you'd come," Arthur said. His voice was strained, like he was trying to talk while lifting weights. Really heavy weights.

Abby, Gina and Sally came into the room, collectively caught their breath. Hines held up one hand so they came no further.

He crouched by his father's head. "What's happening here?"

"Someone had to look after Cleveport while you were gallivanting about." The old man's eyes moved to stare hard at Hines. "You're welcome."

"I don't understand."

Arthur hissed through his teeth. "Of course not. You never did. Nothing for it now though, I've protected you for as long as I can. Now I've had to give myself over to her and I don't think you have much time."

The man's talent pulsed in waves and Hines realized he was pumping magic into the city through their bond. But the nature of his activity was opaque.

"I don't understand," Hines said again.

"You'll have to come in so I can show you." Arthur shut his eyes and his attention was gone, focused once more entirely on his magic and his strange physical connection to the ground.

"What's he talking about?" Abby asked.

Hines swallowed hard, reluctant to do as his father asked. But he had to know. "I need to do something here," he said. "Might take me a few minutes and I'll be kind of out of it for the duration. Just wait for me, okay? Don't interrupt me."

"But Steven…"

"Abby, I don't have time to explain! I'll be okay. Just give me a minute."

He sat cross-legged beside his father and took a deep breath, let his talent swell.

Well, lover, he said to Cleveport. *I'm coming in too. Be gentle, yeah?*

He put his fingertips to the place where his father's flesh became the stone of Cleveport and let his talent out. His fingers slipped like tree roots into water and Cleveport flooded his senses. He heard his own gasp as if from a great distance as his mind rocketed out across the city, spreading like a giant net to land across every part of the sprawling town. The power of the magic was something he'd never felt before, all-encompassing, all-invasive. His mind expanded and he *was* the city, he was all her millions of inhabitants. He was her pulsing electrical veins and her flooding arteries. Every building was a beating heart, every heartbeat erratic and arrhythmic. He was her bones, aching and infested with age, waste, decay; he was her ever-repairing recovery. He was her thousands of maintenance workers, grooming her like a prized beast. But right now they were silent. Absent. The rust and concrete rot was nothing compared to the faster, more virulent deterioration that wormed through her darkened places. He heard and felt and saw her cries for help, her dismay at the infection running rampant through her artificial flesh, corruption she was incapable of resisting. From somewhere deep beneath her it rose, finding its way through her most profound roots. Even though it had no direct effect on her, it stained all her inhabitants and that pained her.

And Hines felt his father. The man's power was massive, stretching through every part of the city, massaging here, gripping there, staunching an outbreak in one place and breaking a blockage in another. Like a god, Arthur omnipotently held Cleveport together.

The incessant rain had every inch of her drains rushing,

every roadway running, with detritus carried along gutters. And that constant flood was exactly what the disease needed. It could only survive where there was copious water and now there was, washing down the mountains, bursting up through overworked storm drains. But even if the rain stopped, the lifecycle of the thing was underway, unstoppable. It would take a drought to slow it now and inevitable truth shuddered through every layer of Cleveport's being.

Arthur fought. Wherever he detected a fungal bloom, he collapsed the roadway beneath it, or toppled a wall onto it. Wherever a person leaned forward and was caught by the exhalation of those foul spores, he did the same. He blocked waterways to contain the spread of infection, while at the same time opening others to prevent the city from being swallowed by floods. But he was one man, however far his power spread, and he could not contain it all. He fought hard and had clearly retarded the rampant spread of whatever tried to infest Cleveport, but was one man against an army. If not for him, the city would have succumbed in no time. Against the scale of the attack, the relentless rain and the virulence of the contagion, he stood little chance of holding out for long.

Cleveport was desperately clinging to Arthur like a child to her father's leg. His city had never seemed so needy before, so dependent. And yet she was still powerful, fueled more than ever before by the fear and concerns of her populace. The breath in her concrete lungs had never been stronger, but nor had it ever been so toxic. Nothing in this fine balance could last.

You see, Steven? Arthur's voice, strained and struggling. Surely the man had little left.

Yes, I see, Hines replied. *But I see symptoms. I see effect. We need to fight the source!*

Hines's will was drawn west, as if along a deep shadow beneath the city herself, out of the suburbs up towards the mountains. Where the city's density became wider her influence weakened. When the suburbs split apart at the hills, her attention ended. Cleveport was blind beyond her own boundaries and only aware of the one thread of disease snaking into her from somewhere over there. Whatever rose into her came from there. And every bit of infection in the city was connected back through that thread, everything soaked in a level of magic he hadn't known before. As if the power emanating from the hills was a remote beacon of life for the fungal satellites it cast forth. But the magic was indiscriminate. While it fueled that rampant spread of whatever infected the city, it amplified everything else too, irradiating every molecule of Cleveport with puissant energy. It made misery deadly, it made weak citymages strong. Like the queen of a hive, the power lay at the heart back there in the mountains and it pulsed stronger and stronger as its influence grew, an energy feedback loop. The more it powered its impact across the land, the more that impact fed it, engorged it, and its own power increased. If Hines could corrupt the source, he would weaken the whole network. And he would have to do so or Cleveport was only the beginning of its dominion.

That's where you should be, son. I am the city right now. You need to go further.

Hines remembered what Rundle had told them. *We think we know where it's coming from,* he told his father.

Then get there! You're no use here, we'll only fail together eventually. If you destroy the cause, we might have a chance at ending the spread of symptoms.

Okay, I'll go. Hold on for me, Dad. I'll do all I can.

He began to withdraw his mind from the vastness of Cleveport, to return to himself. As he went, he called out to the city, *Why did you bring me here? You're just slowing me down. You could have shown me this from afar. You knew we had a clue where to go.*

As his mind traveled he felt her intent, read the communication in that unique way she used, felt her love for him. And for Arthur. And her sacrifice for them both. Tears burned from his eyes, running across his cheeks. He was back from the communion, back to the world and the fetid room around him. He pulled his buried fingers free and the connection severed and he sobbed.

He leaned forward, kissed his father's forehead. "After all this," he whispered, "she brought me here to say goodbye."

"Like a mother fucking hen," Arthur rasped. "Now go, quickly. I'm dying here, haven't got long. When I fail, the infection will get more powerful. We don't have to love each other, son. We don't even have to like each other. But we have this. We have her. So let's do this, at least, yeah?"

Hines nodded, laid a hand gently on his father's bony shoulder. The man's skin looked as gray as stone beneath Hines's vibrant flesh.

"Steven, don't look for some kind of closure now. You owe me nothing and I have no excuses. *She* needs us. Go!"

Hines patted his father once and stood. "Seeya, Dad." He turned to the others, wiped a hand across his cheek.

"You okay?" Abby asked. "Your eyes kinda rolled up and I thought you were having a seizure or something. I didn't know what to do."

"Nothing you could have done. But I've learned something here that maybe we can use. I don't know. We have to get to the place Rundle told us about. Quick as we can."

They turned and hurried back through the dim house.

"What about him?" Gina asked, glancing back over her

shoulder in dismay. "We can't leave him like that!"

"We have to," Hines said. "That's necessary."

"Not going to survive this, is he?" Abby asked.

Hines shook his head. "She's got him. But if we're not quick, she's not going to survive either, and nor will any of us."

"She?" Sally looked confused.

"Cleveport," Hines told her. "Everything and everyone."

36

Hines slowed as they approached a military cordon. Every road out of the city was closed and after trying half a dozen times to find a gap only to double back and flee, they had resigned themselves to facing the soldiers and stating their case. "I'm the goddamn police," Abby said. "I still have some authority in this town." But Hines doubted her resolve.

Two men in full combat fatigues, heavily armed with automatic weapons, stepped in front of the car. Another approached the driver's side. Hines rolled down the window. "Hello there." It sounded absurd but what else could he say?

"No one in or out," the soldier said. "You'll have to turn around and go back to wherever you came from."

"You don't understand, we have to..."

The soldier raised his weapon to window height. "You need to turn around and go back."

Hines stared into the narrow, shining barrel of death only inches from his face. One touch from the soldier and that tiny aperture would bark instant death. The aperture didn't seem so small after all, yawning coldly to engulf him, to swallow him before spitting him out with the volley of lead. He leaned back, as if another six inches might somehow save him.

Abby leaned across from the passenger side, flashed her police ID. "Sergeant Jackson, I'm Detective Abby Jones, Cleveport PD. We have to go through here, it's police business."

Hines smiled. She really was a detective, had managed to spot the man's stitched-on name badge from her seat.

Jackson nodded towards the other men standing at the

cordon. They moved to either side of the car and two more equally armed men appeared from the shadows of the buildings. The night was dark and wet, rain occluded the view and the four of them in the car caused condensation to blur the windows. Hines felt suddenly very vulnerable.

"This is not open for discussion," Jackson said. "We've been told no one goes anywhere, not even police. Please, I do not want to shoot any more people today. And you don't look infected. But I have orders and they are not negotiable."

"You don't understand, Sergeant…" Abby began.

Jackson took a step back and braced in a crouched position. "Threat imminent!" he yelled. "Take aim!"

The other soldiers all raised weapons, four more barrels in an arc from passenger door to driver door. Their eyes, even through the dark and rain, showed nothing but the plain intent to fire.

"We're going!" Hines yelled and slammed the car into reverse. He hammered the accelerator and the car wheelspun on the wet road and rocketed backward, snaking dangerously left and right. The automatic weapons traced the movement perfectly, unwavering. Hines turned the wheel hard and bootlegged the car. Over Abby's curses and protestations he drove hard back the way they'd come and turned a corner to put at least one building between them and the army personnel.

He pulled over and let the engine idle.

"What the actual fuck is wrong with those idiots!" Abby spat. "They were about to riddle this car with bullets. Clearly four normal people inside."

"I think normal is being redefined by the minute," Hines said.

"They had no problem letting me out earlier," Sally said from the back. "They just warned me I'd be unlikely to get back in. But I managed to avoid them then."

Abby shook her head, slipped her ID wallet back into her pocket. "I think things have progressed. What they saw as a threat in the city they now recognize as an infection that's spreading fast. They're not risking any movement. Standard containment procedure, I guess."

"So what do we do?" Hines asked. "We have to get to the source and we really don't have much time. The longer it takes, the more the infection takes hold. That lot will lose control."

Abby looked at him, her face hard in the dashboard light. "And if we do get to the source, you can prevent that?"

"I can try. I think I have some idea of how to help. I have to! No one else seems to be attacking it. Regardless, this is all the product of something else, something bigger. Cleveport can't feel what it is, no one else has figured it out yet, except Johnson. And that prick will just sit and watch. We have to go there."

Abby drummed her fingers on the dash, scowling. "Well, the army certainly aren't about to let us out and by now they'll have every road blocked. This city is wrapped up tighter than a drum. So how do we get out?"

Silence descended, but for the constant tattoo of the rain. "This fucking weather, honestly," Gina muttered.

Hines snorted softly. "If it wasn't for this rain, nobody would be in this mess."

"Really?" Abby's brow furrowed.

"Well, we would one day, I guess. I mean, sooner or later this kind of rain would happen. But this is a record-breaking downpour, we haven't seen rain like this in Cleveport before."

"Climate change?" Gina asked.

Hines laughed, but without humor. "Sure, I guess. Significant weather events are on the increase, apparently, thanks to the changing climate. Go Team Humans, eh? But anyway, it's the relentless rain that's caused this outbreak in a way. Facilitated its spread, at least. That's part of what my father was showing me."

"Still gets us no nearer to getting out of the city," Abby said. "Focus, people. We need a solution here."

"If the army is blocking all the roads," Sally said, "could we go through the buildings?"

Abby turned in her seat as far as her injury would allow. "What do you mean?"

"Well, if we went into a building on one side and came out on the other, could we avoid the cordon on that block?"

Abby pursed her lips. "Possibly. But then we'd be on foot and have to steal a car…"

"I can, er, help there too."

"Lockpick *and* hotwire specialist, eh?"

Sally grinned crookedly. "I have a colorful past."

"Right. Well, one problem is what if we can't get out of the building?" Hines said. "Or we do and the army spot us leaving or something? We're in trouble then. They'll be happy to gun us down in an instant."

"This car smells like a fucking latrine," Abby said.

Hines frowned at her. "Yeah, well, it was the only way to escape…"

She grinned. "No, no. It's given me an idea."

Gina hissed from the back. "You wanna go back in the sewers and go under the cordons?"

"Can you think of a better idea?"

Quiet swelled in the car again. Raindrops ran races down the windshield. "Godsdammit," he said at last. "It probably is the only way through. But we have to hurry."

"How will we know the way?" Sally asked. "Last time we just had to get out and find a ladder to the street. How will we know we're past the cordons?"

Hines sighed. "Cleveport will show me. Come on." He

put the car into gear again and drove slowly along the slick, glistening road. Streetlights reflected yellow off the asphalt as they scanned for an entrance. Hines made a left turn, further from the cordon and pulled over. "There we go."

A metal plate in the middle of the road gleamed under halogen light.

"At least it won't be raining down there," Gina said with a grin.

"Right little optimist, aren't you?" Abby said.

They got out of the car and Hines dug around in the trunk until he found a tire iron. He bent his back to the task, finding a place to dig the iron in and lever up. With a little help from the others and a gentle nudge to Cleveport to relax her grip, they uncovered a wet tunnel, metal rungs leading into darkness. Foul odors rose to meet them.

Hines led the way and they climbed carefully down onto the brick ledge to one side of the sewage channel. A matching ledge ran along the opposite side. Gina used her illusion magic and cast a light for them.

Abby did remarkably well with two hands and one leg after dropping her crutches ahead of her. "Useful skill," she said, looking up at Gina's glowing orb. She reached the bottom and retrieved the crutches to hobble alongside.

"Go team," Gina said, but did nothing to hide her sarcasm.

Dripping echoed along the tunnel, squeaks and scratches with it. Hines pressed one hand to the brickwork of the wall and asked Cleveport for help. Her presence was sickened and unhappy, confused and angry.

Settle, girl. We're doing our best. Show me the way to Callum Street.

That should be far enough, a good three blocks beyond the cordon where they'd nearly been shot. Images flickered through his mind and sensations of movement. She guided him gently, but desperately.

"This way," he said, and moved off along the ledge. "Watch your step."

Hines laid a palm against the wall periodically, reading their best direction. Along with the flowing water and sounds of unseen animals, occasional groans and grunts they couldn't identify floated to them through the dark.

"This place is creepy as hell," Gina said. "I'll actually be glad to be back out in the rain."

"Just keep your eyes peeled and keep moving," Abby said.

After ten minutes they came to a large crossroads in the tunnels. Hines touched the wall, nodded forward. "We gotta jump the flow here and go straight ahead. Then we can look for a way up. I'm pretty sure we'll find Callum Street once we..."

Sally screamed from the back of the group, shrill and terrified. They spun to see her beating at a large naked man who held her in a bear hug, lifting her feet off the ground. She kicked and thrashed and howled.

"The fuck?" Abby pulled her gun, even as Hines raised the shotgun. "Don't shoot Sally!" Abby yelled.

Gina cried out, fumbling for her own weapon, and everything dropped into pitch darkness.

"Gina, the light!" Abby shouted.

There was a sob and a flicker, then the tunnel burst into too bright technicolor again, like a flash gun going off and not going out. Sally staggered forward, tears streaming, hands feeling blindly in front of her. Her face and neck, chest, arms and hands, were covered in a thick, short forest of dark bristles that wavered and shimmied. Everywhere they touched bare flesh they burrowed in rapidly. The huge, fat man who had grabbed her stumbled forward, trying to reach past her for the others. Abby fired, four, five, six quick and expert shots, deafening in the confined space, rising from the man's chest to his neck to his face and head. Every shot hit, but no blood came and his step didn't waver.

Gina grabbed Sally and pulled her to one side, staring with disbelief as the thorns disappeared beneath the girl's skin. Hines stepped past them both, put the barrel of the shotgun right into the attacker's left eye. As the man reached for him, Hines pulled the trigger. Sound vanished in an explosion of thunder and the man's head burst in a spray of blackened vegetation. He staggered backward. Hines pumped the action and put the barrel to the man's chest, fired again. A hole ripped right through, blasting out behind the attacker. He put one foot over the edge of the channel and toppled backward into the effluent and was carried along. Hines and Abby both tracked his passage with their weapons. Hines couldn't be sure if the headless body was still moving, or the flow of sewerage undulated slack limbs, but either way the man disappeared into the darkness beyond the reach of Gina's light.

Sally sat against the stone wall, sobbing, face twisted in pain. She held her arms out before herself, fingers curled into claws. Hines grimaced in horror as the last of the black spines shivered away into her flesh. She began to settle, gasping slightly. Gina fussed, stroked Sally's hair, wiped her face.

"What the fuck just happened?" Gina asked. "Will she be okay?"

Abby and Hines exchanged a look of dismay. He remembered only too clearly Jerry Rundle's rambling description of what he'd learned.

Their victims are stabbed fulla nasty, painful spines and they melt down and become a singing pool of fungus stuff waiting to attract some other poor schmuck and I honestly can't believe I'm telling you all this like it's a fact but it is and there you go.

That conversation seemed like it happened a lifetime

ago. What Rundle hadn't told them, if he even knew, was how long before the person melted down. Hines had no idea how. He looked into Abby's eyes and saw the same dilemma reflected there. They couldn't leave Sally here. How much could they tell Gina?

"I feel weird," Sally said quietly. "I feel kinda drunk."

Gina looked up from where she crouched beside her friend. "What's happening? What do you know?"

"We don't really know, that's the trouble," Abby told her gently. "We know so little about any of this."

"Am I going to be okay?" Sally asked.

Abby drew breath to speak, but paused. Hines held his silence. Gina started to cry.

Sally shook her head. "Really, this day has been a bastard from the very moment I got up." She stood, staggered slightly and Gina caught her. She righted herself and looked across the flow of sewerage. "This way, yeah?" She took a deep breath and jumped across, stepped drunkenly a pace or two, then righted herself. "Come on. Let's at least get out of this stinking hole. You need me to get a car for you, right?"

The others followed. Gina put a hand on Hines's shoulder before he jumped across. "She's going to die, isn't she." It wasn't a question.

Hines nodded. "Pretty badly. But honestly, I don't know how long…"

"But not very long."

"No. Not very long, I guess."

Gina wiped one hand across her cheek to drag tears away. "This is all my fault. I called her and everything is my fault – the crash, that Crater fucker, now this."

Steven put a hand over hers. "You can't go looking at things like that. Everyone's life is a million what-ifs. You start to track them back and that way lies madness."

Gina shook off his touch. "No. This is very simple. I

called her for help and she came. That makes this all my fault. You have to promise me something."

"I will if I can."

"Don't let her suffer."

"What? Me? I don't…"

Gina turned hard eyes up to him. "I certainly can't do it, but somebody has to. I need you to promise me."

Hines blew air out. "Jesus, okay. I'll do my best."

It wasn't much further before they found a ladder up out of the dank and stinking sewers. Like before, the pouring rain was a blessed relief, but at least they hadn't fallen in the waste this time. Though Sally was far worse off than if she had.

Abby tipped the girl's face up into the street light, looked at her eyes. "How do you feel?"

Sally half-smiled. "I actually feel pretty good. Like I said before, I almost feel drunk." Her expression sobered. "But I'm guessing that's not good, is it?"

Abby's face twisted and she shrugged. "I, er…"

"Fucking tell me!" Sally shouted. "I'm fucked, right? As good as dead? Just a matter of time?"

Abby straightened. "Yes. Yes, you're dead. I honestly don't know how long."

Sally nodded, lips pursed. She smiled again, broke out into a small laugh. "Well, just as well I feel good. Nice of them to include a little high with their death sentence."

Gina moved to hug her friend. "Oh, Sal."

"Don't touch me! No offense, but I don't want you to catch anything. Let's find a car." Tears breached her eyelids, evident even in the rain. "Just don't leave me, okay?"

"Sally, we don't know…" Abby began.

Gina spun to face Abby, eyes furious. "You are not fucking leaving her! I don't care how dangerous she is, we're not animals!" Her voice cracked, more tears came. "We can't leave her," she said softly.

"Just watch me," Sally whispered, barely audible over the hiss of the downpour. "I can be helpful for now. As soon as… as soon as anything happens, promise you'll shoot me. Don't let me become something else."

Gina grabbed her friend's hand. "Sal!"

"But please don't leave me. I'd rather you shot me now than left me to whatever is gonna happen. *Please* don't leave me."

"We won't," Abby said. "I promise."

Sally drew a ragged breath, nodded. "Right, we need an old car. New models are too damned well designed, too many immobilizers and shit like that. Something mid-nineties or earlier."

They looked around. Quiet buildings and rain-soaked streets. Hines pointed. "Parked cars on both sides of the street up there. And that's the way we're going. Let's keep an eye open for army patrols."

No one spoke while Sally scanned their choices. She pointed to a battered Toyota. "There we go."

With her lockpick kit she had the door open in seconds. Inside she spent a bit longer, but had the steering column cover removed in no time and busied herself with a pocket knife and a cluster of wires she had pulled free. The cough and kick of the engine was surprising in the quiet street where before there had only been the murmur of rain. Sally sat back, revved the engine a couple of times and nodded. She tucked the wiring away carefully, left the steering column cover in the passenger footwell and got out.

"You'll have to keep it running, obviously. If it stalls or you stop for any reason, you can see the wires I've cleared. Touch them together for ignition, but don't get a shock." She reached around and unlocked the back door, climbed in. "Come on then."

The others exchanged a look, mixed pity and respect in eyes. Hines was impressed with Sally's sudden stoic acceptance of the situation. Perhaps that feeling of drunkenness was a benefit after all. He hoped it wasn't a terrible error to bring her along any further.

37

Hines and Abby did their best to ignore the hushed conversation between Gina and Sally in the back seat. Gina's voice was tear-soaked, full of apology and guilt. Sally's was soft but deadened, calm but resigned. In the rearview mirror, the sky lightened over the ocean. The rain still fell, the sky a closed lid of solid gray cloud, but he was thankful for the light of dawn, however subdued. The darkness ahead shaded into indigo and violet over the mountains, striated with the black and gray of rain.

They left the skyscrapers and traffic lights of the city and traveled into the suburbs. Pathways had trees along them, blocks of units only ran to a few stories high. Terraces gave way to one and two-story homes with front yards, clipped grass, picket fences, ponds and gnomes. Yet still there was no one to be seen. Cleveport, from her heart to her extremities, was a ghost town and they hadn't seen a military patrol since they'd left the sewers.

Hines turned onto a main artery road that led to the highway out of Cleveport and on inland. The suburbs gave way to industrial parks of giant warehouses and huge concrete aprons for the loading and unloading of trucks. He grimaced at the deep ache of leaving. As the distance from Cleveport city increased, so did his discomfort. Enormous department stores bigger than football fields glared into the soft dawn light with their inviting neon in all the primary colors and Hines's ache grew. It was like someone had a thousand hooks throughout his internal organs, attached to a thousand filament wires, and the further he drove, the harder they pulled. He grit his teeth. It wasn't like he had any choice in this.

Sally began to moan quietly.

Hines's heart hammered at the sound. Gina and Sally had stopped talking a while before and only the whirr of tires and the rain on the windshield accompanied their journey.

Sally moaned again, louder.

"She fell asleep," Gina said, her voice taut. "But she looks very uncomfortable now."

Abby turned in her seat to see. "We should check on her."

Hines pulled over in the empty, wide street. Sally's eyes were closed, but squinted tight, her teeth clenched.

"Wake her," Steven said. "See if she can tell us what she needs."

Gina gently shook her friend's shoulder. Sally moaned, didn't wake. Gina shook her again.

Sally's eyes burst open and she screamed. She looked wildly about the car. All three of them cringed back from her sudden animation.

"Oh fuck oh fuck oh fuck it hurts!" Sally reached down, grabbed at her legs, screamed again. She fumbled at the door and swung it open to fall onto the grass verge beside the sidewalk.

The others jumped out. Sally crawled across the grass with only her arms, fingers hooked into claws grasping at the earth, legs dragging uselessly behind.

Gina ran to her, crouched. "What can we do? Sally, tell me what we can do!"

Sally arched up and screamed again. She sat back on her heels, grabbed her face between her palms. "Oh, fuck, it hurts so much!" She shifted strangely against the ground, one leg of her jeans flattening out. She sank to the other side, her knees deflating. Her shoes fell over, empty, as a black viscous pool emerged from the ankle cuffs of her pants, dissolving the material as it spread.

Her hands fell to her sides and she slumped, chin to her chest, all energy gone. She groaned weakly. Her head rose, wobbling on her neck, and her eyes beseeched them before her chin fell to her chest once more. She sank lower as her thighs collapsed flat.

"She's fucking melting!" Gina yelled at Hines. "You promised!" Tears streaked her cheeks.

Hines stared at Sally, bile rising like a rock into his throat. What a horrible thing to see, he couldn't imagine what it was like to experience. But could he kill her? He'd never killed anyone in his life, he'd barely even had a fight. Hell, he'd been beaten up often enough but… He remembered the man who had attacked Sally in the sewers. Hines had put a shotgun in that guy's face and pulled the trigger, and he had thought nothing of it. Was that man even a human anymore? Was Sally?

Abby stepped haltingly up behind Sally, all her weight on one crutch as she held her pistol in the other hand. The sound of the shot was shocking and sudden and Sally's face exploded, showering Hines and Gina with blood and brains.

Gina scrambled back on hands and heels, sobbing loudly, mouthing incoherent words. Hines wiped his face, brain flatlining. Sally's corpse slammed face down on the grass and slowly sank. Her clothes collapsed like the Wicked Witch of the West, only to disintegrate into the thick, black fluid that soaked through them. Tiny, wavering sprouts emerged, reached into the rain as a soft green glow pushed forth from each one. A gentle sound of bells began, both miles distant and inside the mind at the same time.

Abby slapped his face. "Move it! Cover your ears and get in the car!"

Hines staggered to his feet and stumbled for the driver's door that still stood open from his rapid exit. Abby stumped on one crutch to Gina, hauled her to her feet and virtually threw her into the back seat, swung her crutch to slam the door. She fell into the passenger seat, wincing in pain. "Fucking drive, Hines!"

He didn't need telling twice. The car skidded and slewed on the wet road. He floored it and hammered west, began to gasp, slowly took back control of his breathing, though his heart showed no signs of slowing. "Gina, I'm so sorry. I… I froze."

Gina lay curled in a fetal ball on the back seat, hands locked over the back of her head as she buried her face and took huge, shuddering breaths.

"Leave her," Abby said in a strained voice. "She needs to let this out on her own, I think."

Hines glanced across at his friend. She stared dead ahead, mouth pressed into a thin line. "You okay?"

She barked a hurt laugh. "Fuck, no. I just killed a beautiful young woman."

"No, you didn't. This infection killed her back there in the sewers. You did the best thing you could have for her. You did her a favor."

"Yeah? Doesn't feel like it right now. Leave me be for a minute, Steve. I need to be quiet too. Just drive, yeah?"

He nodded, turned back to the road, glistening in the suffuse dawn light. "Yeah." He focused on the increasing discomfort of leaving his city. At least the pain told him he was still alive.

Half an hour later, without spotting a single other vehicle on the road, Hines slowed to check the sign at a junction in the foothills outside Cleveport. None of them had said a word since they had left the scene of Sally's dissolution. Gina was yet to emerge from her tight curl on the back seat. "Better call Rundle," Hines said as he turned onto Galley Road. "Tell him we're here."

"No need." Abby pointed. A car sat parked at the side of the road, cigarette smoke curling from the driver's window into the early morning light.

They had not driven far along Galley Road. "I thought we'd be going further up the mountains for some reason," Hines said as he pulled in behind Rundle.

Abby turned to Gina. "How you doing?"

Gina shrugged, sitting up, eyes red and puffy. "I honestly can't believe any of this, you know?"

Abby smiled, nodded. "I do know, yeah. It's not something we can understand. We just have to get through it. You want to wait here?"

"No, I'll come with you. I don't want to be alone. And you might need my help."

"Yes, we might," Hines said. "It'd be good to have you along." He wanted to keep the poor girl's mind occupied. Besides that, he thought her skills might come in handy.

They all got out of the car as Rundle climbed from his. He stretched and stood back to let his dog jump out behind him. Barkley trotted to the side of the road and pissed against a stand of grass there.

They gathered, hunched against the rain.

"The place Johnson told me about is a half a mile or so that way." Rundle pointed up the shallow incline of the road ahead. "But I don't know any more than that. There's a long driveway, not sure how far it goes. You okay?" He pointed to Hines.

Steven took his arm from where it pressed across his chest. "Yeah, fine. It's a city thing, personal discomfort. I'm fine."

"And what the hell happened to you?" Jerry eyed Abby's crutches.

"Long story," she said. "Tell you later."

Two hawks, mottled brown and black feathers with

sharp, yellow beaks, landed on the roof of Rundle's car with a clatter of talons. They sat motionless, heads turned to one side to stare at the group. Barkley growled at them.

"Damned disconcerting, that is," Rundle said. "Johnson's, no doubt." He leaned forward, squinting. "Yep, you can see the camera eyes. Johnson told me that was always the giveaway."

"So he knows we're all here," Hines said. "Better give him a call."

Rundle pulled his cell phone out, dialed the number and hit the button for the speaker. It rang once, then, "Best thing to do is follow the hawks. They'll lead you in."

"Hello to you, too," Rundle said.

Johnson's voice was tight, the syllables clipped. He actually sounded scared and that was enough to make Hines very uncomfortable. "We don't have time for niceties, ladies and gentlemen. Have you lot learned anything of use?"

Hines held up a hand at Rundle's face of outrage. "Yes, I have actually. You're right, this is close to the source, but we don't know what the source is. We need to get in and see what we find. I don't suppose you've got any of these inside?" He gestured vaguely towards the hawks.

"My animus are throughout the area," Johnson said. "But only hawks. It's a hell of a long way for our hounds or any other creatures to travel on foot and we're unable to drive out there to meet you with them."

"Yeah, getting out of the city is a nightmare," Abby said.

"So my birds will guide you," Johnson went on, "and you can find easily enough where we think the source of the infection is. But then you're going to need to find a way underground."

Hines shook his head ruefully. "Great. How did I know I'd end up in the dark again?"

"We've found some caves at the site and they look fresh,

like they opened up with a recent landslide. It's near a water bore, so I'm guessing the farm in question used the bore for water and all this rain has caused some kind of collapse. That seems to be at least a part of the trigger for all this madness. My guess is that you're going to need to go in via the caves. I'm glad to see you have a dog with you. Barkley, wasn't it?"

"Yeah, what about him?" Rundle said defensively.

"Best you take him. He'll alert you to fungal growths and maybe other dangers too. And I'd suggest earplugs."

Rundle sighed. "I've got some. But I've been using an mp3 player and earphones. Worked well for me. And I guess we will have to take Barkley." He was clearly unhappy about the idea. Barkley whined and looked less than pleased himself.

"Let's just get up to the place first," Abby said. "We'll make better plans when we can see what we're up against."

"One more thing," Johnson said.

"Yeah?"

"You'd better be prepared for a firefight. The place is crawling with… well, people seems too generous a word. I hope you're heavily armed."

38

Hines stared at the phone, dead after Johnson had hung up. The man's hawks scrabbled impatiently on the roof of Rundle's car. Two or three more swooped around above the tree line, in and out of sight. "Heavily armed?" Hines said quietly.

Rundle looked at Abby's crutches, Gina's puffy eyes, Hines's hunched posture. "Right bunch of losers, we are. Honestly, are we really the first line of defense here?"

"First and last," Abby said. "The bureaucrats and the army are too busy locking down the city. I'll call in reinforcements, but we don't have time to wait for them. Besides, even if they helicoptered a fucking SWAT team in here to gun down whoever or whatever is waiting up there, how would we convince them to let Hines in to deal with whatever's in the caves?"

"While we're being honest," Hines said, "I have no goddamn idea if I *can* do anything. Really we need a bunch of mages far better than me, but what kind?"

"Do you know anyone else?"

He raised his hands. "Not really. But is a half-assed citymage and a juvenile illusionist really good enough?" He glanced at Gina. "No offense."

"None taken. I know exactly what I am. But I'm going in and I'm going to help fix this. I have debts to pay." Her eyes were hard, defiant.

Hines nodded, chose to accept that and move on. "Right. So here we are."

"Then we have to go in and do what we can," Rundle said. "Shall I call in to HQ and ask for back up or not?"

"Let's just go and see what's what first," Abby said. "I

mean, if the place is swarming we won't have a chance. But if not, maybe we can keep going here."

Gina laughed softly and they turned to her. "You were right, Steven. Not like the comic books or movies, is it!"

"What isn't?" Rundle asked.

"You. Us. We're hardly superheroes or Bruce bloody Willis, are we?"

Her humor in the face of the absurd infected them and smiles broke out. "Well," Abby said, "I fucking am. I've just hurt my leg. You've got mad illusion skills, Hines has, hopefully, something to end this if we can get past whoever's up there. We might look ragged, but we're the fucking heroes, make no mistake."

"You left out Jerry," Hines said. "Don't leave out Jerry."

Abby turned to her colleague. "Oh yeah, sorry. Well, you've got… I mean, you helped with Johnson and…"

Rundle lit a cigarette, shook his head. "Shit on you! You wanna know my superpower? How about this?" He popped the trunk of his car and grinned, smoke curling from his lips into the rain. In the trunk were several pump-action shotguns, a few bullet-proof vests, a box of flares, assorted automatic pistols and boxes of ammunition and, in the corner, a cardboard box of round, green grenades.

"Who says I ain't Bruce Willis? Can I join your league of superheroes now, huh?"

"Grenades?" Abby said.

"I had some time on my way out here, was a little worried about how all this might play out. Started thinking apocalypse and survival thoughts, you know? I intended to head over the hills and far away if you lot didn't come through, but I was worried about how bad things might get, so I made a detour via the riot squad building and stocked up."

Hines slapped him on the shoulder. "Well done."

Rundle smirked. He dragged a plastic bag from one corner of the trunk. "Hungry?" He handed out sandwiches and cans of soda. "They'll be a bit dry and stale now," he said. "These were emergency rations for me, but I figure we'll need the energy now."

"You really are a fucking superhero," Abby said, and took a huge bite of beef on rye.

They crammed sustenance and sugary drinks into their grateful bodies. Rundle threw a sandwich to Barkley, who happily chomped it from the grass.

Jerry held out the bag to collect their trash, threw it back in the trunk. "Get in your car and follow me," he said. "We'll get closer then sneak a look and make a plan. Here, Barkley." His dog whuffed and hopped happily into the passenger seat.

They drove up the hill and Rundle slowed to a crawl as they drew close. Johnson's two hawks flew on gentle wings ahead of the cars before perching on a wooden fence by a driveway. Hines and his friends got out of their cars and stood in the downpour to watch the long gravel track leading away from the road. One hawk flew ahead, then landed on a tree branch and looked back. The other joined it.

"This is the way then," Hines said.

"Let's get ourselves kitted out and have a look," Abby said. "We'll leave the cars here and try to sneak in."

"Can you sneak on crutches?" Gina asked.

"Watch me."

Hines handed out bulletproof vests. He had no idea how useful they would be, but any protection seemed worthwhile. Rundle's wouldn't close over his corpulent gut and he frowned and wore it open. They each took a pump-action shotgun and pockets full of ammo, except Abby who took three automatic pistols and a dozen clips instead. She tucked two pistols in the back of her waistband and held onto the third.

The others took a couple of pistols each as well for good measure.

"I'm not going to be running around much," Abby said. "Put the grenades in that holdall there and let me hang it across myself. I used to pitch little league and I can throw like a motherfucker, so maybe I'll stay back and lob bombs."

Hines eyed her for a moment, then, "Every time I think this day can't get any weirder."

Armed with all they could carry, they crept along the driveway, Johnson's hawks hopping from bough to bough ahead of them. Rainwater ran in runnels it had carved into the gravel, soaked through the grass at the edges of the road and made it boggy.

Hines wiped rain from his face. "What I'd give for a sunny day."

"I might move to the desert after this is all over," Rundle said.

One of the hawks swept back and swooped past their faces, made them jump.

"The fuck?" Abby said. "That a warning or something?"

"Ladies and gentlemen!" a heavily-accented voice boomed out behind them. Russian.

They spun around. Abby spat. "You have to be fucking kidding me!"

Crater, flanked by two heavies to either side, strode up the driveway to within fifty paces of them and stopped. They spread out, a line of five across the rough road. "It took me a while to track you down," Crater said. "And another while to get out of the city and catch up. But here we are."

"The impound yard is wide open, you know," Abby called out. "Just fuck off and take whatever you want!"

"Oh, this has become far more personal than that. You losers have managed to embarrass me and that cannot be allowed to stand."

Gina bolted forward, screaming. "Fuck you! Fuck you to fucking death!" and she began pumping and firing her shotgun. It barked and bucked, sent her staggering left and right. One of Crater's heavies howled and clutched his shoulder as it exploded in blood. Hines, Abby and Rundle leaped to the sides of the road and the cover of trees as the rest of the hoods brought weapons to bear.

Crater, face twisted in fury, gestured violently and Gina lifted off her feet and flew backward into the trees with a crash of branches. Abby leaned heavily against one crutch and fired quick, expert shots. The remaining heavies started shooting and Hines gasped and spun to the ground as a bullet punched him hard in the chest.

Rundle rolled, staggered up firing, surprisingly agile for a man of his bulk. He winged one thug as another took aim and fired. Jerry howled as his right thigh burst with a spray of scarlet.

Crater gathered his power again, Hines tasted the static of it in the air. After all they'd been through, this two-bit mobster was going to screw everything.

And then the hawks came in.

A dark bird slammed feet first into Crater's face. He screamed, high and piercing. The bird's wings beat hard and it flew up, talons pouring blood. Crater stumbled forward, hands rising to cover the empty bleeding sockets where his eyes had been. Other hawks, five or six at least, swooped and harried the hoods. They swung weapons and fired, tried to get a bead on the fast-moving birds of prey.

Abby stepped forward and aimed carefully, perfectly targeting each Russian, shooting them down. Gina came barreling out of the undergrowth to within ten paces of the staggering mob boss, pumped her shotgun and blew a wide hole in his chest. He lifted high and back to slam motionless into the dirt.

From the moment Crater had first spoken, so full of bravado, to the tableau of he and his four associates dead had taken only a handful of terrified, frantic seconds.

"Fuck me," Hines said, pulling himself to hands and knees. The bullet gleamed dully where it was embedded in his bulletproof vest. His chest thrummed with a deep bruise of pain.

Gina stood gasping as Abby crutched over, put one arm around the girl's shoulders. "You okay?"

"Battered, but fine. Fuck. That. Guy."

Abby looked down at Crater's corpse. "Yeah. Couldn't agree more."

"I don't think he expected us to be so well-armed, do you?" Hines suggested and Abby laughed.

"Walked into something a little bigger than he anticipated," she said. "We're the league of superheroes, remember?"

Hines grinned, still rushing with adrenaline.

"A little help?" Rundle's voice was weak.

They turned to see him lying in the rain, one hand pressed to his heavily bleeding leg.

"Is it bad?" Abby asked.

"Right through the muscle. Hurts like a sonofabitch, but not too serious. Assuming I don't bleed out. Who the hell was that anyway?"

"A mobster who didn't know when to fold 'em," Abby said.

Hines moved to Jerry, checked the injury. It took a couple of minutes to make sure it was cleaned and he strapped it with a torn off shirtsleeve. "You'll live," he said.

Abby threw one of her crutches down. "Here. Guess I have to share now."

Rundle stumbled about until he found his balance on the single crutch. Barkley circled his master, whining. "I'm okay, boy. I'm all right." His phone beeped and he checked it, shook his head. "Text from Johnson. Says, 'You're welcome'. What a dick, really."

"Yeah," Hines agreed. "But he did just save our butts." He looked up towards the original two hawks, perched on branches again, waiting for them to follow. He flicked a salute in their direction.

The birds hopped away and the ragged group followed.

Abby pointed. "Be quiet, we're close."

"Surely anyone there will have heard that commotion," Hines said.

"We'll see."

Ahead, the driveway opened into a wide expanse of grass and fences. The edge of a large colonial house, solar panels across its roof, was visible past the thick pine trees that lined the road. A couple of cars and a minivan were parked to one side, a tractor and small truck across the way. As they crept forward, Hines saw a large hay shed and, beyond it, paddocks of cattle and horses. A massive vegetable garden sprawled off to one side, disappearing from view behind the trees.

"Pretty self-sufficient commune," Hines said quietly.

Gina made a small noise, half squeak, half sob. She pointed.

Around the end of the house a group of people appeared. Naked and shambling, staring at nothing in particular, they turned. Their eyes roved as Hines and his friends ducked out of sight into the trees beside the track.

"They know we're here." Rundle said. "They must, given the noise we made."

Hines relaxed his mind and felt for hints of magic. The moment he did so, he was flooded with energy. It pulsed around them, on a frequency like the one that soaked Cleveport and made everyone's talent too strong. He'd got so used to feeling it that he hadn't stopped to noticed how much it had increased in this place. Gina looked at him and nodded, open to it herself now. Within it, a kind of sentience dwelled. A presence, not like any human mind, but a thought process nonetheless.

"It knows we're here," Hines said. "Whatever *it* is. And those things are its minions."

"It knows?"

"It can feel us, feel our magic, Gina and I. Feel the physical presence of all of us. We're not hiding here. We're just waiting."

"Then screw that!" Rundle said. He shifted forward, braced his crutch in one armpit, and jacked his shotgun. Barkley cowered behind his legs as he pumped and fired, pumped and fired, yelling incoherently.

Hines ran to stand beside him and Gina joined them. Three in a row, they fired shot after shot.

Gina staggered with the recoil, but had a far better handle on it after her previous experience. "This is for Sally, you bastards!"

The shambling group staggered and stumbled, limbs flying with the impact of the shots. But still they shuffled forward.

"Aim for the legs and heads!" Hines yelled, struggling with the recoil himself.

"Why are they so slow?' Rundle called out between shots. "They were fast enough in the city."

"Who knows? Maybe these guys have been waiting a while and they're entirely vegetable only they haven't broken down yet. Some kind of rear guard? It's the only advantage we've got!"

Abby moved from the cover of the trees. "Brace yourselves!" she yelled, and pitched something over their heads. There were a few still, silent moments before the explosion right in the middle of the group. Limbs and bodies flew, but no blood. Broken halves of people hauled themselves forward with their arms if their legs were gone, becoming more animated by the second. Among the blacked grass of their wounds, sickly pale filaments writhed.

"They're getting faster!" Gina cried, pointing to some behind, unharmed by the grenade.

The shamblers broke into a run.

"Maybe they've been in a kind of stasis or something," Hines said. "Now they're needed, they're warming up! Wouldn't surprise me if whatever is here sent most of its minions to the city, but kept a bunch here for protection. You know, in case of something just like us."

"All guesswork," Abby said. "Save it. Look to your right."

Another bunch of naked attackers, vacant-eyed, sat along a fence line. They roused and stumbled forward, gaining agility and speed as they went. Abby hurled another grenade and took out at least half of them. The others turned their guns and cut down the rest.

"Reload!" Rundle shouted.

Abby pulled another grenade from her bag and held it up, one finger hooked into the ring. One of Johnson's hawks swooped down and grabbed it, the ring pulling free as it soared up again. It flew over the house and dropped the grenade on the other side. Dirt and garbage bins and limbs blew out past the house with the explosion.

"More that way then, I guess," Abby said with a crooked smile.

Another hawk flew low and circled them, then moved to the north. "Guess we follow this one," Hines said.

"Watch out for more of those bastards," Rundle warned.

They kept Johnson's animus in sight. Three more unclothed lunatics tried to rush them, but four trigger-happy, scared people blew them to pieces. After that, all was quiet and still but for the pounding rain and the worried lowing of livestock. The hawk led them around the house, through a paddock and towards an escarpment some two hundred yards away. They passed a hay shed with roof, but no walls, bales stacked in the meager shelter.

"Looks like I'm going that way," Hines said, pointing to the rock face ahead of them. "Abby, you should wait here where there's shelter and plenty of wide open space to spot any potential attackers."

"You going alone?" Abby asked.

"You can't go stumbling in caves on crutches, Abs. Neither can Jerry. Besides, someone needs to know about everything we've learned thus far if I don't come back." Hines looked apologetically at Rundle. "I'd like to take your dog, if he'll come."

Rundle crouched, scratched behind Barkley's ears. "You help all you can, you hear me. And you come back! We're moving inland, remember? Don't you forget that."

Barkley looked from Rundle to Hines and back again. He licked Rundle's face and whuffed, then slunk over to Hines, tail between his legs. It was tucked so far under, the tip tickled the hound's belly.

"Smart dog," Abby said.

Rundle nodded, lit a cigarette. "Yeah. You look after him."

Hines shook Rundle's hand. "I will. You guys wait here and I'll be back as soon as I can."

"I'm coming with you."

They all turned to see Gina's defiant stare. "Don't try to stop me," she said. "Sally died because of me and I have to do something to put that right. I'm going all the way."

"It's not your…" Hines began.

Gina stabbed an index finger into his chest. "Shut up! I

need to do this. I need to be part of some kind of solution. Besides, you can feel it right? Deep underneath us somewhere? And that Johnson guy on the phone said caves. So if you're going underground, you're going to need my help. Did you bring a flashlight?"

"Ah, no, I…"

"Right, so you need me. I need earplugs or something."

Rundle handed her his mp3 player. "Here. It's got a few hours of battery left."

Gina narrowed her eyes. "What kind of music is on here?"

"The kind that'll keep you alive!"

"Good point."

"What about you?" Abby asked Hines.

He shrugged. "I don't have anything."

Rundle dug around in his pockets and pulled out a handful of bright orange rubber ear plugs. "Honestly, I have to do everything for you guys?"

Hines took the earplugs. "Thanks. Guess we're off then."

Abby took his hand, squeezed it. "Please be careful. Look after those two." She nodded towards Gina and Barkley.

"I will. See you soon." He leaned forward and hugged her, kissed her cheek. Was it for the last time? He had a sinking feeling it might be. This thing was bigger than any of them.

He turned and headed from the shelter of the tin roof, back out into the rain, Gina keeping pace beside him. Barkley looked back at Rundle, barked once, then trotted with them.

Hines scratched the dog's head. "Thanks, buddy. You're a good boy. I want you to know I appreciate this."

Barkley looked up with a face that clearly portrayed annoyance.

39

Johnson's hawk led them into a stand of trees at the back of the paddock where the ground sloped more steeply. It became rocky and difficult underfoot, freshly turned over by a sudden geological shift. Several trunks leaned at strange angles and the rainwater sluiced heavily through every depression. They pushed in between the injured pines, branches dragging wetly at their limbs and clothes. The further they went, the more broken the land, until the trees were lying flat to the ground and the mud was loose and sucked at their feet. Puffing and struggling, soaked and filthy, they finally came to where the rockface emerged, a solid graybrown wave rising up from the devastation. The landslide had made a miniature valley and, at its center, the rock split open like a wound.

"Just as well Johnson had his scouts out here," Hines said, brushing pine needles and detritus from his arm and chest. "We'd never have found this."

Gina turned her face up to the rain. "I don't know. Can't you feel that energy coming out of there? I think we'd have been drawn here regardless."

"Maybe. But in the maelstrom of power soaking through everything, we might have taken hours to pinpoint it. Anyway, promise me something."

"What?"

"If it gets too much down there, you run away. Take Barkley and you two get the hell out." He held up a hand as she protested. "I'll manage somehow without light. I can use that mp3 player of yours as a flashlight if need be and you can have the earplugs. That tiny screen will provide a lot of light in the pitch dark of a cave. Just promise me, okay? I don't want your death or Barkley's on my conscience too." He put a hand on her shoulder. "Enough people have died."

Gina nodded, looked down at her feet. "Yeah. Okay. But I want to help and if I can, I will."

"Okay. Well, let's see what's in there."

They moved towards the black rent in the rock. A hawk perched on an edge of stone above them. "You're staying here, then?"

The bird flapped its wings once.

"Yeah, well, you watch and report. All you're good for, standing back and letting everyone else do the work. I know you can hear me, Johnson. You may think you're some human evolved, but it's us down here in the trenches doing the actual work. I know you think we're your slaves or some shit, but without us, you're nothing. I appreciate the help with those mobsters, but you need us more than we need you. Remember that!" He stared hard at the hawk, but the creature sat motionless, watching him with one impassive camera eye. "Fuck you," Hines muttered and walked into the dark fissure.

"What was that about?" Gina asked as she followed him in.

"Nothing. Personal. Just that Johnson guy pisses me off. I'll explain later, when all this is over. And if you ever hear of a group called Cyberdawn, you run the hell away from them. They give me the creeps."

Gina smiled, lopsided. "Yes, boss."

The weak light of the overcast day only penetrated the first few feet into the cave system. The ground was wet and sloped down at a steep angle, several busy rivulets of rain running ahead of them. Gina's magic pulsed and her illusory light popped into being. The walls of the passage gleamed, widening into a high cave some thirty yards ahead. The ground dropped away towards it.

"Here we go then." Hines walked in front, Barkley at his heels and Gina brought up the rear. As the passage widened, Barkley moved ahead, slinking low to the ground, tail tucked. He sniffed the air constantly, glanced back often. His eyes were sad under knitted brows.

They entered the broad opening of the first cave, Gina sending her light on to illuminate the cathedral-like space. The ground continued downwards and the cave narrowed to another tunnel, an inverted V-shaped split in the stone. The cave floor was covered in puddles and several small streams of rainwater hurried through and disappeared into the far opening.

"Only one way to go so far," Hines whispered. The cave was still and dank, silence hung heavy and he was loathe to disturb it with too loud a voice. "All this rainwater running through here since the landslide. I wonder if it's the first time these caves have seen water in… maybe ever?"

"Can you feel it?" Gina whispered back. "Like… a pulse or something."

Hines nodded, swallowed nerves. "It's slow and kinda massive, huh?"

"Yeah. Hard to imagine just how big it is. It feels… epic."

"You can go back any time."

She looked daggers at him, so he shrugged and headed for the far tunnel. Barkley bounced in front, growling deep in his throat. He put his paws wide and bowed between them, butt high, hackles rippling between his shoulders as he blocked the way.

"Time for ear protection, I think," Hines said. He pulled out the plugs and jammed them in. His voice was strange inside his own head when he spoke again. "I hope these are good enough to cut out the danger."

Gina's mouth moved, but he heard no words.

"What?"

She grinned, spoke louder. "That was normal talking volume and now I'm nearly shouting, so hopefully they'll be good." She looked at the mp3 player and frowned. Then her eyes brightened. She held it up so Hines could see the screen.

"Tool," Hines read. "*10,000 Days*, that's a good album."

Gina smirked. "You and Rundle both got some dark horse musical taste."

"That might not be his. He might have got it anywhere."

"I like to think of him cranking it while he smokes in his car." She put the earbuds in and turned it up, head nodding subtly.

Hines turned back to Barkley, tapped one ear. "We got protection, now. Can we go on?"

The dog stayed low, teeth bared.

Hines crouched, scratched one cheek. "I get it, buddy. This is good, the warning. You keep those coming. But we have to move on."

He stood and moved past Barkley, who slunk alongside, then trotted ahead again. Gina caught up on the other side and they entered the dark tunnel. Hines tapped her shoulder, pointed to her glowing orb, made a downward gesture with his hand. She dialed down the brightness as it drifted ahead of them. A couple of smears of soft green luminescence rose from the shadows to either side. Gina reduced the brightness even more, to a barely visible soft glow, more like the way was backlit, and the verdancy rose in response, the tunnel taking on an undersea ambiance. Their eyes adjusted. Pools and swirls of fungal outgrowths were everywhere, patching the floor in a mosaic of soft gleaming. In places it crept up the walls, shimmering nodules wavering.

The weight of the shotgun in Hines's hand was a hindrance. All he wanted to do was cover both ears with his hands as well as stuffing extra earplugs in. Gina turned up the volume on her music. She moved forward as she did so, head tilting to one side as she crouched for a closer look at a patch creeping up the nearest wall. Hines grabbed her shoulder, hauled her back. He shook his head vigorously and made a gesture with his hand, two fingers to his eyes, then two fingers straight ahead. Gina swallowed, nodded.

Barkley went in front of them, belly low, tail tucked. His brow was creased and Hines felt sorry for him. The poor dog would clearly rather be anywhere but here. And yet, here he was, doing the right thing. Doing as he'd been told. Hines caught up, patted him. "Good dog! You're a really good dog."

Barkley pressed up into Hines's hand briefly then carried on. They followed, carefully picking their way between the growths, staying as far from any of them as possible, walking in the running water as often as they could to ensure they didn't step on one accidentally. In places, the patches showed weakly through the rivulets, drowned and inert. Hines pointed one out to Gina and she nodded.

The passage continued its downward trend and began to narrow. The pain of leaving Cleveport's heart riddled Hines's nerves and organs, yet something else persisted through it all. A subterranean vibration, connected to the pulsing magic somehow, stretching all the way back to the city. He tried to relax, let the tension of it ease. Through that connection, he felt her fretting. He sent waves of reassurance, but she would see right through them. There was no way he could fool her into feeling confidence he didn't have. *We'll do all we can*. She wasn't mollified by his promise.

The way narrowed further and claustrophobia clutched at him as the walls closed in. Before long he had to turn sideways, squeezing through as the rock dragged at his bulletproof vest. He looked back to Gina. Her eyes were wide and frightened. He tried to smile, but it felt like a grimace. She nodded.

The water running through from above was funneled and ankle deep, any fungus well drowned in the narrow passage. Hines prayed there was none creeping up the walls. The flood rose almost to his knees before the passage thankfully opened out again. The impromptu river level reduced, but still ran, deep enough to cover their shoes. Hines's feet had gone numb from cold. He couldn't guess how much effect the huge volume of rain was having on the underground structure, and knew that was at least partly responsible for everything happening around Cleveport. It was also responsible for the landslide above and the revealing of this route they took. With any luck, it wouldn't have any other significant geological effects while they were exploring the dark system of caves and tunnels.

Barkley barked, loud and insistent, the dog's concern clear even through the earplugs. Hines bent and patted the dog's rump, pushed him forward. "Okay, boy, okay. We're ready." He pointed to his ears again and Barkley moved on.

But they weren't ready.

They emerged into a cavern that dwarfed the first. The ceiling vaulted far above into shadow and the floor was undulating, scattered with rocks, and rivulets rushed through it in a hectic pattern, finding every low point to split and run and rejoin and split again. And everything was aglow in deep, shimmering greens. The fungal growths smothered the rocks, coated all the walls. As they stood agape, every glowing nodule seemed to reach for them, as if the entire cavern turned to look, the growths bigger and more developed than Hines had seen before.

Barkley pushed his butt back against them, trying to convince them to turn around. Hines had never wanted to take the advice of a dog more seriously in his life. But it wasn't an option. Gina raised both hands in a gesture of helplessness. He nodded, understanding. The fungus covered everything, no gaps in between for them to pick their way through. Wherever they stepped, they would disturb it and the spores would burst forth and engulf them. Hines wished Rundle had had gas masks in his crazy car trunk stash. The man was smart. If there were gas masks to be had, Jerry would surely have brought them. Regardless, it was too late now.

The edges of that crystalline song, the cajoling tones that dragged at him, tried to coax him forward. The cavern virtually rang with it and his earplugs were not enough to keep it all out. Gina was stabbing the volume of the mp3 player higher, eyes narrowed as if in pain. Barkley pranced and barked angrily. Everywhere Hines looked, he saw reaching green and had to fight the compulsion to go to it.

He put the shotgun under his arm, gripped it against his chest and jammed his fingertips into his ears on top of the plugs. The song sank away and his mind cleared a little. He squinted, tried to suppress the cajoling glow, and that helped a little too. But still the way ahead was a sea of death with no way around.

The energy of whatever lay beneath pulsed up to them, unstoppable. It enhanced Hines's magical self so much he felt he might burst. The drag of leaving Cleveport tore through him in one direction, the pounding of the magic beneath blew into from the other. The deadly music of the mold was only held back by his flimsy fingers. What chance did he have of stopping any of it? There wasn't even a way to cross this cave and survive.

How far had they come? They must be at least half a mile into the mountainside by now, and they'd gone down constantly, hundreds of feet surely. The water rushed past them, splitting around rocks and pooling in places. Could they use the streams to travel? Were any wide enough to be safe? He moved up one side of the passage near the opening they had emerged from, to a chunk of rock unaffected by the spread of fungus, to gain a higher view. Most of the rivulets were only a few inches across, maybe as wide as his outstretched palm at most. Even picking their way along those would put them far too close to the growths on either side.

Then he noticed one babbling stream wider than the others, maybe half a yard across. He strained to see if it went all the way. It would be no good to creep along it and find themselves marooned in the middle of the cave, surrounded by a sea of glowing death. The stream filled a pool about two-thirds of the way across and that pool overflowed in several places on the far side, but the ground dropped away too much to see if the way was clear beyond it.

Gina looked at him expectantly as he returned to her. He shrugged, gestured for her to follow him and keep her eyes only at her feet. He pointed to a patch of straining green globules, then to his eyes and shook his head vigorously: *Don't look, don't listen!*

She nodded.

Hines nudged Barkley ahead and the dog walked into the stream, picked his paws up high with each step, gingerly moving forward. Hines followed, the water icy around his ankles. He kept his shotgun tucked under his arm and his fingers in his ears, stared hard at his feet stepping one in front of the other and did all he could to ignore the brightness clamoring at his peripheral vision.

Cleveport clawed at him, whatever entity lay ahead drew him on with its talent-enhancing strength even as its extrusions all around tried to pull him down and infect him. All he wanted to do was run away. He was a private investigator! He specialized in missing persons cases. He couldn't think of anywhere more out of his comfort zone. Then he sensed the presence of Gina behind, pushing herself onwards, showing bravery he would never have thought her capable of out in the street, with her attitude and angry clothes. He looked down at Barkley slinking ahead, the cold water up to his belly, his face a picture of misery.

Stop feeling so sorry for yourself, Hines.

The stream opened out into the pool. He moved forward to make room for Gina, who came to stand beside him. The water reached their knees, poor Barkley keeping his head high now as it was up to his shoulders. His ears shivered as he trembled from the cold.

The pool was a good few feet across and several small waterfalls tumbled off its far edge as the cavern fell away to a wall far below. The slope ahead of them was at least forty-five degrees angled downwards and no rivulet was more than an inch or two wide.

Hines's heart sank. The glowing death carpeted the way in every direction and at least a couple of feet up the far wall below them. A few gaps and cracks opened onto darkened passages there, but the one he needed was obvious by its emanating aura. It was low and narrow, at the lowest point of the cavern. All the streams and creeks gathered and bubbling in front of it and disappeared into the shadows. They had been following the rain down all along and needed to go deeper, but were thoroughly cut off.

He glanced to Gina who shook her head. She leaned close, shouted into his ear. "Illusions are fucking useless here! I'm useless!"

He shook his head, pointed to her hanging light. She shrugged, face rueful, gestured to the green light all around and doused her glowing orb. They could see perfectly well by the green phosphorescence. Barkley sat in the water, only his head showing and he shivered.

Cleveport tugged at Hines. He closed his eyes. Their lien was fractured, muffled by distance but their connection was unbreakable. She sent cracked images, of him moving the asphalt of her streets, opening the stone floor in Crater's cell, loosening sewer access covers. He frowned, starting to understand, but did he have the power? In truth, he had more power in his talent than he'd imagined possible, but was even that enough? To move her like that?

He gestured for Gina to wait, tapped his head, *I've got an idea.*

It seemed absurd, but they were finished otherwise. He closed his eyes and let his mind flow back to Cleveport. He ignored her clamoring, concentrated on the substance of her. Like stirring the asphalt for Rundle a lifetime ago, he found a strip of road in the suburbs and slipped his consciousness into it, through it, let himself spread out as if he were a twenty-yard section of usually busy street. His talent felt more potent than ever and he gathered it up with the surface, drew it along the connection he had with Cleveport. Through the aether, through some subspace of non-reality where magic lived, where everyone's magic traveled, he willed that one specific part of Cleveport to come to him.

And the road *shifted*.

He dragged it forward and cast his mind to the glowing expanse between himself and the passageway ahead and threw his talent at it.

The pulse of magic slammed through him, tore at his muscles like he was physically lifting weight. It knocked him onto his ass in the icy water and he gasped, his eyes flew open. Chunks of asphalt, incongruous dotted lines of paint on parts of it, crashed into the cave from nowhere. He felt Cleveport gasp in pain and pleasure, his head thrumming like it would burst with the power he wielded.

As the substance of the road hit the steeply sloping cave floor it covered the fungal growths there, but the masses of it either side burst up in clouds of spores. He grabbed Gina's arm and dragged her, stumble-running against his injured knee over the freshly lain surface of broken asphalt, Barkley prancing and barking ahead of them. They squeezed their lips tightly, pinched their noses shut and ran for the tunnel. The water there rushed ankle deep and ten feet wide from wall to wall, and no fungus grew in the torrent. Gina recast her light and it bobbed ahead. They stumbled along until they were a good hundred yards from the cavern.

Hines pulled to a halt, flapped one hand as he gasped for breath. The huge movement of a piece of Cleveport had exhausted him, mentally and physically. He felt torn inside, his body not used to that level of magic coursing through it. Not really up to it. Gina sent her light back the way they'd come. No clouds of spores floated in the air, the only glow was Gina's own. She pulled her earbuds free and looked at Hines as he leaned, hands on his thighs and gasped for breath. His right knee throbbed in bursts of agony, threatening to collapse on him at any moment. He had no time to consider that.

She plucked one earplug from him. "What the fuck did you just do?"

Hines shook his head, grinned. "Something I didn't believe was possible."

"You, like, cast a road, man."

"Well, not really. Just relocated it."

"Just? Well, thank fuck we got out of there. The place was hideous."

Barkley barked again, frantic high yips. Hines and Gina turned to where he looked, off down the tunnel ahead of them. The tunnel widened significantly, the rainwater powering along it like a shallow river, everything from above funneled into this one channel. Gina sent her light that way. She gasped. A horde of people, silhouettes outlined by her dancing brightness, ran up the slope towards them, hands outstretched. They moaned and growled as they came.

40

"Oh, fuck me!" Gina cried and swung her shotgun up.

Hines no longer had his, he must have dropped it in their flight from the green cavern. He pulled both pistols from his waistband and fired two-handed, pumping bullets into the crowd. Gina's shotgun boomed thunder and blasts of light, heads and arms exploding in grassy masses.

"Take out the legs!" Hines shouted. "We have to slow them down."

Barkley cowered behind them, pressed low to the rushing water, as their weapons lit the tunnel with fire and sound.

"Too many of them!" Gina screamed even as several fell.

"How many hippies lived in this goddamn commune?" Hines yelled, staggering slightly on his weak knee.

Dust and chips of stone rained around them, disturbed by the sonic blasts of the weapons. A chuck of rock the size of his head dropped right beside Hines.

"Be careful, we'll bring the roof down on ourselves."

Gina dropped her shotgun and drew both her pistols. "I'm out of ammo anyway, no time to reload."

They'd briefly slowed the horde, but less than ten yards remained between them. Stumbling over their fallen comrades, who even now clawed by broken hands through the rushing torrent, a dozen or more moved forward once again.

"You have to run," Hines said. "Don't let them get you. Take Barkley."

Gina glanced at him. "And what about you?"

"I… I don't know. Maybe this is as far as we get."

"Only to fail now?"

Was this where it ended? The mindless, vegetative people surged up the steep passage, slipping and sliding on the wet rock as they came.

"I can give you one chance!" Gina said suddenly and shoved Hines against the tunnel wall. "Stay absolutely still, I'll lead them away! Hopefully this is the last of them."

"What?"

Before he could protest, her magic pulsed. Whatever illusion she cast was invisible to Hines beyond a strange shimmering in the dim air between him and the advancing attackers.

"Don't move!" Gina said. She ran into the middle of the tunnel and waved her arms, fired a couple of shots at the marauders. "Come on, you fuckers!" She turned and raced back the way they'd come.

"Go with her, boy!" Hines said to Barkley. "Protect Gina! I'll take it from here."

Barkley looked around, tan eyebrows knitted, then barked once at Hines and ran. He quickly got ahead of Gina as she jammed her earbuds back in and they fled towards that hellish, glowing cavern, Gina's dim light bobbing ahead of them.

Hines froze, pressed into the wall, his twin guns held up before him. They felt about as useful as water pistols. He braced for the agonizing attack of the mob. They scrambled on, barely hampered by the incline and the flowing rainwater now they'd found their stride.

Hines held his breath as they drew alongside, but they looked only ahead, clawing at the air as they passed. Small fungal sprouts protruded around their eyes, noses and mouths, the rippling lumps all over their hands and arms. Hines counted eleven of them, some with limbs missing or chunks of torso blown away. Moments later, three more came crawling past, hauling their broken bodies in strange parodies of running. Then he was alone in a dark torrent. He finally released his breath.

Gina's light illuminated the huge cavern up the slope, the glow leaking weakly back to him. It faded as she made her way towards the surface and he gasped as the sensation of her magic dropped away. He stood in absolute blackness, icy water almost to his knees.

Whatever illusion she'd used to conceal him was gone and he was truly alone. And that was probably for the best. She had certainly saved them and he hoped she would make it out alive. With any luck she could use her illusions to protect herself and Barkley. It was all down to Hines now. At some level he had always known it would be, since these strange events began, a very personal fight. He'd needed the help he had received thus far, but it was his city under threat. Now it was time to face whatever else lay ahead on his own. Hines against the thing that threatened *his* Cleveport.

He turned to look down the slope. It wasn't entirely pitch dark. His eyes had adjusted to a soft glow far in the distance. It was something to focus on. Maybe it was the end of this journey, as he was fast running out of chances and options. What he might do when he got there was still a mystery, but he needed to get there at least. Keeping one hand trailing along the wall for comfort, stepping slowly and carefully in the streaming water, he started towards the feeble green smudge in the blackness.

41

Gina ran through the green cavern, Tool blasting in her ears. She watched her feet as she ran the narrow stream from the pool back to the far side. Scrambling up Hines's recently delivered roadway had been nerve-wracking, cracked and broken and steep as it was, wet with rushing water, she'd slipped and nearly tumbled several times. Barkley had scrabbled and scratched his way up by determination alone. Gina had to drop her illusion of rock walls concealing Hines and could only hope she'd bought him enough time. She made it across the cavern as the moaning coughs of her pursuers echoed through the space. Barkley bounced and barked ahead of her, regularly looking back to check she was with him.

She sent her light up the tunnel and followed it, thankful to be leaving the toxic cave behind. She risked a glance back and saw the shambling, reaching horrors spread out across the rough floor, heedless of the fungal patches bursting with spores all around them in swirling luminescent clouds.

The mob traveled fast and had nearly crossed the wide cavern as she ran into the narrow mouth of the passage leading up. She pictured a waterfall of tumbling rock, an internal landslide, and her illusion piled ragged chunks of stone across the cave wall, built up in front of the tunnel mouth.

Her talent let her see both the solidity of her illusion and through it at the same time. She saw the mob slow and look left and right, up and back. Clearly they still relied on vision to some degree, though how those gleaming greenblack eyes worked was a mystery. It gave her hope that Hines would be safe and she had time to run. She turned and rushed on, slipping and cursing. The way seemed steeper than she remembered, but presumably a careful descent was far easier than a rapid ascent. Running up the wet stone against the flow of water was treacherous.

She reached the narrowing of rock and squeezed in, Barkley wriggling ahead of her, his tail whipping in silhouette as her light bobbed above. She pushed through into the wider passage as a sharp cracking sounded from somewhere nearby.

She skidded to a halt, pulled her earbuds free, looked around. Had she really heard that? Water jetted from several splits in the ceiling of rock above her that had not been there before. The loud cracking came once more. Barkley turned, barked furiously. Gina nodded. "I hear ya, boy. Let's go!"

She ran again, but Barkley continued to bark, facing the way she'd come. The rock above creaked and a huge, wedge-shaped chunk dropped free. Torrents gushed behind it.

Gina ran past the dog. "Come on, boy!" She looked back and screamed as a huge naked man, muscles swollen and skin scored and grazed by the narrow passage, pushed through. Where his skin was broken, pale fibrous lines sprouted out. He opened his mouth and inside was a forest of writhing mushrooms that reached out past his lips.

The rock groaned again, Gina staggered and slipped, fell to her hands and knees, clawed her way upwards on all fours. Another crack, another falling chunk of stone, more gushing water. Gina gained her feet. The fungal man was nearly upon her. Then Barkley was snarling and flying through the air. His front paws hit the man square in the chest and sent his balance back. He sat down, waist deep in the flood, and slid backward on his butt. Barkley snapped and barked, standing against the man's chest and then everything was spraying icy water, deafening cracks and tumbling stones.

Gina ran back up the treacherous slope, crying and

shouting, calling Barkley's name. Fallen rock filled the tunnel. Attacker and dog were nowhere to be seen, where they had been was only broken stone, and torrents pouring down from myriad fissures above.

Sobbing, Gina turned and ran up, up, up until she burst out into the pine-fresh air and drenching rain. The downpour was bigger than ever, obscuring everything beyond a few feet ahead, roaring through the nearby pines. She slipped and slid on the landslide until she reached the shelter of the trees, but they barely slowed the deluge. Gasping for breath, she leaned against one wet, sappy trunk and looked back to the cave's entrance. The landslide above had increased, more substrate shifting to either side. She heard boughs breaking and saw another slide beginning to the north. The monumental weather was changing the geography around her.

She stared hard at the dark mouth of the rock above, willing a sodden and battered dog to appear, but it didn't happen. "Barkley," she sobbed quietly. "Oh, Barkley."

42

Steven's eyes adjusted, distant green growing into a glow that outlined the edges of the tunnel ahead of him. The rainwater rushing past was higher than his knees, threatening to pull his feet from under him and send him flying like a whitewater rapids canoe. His old injury stabbed with every step. More than simply aggravated, it seemed to be reinjured. Would he collapse and drown before he reached his goal? There would be a sick irony in that.

He concentrated on the luminescence and kept moving. The channel steepened and narrowed and after five hundred yards or more the water had reached his hips and the glow seemed no nearer. Patches of the cruel fungus were visible here and there through the rushing stream, still pale with phosphorescence, but thoroughly drowned. Harmless, for now at least. Thankfully the torrent was still slow enough that he could stand against it, but he didn't know how long that would last. He moved sideways, both hands against the tunnel wall for stability.

How far had he come? He must be a mile or more into the mountain range, maybe half a mile or more down. Possibly much more. He trudged on.

As he progressed, the sensation of magic became less a general presence and more a burning insistence. What had been gently increasing people's talents in Cleveport was pushing his skills out through his bones in the darkness of these caverns. He'd remotely shifted his consciousness into Cleveport, carried a piece of the city through the aether to smash into the cave floor. The degree of magic required for such an act was inconceivable, yet he *had* done it. Worthless citymage, Steven Hines, had done that. But not without cost.

It had taxed him. He was frayed, stripped by the process. A body was not supposed to manipulate power like that and it had physically injured his muscles, even his bones. And yet the further he went, the stronger the influence and the stronger his talent seemed. It felt as though he could move the Earth itself, even though the act might tear him apart.

The glow increased as the passage steepened even further. He slipped and staggered regularly, the water trying to drag him along. Then the way began to widen and level off. The radiance pulsed until it was a swollen luminescence filling the space ahead of him. He saw the outlines of cave edges only a couple of hundred yards away.

The rainwater had reached his buttocks by the time the tunnel floor flattened, then the walls receded to either side and the river sank below his knees once more. The relief was massive, he allowed himself a moment to relax. Everything was lit as the tunnel widened into a plateau at the edge of a huge cavern. No, not the edge. Halfway or more up the wall of a monumental space. The ceiling arched high above, stark relief of green light and sharp shadows. The water tumbled over the lip of a natural rock ledge and poured into the depths below and onto the source of the radiance.

Steven's mind repulsed and flexed. A huge, globular mass, pulsing with life and magic, emanating a brain-blistering arcane heat. Its surface – its skin? – was taut and black and rippled with coruscating striations of green light and palpitating lumps and waves. In random patterns, as the exterior rippled, tentacular appendages sprouted forth and spat clouds of verdant spores and spines that floated and drifted in the air far below Hines's feet. Viscous patches of the fungus that had riddled the city climbed the walls and crept over the ceiling. Only the rushing water protected him from a thousand bursts of spores.

And as he looked upon the thing he began to conceive of

its monstrosity, its behemoth size. This was only the end of it, the focal point. Something he was reluctant to consider a head or a brain, but that was the nearest analog, and that shadow deep under Cleveport, where her furthest roots reached, was its body. Its Leviathan mass, stretching from the hills out into the ocean, with a city of millions perched on its back, leaching its power, taking strength from its presence. No wonder Cleveport was a more sentient, a more magical city, than most.

As the flood poured into the cavern, the thing down there throbbed and sucked, breathed the water in and expanded itself, swelled up to fill the space, but so very slowly. The rains had engorged the dried and desiccated thing. Every vibe he got from it was one of slow awakening, a behemoth gently shrugging its way up from slumber, taking shuddering early breaths, yet to even open its "eyes". It had no eyes, though, no organs, nothing he could see that would clarify it as any known form of life, and yet Hines was under no doubt that it was a living entity. A massive, ancient, terrible living thing of a kind he could barely comprehend. And the water roused it and it shifted. Hines felt Cleveport cry out as her streets split and buildings cracked in the earthquake of this being's awakening.

All the devastation thus far had been caused before this creature had truly taken its first blink of arising. The rains it consumed had barely begun to shudder it into consciousness. What kind of effect could it have on the world if truly revived? Cleveport would be brushed aside like a bug as it rose if it was allowed to emerge and then what? How much might magical ability in the world enhance if its influence became fully manifest? Already Hines winced at the burn of energy coursing through him. It would surely destroy everything with even a hint of talent about it, burn them up in its aura like a meteor on hitting the atmosphere. And it would crush thousands with every step of gargantuan limbs that even now stirred the silty bottom of Cleveport harbor. A monster a hundred miles high and incandescent with raw magic, it would devastate the planet.

Hines could piece it together, the pattern of events laid clear around him. These caves, sealed up for millennia, locked away, forgotten. How this thing found itself here was a mystery, but the ground had closed over it here and it slumbered, dry, waiting. The Earth changed. Weather patterns and geological shifts occurred over hundreds, thousands of years. And eventually, something cracked, far above. Landslides on the surface, movements beneath, and unprecedented rains began to wash down the slopes and flood the land. That life-giving water found its way through dehydrated passages and trickled down, down, down until it began to tumble into this enormous, forgotten cavern and drip onto the entity that had lain here in its millennial sleep and that entity had *gasped*. It began to breathe in and it was still breathing in and perhaps only just beginning its first outbreath. And with that dread exhalation came the traveling spores of its procreation. And the commune above, full of inquisitive humans, their unstoppable curiosity, had noticed new gaps in the rock faces. They had gone looking, exploring as humans will, and they had found apocalypse waiting. Was that this thing's plan all along? Did it even have a plan?

Before the torrents had become too strong, those spores would have risen up, infected the curious, turned them slowly into mindless attackers and they had gone forth, slowly directed by the slumbering mind of this thing to the heart of the nearest food source. To Cleveport and its dense population, and the entity's legacy was begun. The waters awoke it, humanity attracted it and the chain reaction was set in motion. The thing that frightened Hines the most was the simple fact that it had barely started. This unfathomable monster meant nothing but devastation to the human race. He couldn't begin to understand it, but he could conceive of its impact.

And even as he tried to parse all this, it seemed to sense him too. It flexed and rose, Cleveport howled again against giant tremors through her streets. From the rounded bulk below extended a questing column, reaching up from the depths like a finger pointing to his soul. Was this how it had first tainted those initial explorers?

As that accusing finger rose, its end bifurcated again and again into bristling tendrils that quested directly for Hines as he stood mesmerized on the ledge, a river coursing past his legs in a waterfall of life for this leviathan. A torrent of death for everything he knew.

Cleveport cried out, begged him to save her, and in her lament he heard the cries of four million souls. And beyond that population, the yet to be uttered shrieks of fear and need from every soul beyond, across the country, around the world. This destruction was just begun and he had to stop it.

He sent his will back towards his city. *I need your help. I need you.*

And she answered with every vibe of acquiescence she could muster. Though her fear was all-encompassing, her sickness debilitating, her surfaces breaking, she would give him everything she could to save herself. And Hines would take it. The seeking appendage closed the space between them and Hines closed his eyes on it.

He pictured a section of street outside the office building of a large law firm, two lanes each way and flat. He wrapped his mind around a thirty-yard section and shifted it. His muscles swelled and tore, his bones creaked, but the piece of Cleveport fell from the nowhere space between and slammed the reaching arm of the entity back into the depths. A deep, resonant moan vibrated the cave. As the lump of asphalt crashed down onto the thing, suddenly minuscule against the mammoth bulk, several more arms burst up around it and shot skyward, faster, more urgent than before, writhing hungrily.

Roads weren't enough. Hines needed to think bigger. And he risked many more lives, but what choice did he have? He would have to stay in the central business district in the hope it was the least populated part of Cleveport right now.

He shifted his attention from the roadway to the legal building itself, seventeen stories of cement and steel and glass and furniture. The entity's own presence empowered Hines, gave him exactly what he needed to fight it, if only he could survive the process. There was a beautiful justice somewhere in that.

He gathered Cleveport to him and a tower block dropped through the air before him, the wind of its passage tugging at his sodden clothes, threatening to suck him away with it.

He fell to his knees, pain lanced up his thigh and he sat back into the rushing water that flooded past at chest height. He braced his feet against lumps of rocks as the thing down there moaned again, and hundreds of tons of city crushed into it from above.

Another presence filled Hines's mind, buoyed him up like a father steadying his young son on his first bike ride. And a father it was. His father, offering strength and assistance from his bond deep in Cleveport's body. Weak, almost gone, but still clinging on, Arthur Hines threw his will behind his son's.

With desperate gratitude, Hines drew on that will, on Cleveport's need, used the entity's own massive enhancement of natural magic against it and hauled through the building next to the one he had dropped before. His muscles tore, his mind threatened to split and spill out of his ears, but he grimaced against it and took the next building and the next. He didn't need to survive this. He just had to make sure that whatever it was down there didn't either.

Massive holes tore open in the fabric of his city and thousands of tons of human endeavor fell from the null space of in-between. One moment part of a vibrant city, the next traveling with his will to crush the throbbing, swelling abomination that filled the gargantuan hole below. Its moans turned into deafening subsonic roars, its reaching tendrils snaked and writhed, trying to find the tiny, irrelevant thing that harried it. Spines and spores jetted up, riddled Hines's flesh and lungs, but he ignored them and fought on.

He was not insignificant. He *was* Cleveport. He was hundreds of years of human industry. He was four million souls who refused to be beaten. He was an entity at least as large as this horror from prehistory trying to take away everything he was.

He tore again at the city and she gave of herself gladly, excising a part of the infected body to destroy the source of the disease. Hines heard his bones cracking and flesh ripping with the pulses of magical energy passing through him, but didn't care. He didn't matter. She mattered. It was Cleveport who needed to survive.

Wind rushed past him as buildings and roads ripped through the space between space to crash onto this unimaginable enemy. He dropped entire city blocks onto it and those blocks collapsed and fractured under their own weight. They broke apart and compressed into themselves, a massive substrate of everything man-made that crushed the furious nemesis below. It split and burst, its green phosphorescence became a searing incandescence and its roar became a scream that punctured Hines's ears. Its body bucked as more of Cleveport fell. Its gargantuan form writhed, the earth split with its throes from mountains to sea.

Wharves broke and fell, roads and buildings heaved and tumbled, sinkholes opened like gaping wounds as the enemy thrashed.

Blood ran down Hines's cheeks, his bones split, his muscles tore. But he ignored the pain and slammed more and more of his city, of himself, into the hole beneath him. The city crashed and crumbled, became like gravel as it smothered the groaning creature and smashed it flatter and flatter. Compressed it down into the cavern floor and built upon it a new land of impenetrable pieces that became thicker and thicker as Hines brought more of his city to bear.

Before he realized it, the shattered city had risen almost to meet him, and the thing below was silenced. Hines's magic drained away. The influence of all the spores he had felt invade him flickered out.

His connection to Cleveport was there, but weak again with distance. She had a mighty hole in her heart, her voice frail, but the stimulus of the thing that tried to take her into itself was gone.

Hines sat and gasped, almost blacked out with his efforts, his body ruptured and broken. He managed a crooked smile. "Well, fuck me," he muttered.

The rainwaters didn't cease and with the city filling thousands of cubic feet of cavern below him, they rose and the flooding from above continued to feed it and Hines found himself floating and spinning, carried on a tide towards the vault of the cave. A giant Archimedean experiment.

The roof was covered with patches of rippling green fungus, but the failing light was not just his mind shutting down. The glow had faded, the arcane energy that powered that fungal life was extinguished and everything it created was dying along with its progenitor.

Hines laughed, not entirely sane. He would at least have the pleasure of death by drowning rather than fall victim to this hideous thing. That was an achievement of which he could be truly proud.

He saw a split in the rock, runnels of water pouring from it and realized the passage he had traveled down was not the only one leading in. He paddled weakly towards the hole and, as the levels continued to rise, let himself be pushed into it, up through the mountain. He had no idea where he would go, but at least away from this place so he could die somewhere else.

43

Gina sat with Abby Jones and Jerry Rundle in the inadequate shelter of the hay shed as the downpour continued unabated. She couldn't meet Jerry's eye after telling him about Barkley. He said he didn't blame her and she could see he meant it, but his grief was palpable.

Abby stared into the veil of rain with an expression somewhere between fury and sadness. "I should be with him," she said and bashed her crutch angrily against the ground.

"Not your world," Gina said. "I can feel massive fluctuations in the magical energy here. I don't know what he's doing, but I can assure you he's alive and he's doing something fucking huge. The aether is almost tearing all around us. Can you really not hear it?"

"I can only hear the rain," Abby said.

Rundle maintained his silence.

Over the thunderous drumming of the deluge on the tin roof, Gina listened to huge magics. She had never heard it before, had no idea there was anything to hear about someone exercising their talent, but sound was the best description for the roaring that vibrated through her. And underlying that, a deep, resonant moan and lament, as of something in pain inconceivable. All she could see it as was a life of some kind slowly being extinguished. Or was she projecting that? Hoping that whatever was happening down there under the mountain, what she heard, might be Hines succeeding. She pleaded silently for that to be the case, that something terrible was dying at his hand.

They cried out as the ground suddenly shifted and cracked, the hay shed tipped and halted at a new angle. A fissure ran randomly from one side of the paddock to the other and the house crumbled on one side, solar panels crashing to the driveway.

"The fuck is this?" Abby yelled as she ducked away from a falling bale.

The essence of magic drained away.

Gina had grabbed one corner post of the roof for support, and she gasped and staggered forward, stumbling out into the downpour in her shock before scurrying back under cover. She drew quick breaths like she had just run a sprint. The earth tremors settled and the roaring of magic and howling of the thing she could not explain leaked out of the air. The aether became insubstantial and distant again. Her talent had slipped away to nothing. No, not nothing. It was there, but so very weak and feeble. Back, in fact, to what it had always been before. Untrained and new.

"You all right?" Abby asked, leaning forward on her crutch to put a hand on Gina's shoulder.

Gina nodded, turned to face the policewoman. "Yes. You can't feel any change can you?"

"No. Is it a big change?"

Gina grinned. "Yeah. The biggest. I… I think he's done it."

"Done what?"

Gina's grin became a laugh. "Saved us. I think Steven's succeeded. Everything that was wrong with the world has gone away."

Abby popped one eyebrow up.

"Well," Gina admitted. "Not everything. But everything that was awry with the magical world seems to have died out."

"Just like that?"

"Yeah."

Abby crutched forward to the edge of their shelter,

looked up at the mountains rising from the far side of the paddock. More land slipped and shifted before her eyes, pines splintering and falling. "Well, fuck me." She turned to look back at Gina. "And Hines, is he..?"

Gina shrugged. "I don't know. No way I can know. I guess we wait?"

Abby moved back and sat on a hay bale again. "Yeah, we wait."

"For how long?"

"As long as it takes."

They waited all day and nothing changed except the rain. It became lighter and lighter until it was eventually little more than a gusting drizzle. As the light began to fail, Abby sighed and stood. "Well, I don't know whether to laugh or cry. It's over, but I guess Hines isn't coming back."

"You can laugh *and* cry," Gina said. "He saved us all."

"Very mature," Abby said, with a half-smile.

"Same goes for Barkley." Gina put a hand on Rundle's shoulder. "I'm so sorry, but he really saved my life. He protected us all the way in and he's the only reason I got out. I hope that's some consolation. I'm sure you'd rather have him here than me. But I'll never forget him."

Jerry nodded. He hadn't said a word all day and still didn't seem inclined to speak.

"Let's get back to the city," Abby said. "No idea how the hell I'm going to report all this, but maybe I just won't. If it's over, perhaps that's enough." She looked to the hills once more. "See ya, Steve, you big idiot." She threw a two-fingered salute. "And thank you."

They turned to head back across the paddock, through the commune and farm, back to the cars. Rundle dragged himself to his feet and turned to follow as a sound came to them through the drizzle.

Rundle froze, looked over his shoulder. The sound came again, a weak whining. Through the scattered trees to the far north of the paddock, a shadow emerged into the gloom. Low and limping, Barkley dragged himself onto the grass.

Rundle ran faster than Gina would have thought possible for a man on a crutch with a bullet wound in his leg. She sprinted alongside. Barkley panted and grinned, his tail wagging weakly despite his battered state, thumping wetly against the ground. He was cut and bleeding, patches of fur missing and his left back leg was horribly twisted, clearly broken. He barked once, a high yap of greeting. Gina had never heard anything more beautiful in her life.

Rundle crouched and gathered the dog gingerly into his arms. "Barkley, you amazing hound!" he said, tears pouring unashamedly. He pressed his face into Barkley's neck and the dog twisted his head to lick all over Rundle's cheek and ear.

"Where did he come from?" Gina asked. "How did he escape?"

Jerry grinned up at her, his demeanor entirely transformed. "Followed his nose and found another way out! Clever boy!"

"Come on," Gina said. "Let's get him to a vet. In fact, I think we all need doctors of one sort or another."

44

Hines drifted in a haze, his mind like a flag shredded by too much time in the wind. His entire being, in fact, tattered and used up. He only realized he was still alive when the motion stopped and ice cold ate through the pain. It was darker than night, darker than death, but he lived and floated in some underground lake. He'd been carried up, away from the chamber of… whatever that thing was, and he reveled in the silence and stillness of its demise. The noise of intense magic was gone. All the energetic levels he'd grown used to had returned to normal. Even though his time was spent, he could at least enjoy that before he died. But something else tugged at him too, relentless, insistent.

Cleveport.

He didn't want to expire here in the dark bowels of a rain-drenched mountain. He needed to die there, in her arms. And she needed him back. What vestige of power he retained she needed, drained as she was by the death of the thing she had been built upon. He forced himself to move, grit his teeth against the grinding agony. His bones felt like they had splits along their lengths, his muscles as though they had razors inserted through every millimeter, but his body worked, after a fashion. He turned onto his front and painfully paddled. He had no way to make light, probably no chance of escaping these natural catacombs, but he had to try.

As he swam, he felt something wonderful. Fresh air blew into his face and carried with it the scent of pines and dirt. He laughed. *You're a lucky son of a bitch.* But perhaps it was fated this way. Who was he to question it?

He swam towards the breeze, his hands and knees hit rock and he began to crawl. It took what felt like hours, but he dragged himself up passageways of wet rock until he finally emerged into a different darkness. Into the night. Rain still fell, though lighter than it had in weeks. Here and there, patches of stars peeked through the incessant cloud cover. Hines hauled himself to his feet, ignored the sensation of knives through every inch of his body, and staggered forward to look around. His injured knee wouldn't bend and he dragged his leg behind him like deadwood, using it as a prop with every painful step.

Far below, he saw lights on in a farmhouse. With a crooked smile, he headed towards them. More seeming hours of pain-filled, interminable staggering finally saw him reach the house. A battered pick-up truck sat in the driveway and the keys hung in the ignition. Country folk never expected a vehicle theft from their own property. Hines fell into the driver's seat, started the vehicle and drove away, before anyone inside could react to the engine gunning into life.

He was more tired than he had ever been, pushing on despite the fact that he was pretty much already dead. He just needed to get back to Cleveport. And Abby. He needed to get word to her. He owed her that, but not in person. She wouldn't understand.

The road towards town had a smattering of traffic on it. Wide cracks here and there in the asphalt gaped as testament to his recent battle, cars carefully navigating around them. It was strange to see life happening when Cleveport had so quickly and thoroughly ground to a halt. Almost every other vehicle was military, their presence still strong, though they were letting other people move again.

He pulled into a service station just as a wide-eyed, pimply teenager opened it up and the overhead fluorescents flickered into life. He found a few dollars of change in the pick-up's ashtray. He bought a pad of paper, envelopes and a pen from the station attendant.

"Been a long day," he told the young man.

"No shit. You okay?"

"Not really, but that's fine."

"I wondered if I should even come to work," the kid said. "But thought I should check in, just in case. What's been happening?"

The obliviousness of youth. "Oh, the end of the world was narrowly averted, that's all," Hines said with a grin.

He sat in the pickup cab and wrote a letter to Abby, addressed it and shuffled back into the service station. "Do me a favor?" he asked the young man.

The kid's eyes narrowed. "Like what?"

"I really need for this letter to be delivered. Can you help?" He put the few remaining dollars on the counter. "That's all I have, but could you buy a stamp and drop it in the mail?"

"Sure, I guess."

"Seriously, it's incredibly important."

The kid shrugged, nodded. "No problem. I'll make sure to post it."

"Thanks."

Fighting nausea from exhaustion and pain, Hines drove into a town that was cracked and broken, buildings crooked here and there with emergency services buzzing around, but that appeared to be waking up, people and vehicles moving cautiously.

As he entered the center of Cleveport, a profound calm overlaid the hurt through his mind and body. She sang weakly to him, welcomed him back and saturated him with thanks. He also felt her grief. It was, at least in part, for his father. Sometime during that insane effort to destroy the thing, his father had died. He hadn't even noticed. The man was at peace now, he supposed. One way or another. And some of her grief was for Hines. And a large part for herself.

She was no longer as she had been and knew she never would be again. At least he could give her back some of it, the part he carried in himself.

He drove on towards the section of downtown he had so unbelievably removed and dumped inside a mountain. From a block out he could see fervent activity and bright yellow tape around a massive area of devastation. He parked the stolen car and stumbled along the shadowed street. City workers and police buzzed around the site. It was a giant hole, as if some unnatural hand had reached down and scooped out several entire blocks. Which was pretty much exactly what had happened.

Underground train lines and sewers and cabling pockmarked the huge indentation below the ragged edges of road, a cross-section of the underside of Cleveport. Her workings were exposed like an open wound and it hurt him to see that, but it was a price she had gladly paid. No one was coming out of this situation unscathed, but Cleveport would bear the least of the scars in the end, of that much he was certain. People always rebuilt their cities.

He moved towards the devastation. He waited until people nearby were distracted and slipped under the tape, to the edge of a ragged building only half stolen away. He could barely walk, but he was nearly there. The broken structure was a dangerous and unstable monument to his efforts, which was exactly what he needed.

Movement above caught his eye as a dozen tan and speckled hawks settled in a uniform line along one exposed metal beam. They opened their wings and bowed to him like a chorus line, heads dipping low and rising again three times. Hines couldn't help a wry laugh. He shakily raised one hand and extended his middle finger. "You're welcome!" he mouthed, no strength left to shout. The birds dipped once more and took to the air.

Hines looked into the broken city below his feet. "I'm yours, darling," he whispered. "Time to start repairing yourself." And he stepped off the edge and tumbled into the gaping wound below.

Cleveport sighed and shifted and the unsteady building came down. Cleveport's love wrapped him in arms of concrete and steel.

EPILOGUE

Gina Baker approached her family home cautiously. As she made her way along the driveway, Rufus came bounding out of the still open front door, grinning and barking a greeting. She crouched and he barreled into her, licking kisses all over her face.

"Roofie, Roofie, Roofie!" she sang. "My beautiful boy! You're okay!"

He bounced and wagged beside her as she entered the house. The marks on the kitchen floor were dark, flat stains now, fading to a dull charcoal, inert and harmless.

"Mum," she whispered. "Dad." Tears came again. Was this really them?

She opened the fridge, suddenly starving, and began to mechanically fix herself and Rufus something to eat.

"We've got some tidying up to do," she told the dog. "And I have no idea of the legalities surrounding the house and everything else. Guess I'd better look for their will or something. I suppose a lot of people have shit like this to deal with now, eh, boy?"

How would she explain anything to an insurance company? How would anybody affected by the ridiculous events of the last two days? But at least she had Abby and Jerry. The three of them alone knew the truth of what had happened, regardless of what else may or may not come to public light. And they'd agreed to stay in touch, meet regularly and help each other deal with their experiences. It was as good as place as any to start.

For now, she would eat until the hunger that tore at her gut dissipated, then she would curl up with Rufus and sleep like the dead. Everything else could wait.

Jerry Rundle had driven for hours. Barkley lay on the back seat, one leg heavily cast, bandages wrapping other parts of his battered body, but his tongue lolled in a doggy grin all the same.

Rundle came down the other side of the mountains, his own leg bandaged tightly, and headed southeast. The land became wider and drier as they went. It had still been raining in Cleveport when they left, but nothing like as heavily as before. Maybe it would stop one day, but he didn't care. He'd be happy to never see rain again.

They passed a sign. "See that, buddy?" he asked the dog. "About another four or five hours drive probably and then we'll have to find that motel we looked up. I reckon my early retirement money will buy us a fine house in that back of beyond shitheel town when it comes through, eh? Lowest rainfall in the country, according to the internet. Sounds good, right? I'm going to try to grow veggies, but we'll probably end up eating cactus."

Barkley whuffed happily.

Rundle nodded. "Yeah, we made the right decision. Nothing but peace and quiet for us. Maybe Abby and Gina will visit from time to time."

He reached into his jacket and pulled out a battered, nearly empty pack of Lucky cigarettes. As he shook it to free one, Barkley yelped from the back, high and sharp. It was clearly a bark of admonishment. *You promised!*

Rundle laughed. "Yeah. Yeah, I did, huh?"

He crumpled the pack and threw it onto the floor on the passenger side.

Barkley struggled up, licked Rundle's ear. Jerry laughed and reached over to pat his friend as the dog fell back to the seat and curled up happily. Jerry turned up the radio, country music blasting out, and put his foot down.

Detective Abby Jones sat deskbound, her leg in full plaster. It restricted her so much that she was beginning to go stir crazy after just two days. But perhaps it was the reading more than her forced confinement that frustrated her so much.

Reports from the city officials, the police and the army congratulating themselves on containing and ending the outbreak in Cleveport. Unprecedented rain had caused earthquakes, landslides and sinkholes to open up in the city, the word went, and that had released a dangerous and strange chemical spill. It made no sense at all, but that was the official line and they were sticking to it. Accounts of an infection causing citizens to go mad were unfounded and exaggerated, they said. Social media was being purged, even video she had seen that morning was no longer online. The truth was quickly moving from the front page to the conspiracy websites and Abby wondered just how far up it all went.

She knew the biggest "sinkhole" in the city had to be somehow connected to Hines's magic. But repairs were underway. Bigger powers were clearly covering up things they didn't really know or understand, and Abby was resigned to the fact that they probably never would know. And they certainly wouldn't reveal what they might manage to figure out. The real truth was known only to a very few and all of it only to one.

She grimaced against tears again, wishing Hines had survived. Her only real friend, he'd turned out to be quite the hero and would go forever unrecognized. But she wouldn't forget. She would honor his memory always. She had already agreed with Gina and Jerry Rundle that every year, on the date he saved Cleveport, they'd get together and drink to his memory. Even though Jerry had already left town, he'd come back for their pact, he had promised. Abby couldn't blame him for leaving, but she wouldn't ever quit the city. Not now. She might not be tied to Cleveport in quite the way Hines had been, but it would always be her home. And it was a monument to Steven too, one she intended to stand by.

And Abby knew now, beyond any possible doubt, that magic was real, in Cleveport and beyond. She would not be blind to its existence anymore. No doubt the misery trade was back on track. She vowed to find and bring down any more bastards like Crater, one way or another. That, at least, would be a vendetta she carried on from recent events.

"Letter for ya."

Abby looked up from her reverie, saw a young man holding out an envelope. "Thanks."

She took it and her heart skipped. Hines's handwriting was recognizable even though it was shaky and uncertain. Her hands trembled and she tore it open and read.

> Dear Abby
>
> Firstly, please know how sorry I am. I don't want to go, but I have no choice. What happened down there has broken me, inside and out. And Cleveport still needs me.
>
> I can't begin to explain what happened, but I'm fairly sure it's over. I can only hope it'll never happen again somewhere else.
>
> My whole life has been borrowed time. I've always been part of the city, could never leave. Remember when you invited me to Miami that time and I made excuses... Ah, but this is not the time. I'm truly going home now, just think of it like that.
>
> I've gone to my city. I can't expect you to understand what that means, but I think you managed to know me properly at last, right before everything turned to shit. We did good, you and I.

We're the fucking heroes of this piece, Jones, so remember me like that, yeah? No one else will, but that doesn't matter. Cleveport knows. She's safe for now and I'm okay with that. And try to not grieve for me too much. I'll be around all the time you're in Cleveport. When you put your hands to a building, you'll feel me. When you look through a window, I'll be looking back.

Protect yourself. Look after yourself and look after the city. Don't hide from the things you've learned. Embrace them. And do me a favor. When you've read this and wiped the tears off your stupid face, go look in a mirror.

You know I love you, always have. We've always been so much more than lovers or family or whatever the hell else is possible. So shut up, stop crying and go get wasted in my memory on the best scotch you can find. Hurts too much to keep writing. Stopping now.

Love ya, doofus.

Steve.

PS Do me a favor and check in on old Maeve in my building for me. She's a sweetheart.

PPS MIRROR!

Abby laughed, wiped a sleeve across one cheek then the other. "Fuck you, Hines," she said quietly. She read the letter again before folding it and putting it in her bag. She hobbled out from her desk and pushed up on her crutches. Not sure what to expect, she made her way to the bathroom and checked no one was in there before standing in front of a sink. She leaned forward, staring hard into the mirror. Her face looked gaunt, bags under her eyes. It was going to take a while to recover from the last few days.

What was she looking for exactly? She imagined Hines's voice in her head. *Stop looking at your stupid self. It's not all about you.*

She grinned, scanned around the rest of the mirror. Movement caught her eye and she froze. Just at the periphery of her vision, two vaguely human-shaped shadows shifted. She looked slowly towards them. They phased and faded, clearer if she looked not quite directly at them. A man and a woman.

Steven and Jenny.

Hines raised one hand. She thought he was waving before she realized he had one finger up. She laughed and flipped the bird back at them. Unclear and shadowy though they were, she could see them laughing. They both moved, both waving this time and she held up one hand as they faded back into silvery nothing.

Abby Jones stared at herself crying for a good ten minutes before she felt composed enough to return to her desk, but there was a deep sense of satisfaction and happiness mixed in with her melancholy. It was time to get back to work.

THE END

ABOUT THE AUTHOR

Alan Baxter is a multi-award-winning British-Australian author of horror and weird fiction. This Is Horror podcast calls him "Australia's master of literary darkness" and the Talking Scared podcast dubbed him "The Lord of Weird Australia." He's also a martial artist, whisky-soaked swear monkey, metalhead and dog lover. He writes his darkly strange tales deep in the valleys of southern Tasmania. Find him online at alanbaxter.com.au

ALSO BY ALAN BAXTER

BLOOD COVENANT
SALLOW BEND
RECALL
DEVOURING DARK
HIDDEN CITY

BOUND (Alex Caine Book 1)
OBSIDIAN (Alex Caine Book 2)
ABDUCTION (Alex Caine Book 3)

REALMSHIFT (The Balance Book 1)
MAGESIGN (The Balance Book 2)

SERVED COLD – Short Stories
CROW SHINE – Short Stories
AND FIRE POURED FORTH – Short Stories

THE GULP: Tales From The Gulp 1
THE FALL: Tales From The Gulp 2
THE RISE: Tales From The Gulp 3

THE LEAVES FORGET
THE ROO
THE BOOK CLUB
GHOST OF THE BLACK: A 'Verse Full of Scum
GOLDEN FORTUNE, DRAGON JADE

Co-authored with David Wood

PRIMORDIAL (Sam Aston Investigations Book 1)
OVERLORD (Sam Aston Investigations Book 2)
CROCALYPSE (Sam Aston Investigations Book 3)

SANCTUM (Jake Crowley Adventures 0)
BLOOD CODEX (Jake Crowley Adventures 1)
ANUBIS KEY (Jake Crowley Adventures 2)
REVENANT (Jake Crowley Adventures 3)

DARK RITE

alanbaxter.com.au

www.ingramcontent.com/pod-product-compliance
Ingram Content Group UK Ltd.
Pitfield, Milton Keynes, MK11 3LW, UK
UKHW041631190726
13854UKWH00006B/2429

9 781950 920037